THE SUP

CONTENTS

INTRODUCTION

THIS IS MY FIRST ATTEMPT WRITING A NOVEL. I HOPE YOU ENJOY READING IT AS MUCH AS I ENJOYED writting it while RECOUNTING MY EXPERIENCES IN MY FIRST JOB. I HAVE TOTALLY EXAGERATED AND GLORIFIED WITH A FEW major additions TO MAKE IT MORE INTERESTING, especially the final scene.

PROLOGUE

The Super Rat

A Novel by D.J Pullar

"Though a good deal is too strange to be believed, nothing is too strange to have happened." Thomas Hardy (Novelist and Poet).

"There are better things in life than alcohol … but alcohol compensates you for not getting them." Terry Pratchett (Novelist).

"There is no substitute for doing it correctly the first time". - DRD Ainslie

CHAPTER ONE

A New Beginning

Allan sat anxiously at his desk in the corner, looking outside at the stormy weather, and glancing at his watch, frequently. Amidst the lively discussion among his colleagues, he was alone in his private, yet eager thoughts. There was still fifteen minutes until his shift ended, so he reached over, and lifted the telephone to call home.

'On second thoughts, it's too good to tell over the phone; it's much better if I do it face-to-face. This is the best thing to happen to me for ages or probably ever. I won't be able to control myself'. Although, inside, he was bursting to tell someone.

'Right, Allan, that's us finished now!' someone shouted, but Allan didn't hear them. 'We're all off down to The Red Lion for a quick one before we go home. We'll meet you there!'

Everyone shuffled out, except Allan, who thought to himself, 'It's a pity I will never see any of them again; I've really enjoyed working here. Shame, I never got to grips with those new secretaries, but who knows what's just round the corner for me.

Replacing the telephone in the cradle and sliding it over to corner of the desk, he put in his briefcase the silver pen he had been given for his 21st birthday by his girlfriend Celia, a few cheaper pens, some Tipp-Ex, his newspaper, his diary, and finally, some self-adhesive reinforcement rings – or teddy bears arseholes as his colleague 'Stuart' called them. A quick look over his desk to ensure it was neat and tidy, as he usually left it every night, before he grabbed his drolly, and switched his office light off.

One last glance at the office he had gained so much work experience in, left him glowing with happiness inside but tinged with a modicum of sadness, nevertheless: 'I'm glad I haven't told everybody that I am leaving; I hate goodbyes, and they always make a big fuss of a leaver and give a good leaving present. It's probably for the best that only the Boss and the Directors know my news'.

He briskly walked from the office to the elevator, to the ground floor, only smiling and nodding to his fellow occupants; none of the usual chit-chat about the weekend coming up or the weather. He was just keeping his good news safely inside himself until he got home.

Outside the elevator, he could see through the transparent entrance doors that the weather was still very wet. With his umbrella reassuringly ready for action, he went over to the uniform man at the front door and mumbled acknowledgement at him: 'Typical weather for the weekend, huh?'

As the doorman opened the door for him to brave the weather, Allan went straight outside before looking up to the sky. Frowned, then smiling, he shrugged his shoulders and opened the umbrella. With a sprightly skip to his step, he bought an evening paper and stuck it under his arm as he always did, not caring that it would be sodden by the time he got home.

The number 20 bus was just pulling into the bus stop, so Allan quickly ran to the stop. Getting in quickly, he climbed the stairs because he preferred the view up there to read his paper and have a well-deserved smoke. 'Hi, Davie', he said to his friend Davie Brenson, joining him in the seat near the front.

Davie was an old school friend of his who lived in the next street to Allan, so they chatted. 'So, what's new with you, Davie?' 'Nothing new, going to a concert tomorrow night. What's been happening in your life?'

Desperate to tell Davie of his news, he said, 'Well '– but decided not to reveal anything until he told the family. 'Nothing much, really, just the same old, same old. A few things may be on the horizon, but the work's all looking good'.

The bus reached their stop, so they went down to the door, said hello to a few fellow passengers they often saw at this time, and looked in disgust at the weather. With brollies at the ready, everyone got off the bus and went their separate ways, leaving the smell of damp clothes, used tickets, and smoke from upstairs behind them.

Davie and Allan walked a short distance towards Allan's road, then said, 'See you soon', as they went on to their respective houses.

Another thunder clap made Allan eventually put up his collar, tighten his scarf, and ran the final few yards to home.

Stopping at the gate to get his key, he decided to go in through the back door which would be unlocked, as his mother would be making the tea.

He opened the door to a blast of warm air and the delicious aroma of roast chicken. 'That smells great, Mum'. He smiled at her, and went through the porch, saying, 'I'm glad to have gotten out of that rain, Mum. Can't wait for tea, and have I got news for everyone at the table'. He then went straight to his bedroom to change out of his wet clothes into what he called his civvies and slippers.

When Mum shouted, 'Tea's up!' he took a deep breath and ran downstairs to join the rest of the family, who by this time were all waiting for their dinner, and to hear what everyone else had been up to that day.

Allan took his place at the dining table, and jumped up again when his mother said, 'Okay, Allan, come and bring these through'. Smilingly, he quickly went through to the adjoining kitchen and took two plates through to the dining room. 'What are you looking so pleased about?' his Mum asked. 'Just wait. I'll tell it all when everyone is here, but it's good news'.

He went back to the table, followed by his mother and younger sister Tilda, with the rest of the food. They sat down and joined the rest, as everyone began to tell each other about their day. Nobody paid much attention to anyone else; each just waiting for an opportunity and a lull to continue their version of their day's events.

His brother seized a quieter moment, and said, 'Right, what's this good news Mum was saying? Tell us, then' okay, I've good news and bad news. So, which do you want to hear first?' he asked, whilst pouring himself a cup of tea. 'The bad news for you all is I'll be moving out'. This was followed by a stifled cheer from each of the brothers and a grunt from his father.

'Why, what's up?' asked his mother. 'Well, it's really good, Mum. Only my Boss and the Directors know, but no one else. You'll be the first to know'.'Well, get on with it, boy', said his father curtly, while chewing and splattering mouthfuls everywhere.

'Right', he said, 'I've been offered a job in Strathmanor – that's near Stoopchurch. I'll have to move through there permanently, as I start next month'. Allan explained to attentive ears that the job was a promotion for him and he would be an important part of the new office the company was setting up.

'Well, you'll need to have somewhere to stay', said his mother. 'No shit, Sherlock', said his brother Ronald. 'Oi, cut that bloody language out right now', said his Dad.'I know that', Allan said with a frown.

'Do you want that last potato? No? Good, I'll have it', he said quickly without waiting to hear any reply. 'Yes, mother...' he said slowly. 'I've spent most of the afternoonlooking for a house, and there is one at a remarkably cheap price by the road into Strathmanor'.

'Well, that'll be why it's so cheap; it's by the road, so it'll be noisy', said Dad 'another piece of useless information' said Tilda mockingly.

'Yes, maybe, but the price is good, it seems like a really good deal. And if I don't find a house immediately, I'll have to take bed and breakfast or travel daily while I look for one'.

'Well, I hope that old car of yours is up to the job. It's not like here where you can just go by bus during the week', said Mum.

'We're ahead of you', said his Dad. 'I serviced it during the week'.

'Yeah, he filled the windscreen, water bottle, and checked the radiator'.

'Shut up, Alistair, and get on with your tea', said Dad.

'I'd be happier if you had somewhere sorted before you go. I'll only worry that you are okay', said his Mum.

Allan, nodding his head, agreed with her, and said, 'I'm going through tomorrow to meet my new Boss, so while I'm down there I'll check out the house I have found'. He thought that if it was suitable he could make an offer, and be back up the road that night. 'I'm sure the seller will agree to a viewing, as they want a quick sale'.

'Well, if you're planning on going down tomorrow and back up at night, I could come with you and have a look', suggested Mum.'Yes, okay, but just you. The rest will all be at work, anyway'.

'What about, What's her name that you're seeing?' asked Alistair. Yea, Thingummy, we'll keep an eye on her when she goes to the clubs while you are away' added Ronald. 'Oi, broke in their father 'Yes, that's what he calls her' they laughed, 'Cut it out you two', he said with a menacing glare 'She is a really nice girl', 'That's enough.

'Yes, you remember to phone that nice wee lass Cecilea', and looking at the other two 'Or Celia at worst' demanded his mother. 'Right Mum, I will go do that right now and leave you two to help Mum and Tilda with the dishes', he said, as he walked through to the phone, with Ronald and Alistair making all the childish lovey-dovey noises in the background.

The next morning, Allan and his Mum were up early, and set off to the new house. As they were crossing the road bridge, they listened on the radio to the road traffic reports, which started well by saying the rain would cease by that night, to be followed by a cold snap.

As soon as they got over the road bridge a bombardment of directional instructions were given by his Mum. 'I know the route, Mum. I've been over it countlessly in dad's AA book, so let me concentrate, as the road will still be a bit slippery even though the rain is off'.

They drove into Kincardine, and decided to nip in for a quick coffee while his Mum wandered around looking for some charity shops. 'Come on, Mum, we must get a move on. We haven't even got there yet. We should look at these on the way home. We need to get back on the road again'.

They got back in the car and carried on down the busy road. Allan said, 'As soon as we get into the town, Mum, it's the

10

third or fourth house on the left. The estate agent said she would wait for us outside'. They kept a close watch for the estate agent but never noticed her frantically jumping up and down; waving to get their attention.

They went all around Strathmanor looking for the road that they had already been on. When they came back up the road, they noticed a very cold and cheesed-off-looking woman. 'That woman is still there, but she's stopped jumping. Oh, that could be her', said Mum.

When they parked the car in the drive and got out, the agent said, 'I thought you were never coming. This is the house, here'. She pointed to the house, and said, 'I'm actually late for another appointment now, so if you don't mind, I will leave you the keys to have a look around for yourselves. Take as long as you want'. Mum apologised, and taking the keys, they walked up the path in the slightly unkempt garden and entered the house.

The first thing that struck them was that it was cold; it was a very cold house and had a stale musty smell, as it had lain empty for quite some time. They wandered from room-to-room taking everything in, with his Mum straightening a few pictures here and there.

'This looks great', said Allan from the kitchen. 'There's lots of room, a fridge, a cooker, and a washing machine included. I could probably just live in this room if I get a portable TV. That'll save on the heating', he said jokingly.

His Mum said, 'It is freezing, but that'll soon warm up when you move in, and if you do your ironing here that'll warm you up because you're not coming home during the weekend for me to do your washing and ironing'. He noticed there was a back garden for the washing, and said, 'Let's check the other rooms'.

They nipped upstairs, and nodded in approval at the two double bedrooms, with his Mum tutting and saying, 'Well, I don't like that picture for a start; what kind of a person lived here before? That girl would have got her death from the cold; dressed up like that.

I have some nice ones at home for you if you want them. But, knowing you, you probably won't, and you'll stick with that thing that would be better in some kind of magazine for men." 'No, I best not say I wish she was real'.'You'd think they'd at least polish all these marks off it', his mother added. Nodding, Allan said, 'Yes, but remember, it has been empty for ages. Now, let's go check the rooms downstairs.

There were two public rooms downstairs: one with a television and the other with masses of old books and a piano. 'Well, he wouldn't be bored at any rate', his mother said from one of the rooms.'Well, for the price that's its going for, I think we're onto a winner here!' Allan called out from the other room.

Allan also noticed there was a doctor's surgery next door, a police station across the road, a pub, and the start of a shopping precinct. That, added to the fact the house was only a quarter of a mile away from the new office, this made him think he probably could have just said yes to the house there and then, but he thought, its best not to let her think he was too keen.

They went out to wait in the car for the estate agent, just as she drove up. Allan told her he was very impressed, and he could let her know, for sure, first thing in the morning, knowing inside that he wanted this house.

The journey home was full of chat about the house and the prospects, with his Mum commenting, 'The estate agent should have shown us round though, but probably thought it would be too cold for her'. Feeling very pleased and optimistic with himself, he drove the wrong way home for a half-mile until they realised the mistake, turned and set for home properly.

The weekend of the move finally arrived, and he spent the Saturday morning making final preparations, checking his suitcases; packing and repacking to make sure nothing was forgotten, and that he had everything needed to relocate.

From downstairs, he heard his mother's voice calling up, 'Have you remembered to pack a scarf and a set of gloves? The weather's on the turn, and make sure you take a hot water bottle just in case'. Wearily, he said, 'Yes, mother, and I have packed fresh underpants too', he added sarcastically.

Ignoring his mother's request for him to take a hot water bottle, he decided to take his squash racquet and new trainers that his brothers had requested he leave behind. 'I'll need these myself', he thought. 'They'll come in handy at that new sports centre they are opening'.

He finished packing, and with the help of his brothers, they squeezed everything into his car so he could leave first thing Monday morning. He went off immediately after dinner to the pub to say goodbye, and explain to his friends there about his   move.

CHAPTER TWO

The First Day

Monday morning came, and so did an early frost on all the windows in his bedroom. Jumping out of bed, he ran downstairs for a quick shower, had some breakfast, and said, 'Mum, that's me off now. I'll phone you when I arrive'. 'Be careful on the roads. You're still not used to that journey'. 'Of course, I'll just go canny'. With that, Allan pinged his Black-Watch-Braces, and said 'I'll be okay', grinned, and left for the car.

Shivering, he briskly walked across the grass deliberately to hear the crisp sound under his feet, got in the car, and closed the door. The first thing he did was turn the radio on to get the battery warmed up; a trick one of his mechanic friends had taught him. He always did this even though he was never sure that it actually served a real purpose. He then pulled out the choke, and hoping for action, turned the key in the ignition.

Allan's hands were very cold by this time, so the heater was switched on as he waited for the engine thermostat to rise. As soon as it started to rise, he turned the heater up, and after a few seconds the whole car was all toasty and the frost began to melt. The heated rear window was by now doing its job, so he nudged the car forward to the main road, picked up a cigarette and set off on his journey.

He was about to light it as soon as he was out of the sight of his mother, but decided, 'No. New job... New town... No fags anymore!' and tossed the packet onto the passenger seat. On the road, his thoughts were shared between the harsh early weather driving conditions and the excitement of this new adventure.

In almost no time at all, he was passing village after village on the road up to Perth. 'Blast, this heavy goods vehicle is slowing me down', he thought to himself. Just at that moment, the HGV that was quite far ahead of him pulled off the road into a lay-by, and the long line of slow-moving traffic immediately sped up to a much more acceptable pace.

'Let's see what's on the radio'. Turning it up, Allan reduced speed abruptly, as every other car in the procession slowed quite sharply. Laughing to himself, he realised it was one of those new wave songs on the radio, that had started with police sirens.

With everybody in the line of, by now, crawling traffic, the trail started to pick up speed. Glancing at the clock on the dashboard, he thought to himself, 'I must concentrate on arriving at the estate on time to get the keys from the agent. No time for admiring the scenery'.

All of a sudden, the car seemed to lose a bit of control. It was a puncture! He pulled into the side of the road and sighed in exasperation as he realised that the wheel had not been repaired from the last puncture, so here he was with two flat tyres. 'What to do now?' I suppose I best run across the motorway to hitch a lift into Perth. I have cousins there that may be able to help get it repaired.'

Halfway across, just as he had gotten to the central reservation, Allan heard real sirens. This time it actually was a police car cruising up the motorway at a reasonable pace, just monitoring traffic. It wasn't after anyone in particular; just trying to get Allan's attention.

The driver started waving and pointing frantically at him to get back off the motorway, which he immediately did. When Allan got back to his car he felt safe, thinking, 'Oh well, at least the police will come back to tell me off, and they may help'.

After a while, he realised they weren't going to waste their time coming back for an idiot like him, so what could he do now. A few hundred yards back there was a house in a field up a slight incline, so he thought he'd best just climb up there and ask for assistance.

He asked the old lady in the house to telephone a garage, who agreed to deliver a new wheel, but at a hefty premium for their inconvenience. Allan thanked the old lady, left her some money for the phone call, and went back down the slope to the car where he met the mechanic, and the wheel was changed quickly. 'Oh well', he thought, 'let's try and make up some time to meet Mrs Lawson the estate agent'.

Hurtling down the road with one eye on the speedometer, he kept checking for traffic cops and the time. Soon he arrived in Strathmanor which he had recognised from a few miles back because of the flare stacks burning up unusable gases.

The first thing he noticed again in Strathmanor was the unusual smell which could only be described as rotten eggs. 'It must be from the refinery', he thought and was vexed to find no estate agent waiting for him.

He phoned their office where he was told that they had phoned his home earlier this morning to tell him that, as it had been a holiday weekend, the necessary documents hadn't been cleared, therefore he couldn't get the keys to his place. Disappointed, he drove to the sports centre where he had arranged to meet someone from his new office...

Arriving in the car park, he looked around for signs of any waiting colleague. There was no one to be seen, and after an hour of waiting, he thought that, as it was a public holiday this weekend, maybe the new office hadn't realised that he wouldn't know this. Wondering what to do now, he went back to his car, and looked at the fags he had discarded which seemed to be crying out for him to have one: *'Please smoke me'.*

Resisting the temptation, and pleased with himself for doing so, Allan found a telephone box nearby and phoned several bed and breakfasts in the area that told him they were all fully booked until, at last, he finally found one which was available for two nights; the owner of which said her friend would take him for the other two nights. This was ideal, as that would take him up to Friday when he would head back home and regale what an adventurous week, he had had, and maybe get his laundry done.

Quite pleased with himself, and not just a little bit relieved that he had found somewhere to stay, Allan went back to the car, looked at the directions, and drove to the old farmhouse bed and breakfast.

Taking his suitcase in with him, he was shown to his room by a young and pretty assistant. Following her up the stairs, he watched her every move, which reminded him to phone his girlfriend, Celia. He immediately felt at home here because of the lovely smell coming from the dining room: steak and kidney pie.

Opening the door for him, she explained, 'This is your room. There's a bathroom adjoining it, and there's a sitting room downstairs where other guests spend their evening. No smoking, though'.

'That's great – no smoking suits me. I'm Allan by the way. What's your name?'

'Leanne McDonald. My mother owns this place'.

'I will probably drive around for a while to get to know the area, pick up a bite to eat, join the other guests, have a bath, and go for an early night. Do you fancy coming with me for a drive later? I don't know this place at all'.

She smiled, but shook her head, and said, 'No, I'm working 'till very late, then I'm up early for breakfast'. Pleased with this initial contact, he asked the assistant, 'I will just make a quick phone call home, where is the payphone?' She pointed to the payphone in the hall, and after making sure no one else was within earshot, he telephoned his girlfriend.

'Hi there, it's me I'm missing you already and totally miserable without you, I don't know when next I will get home, but I will try to phone you every day either from the office or from here'. After talking at length, he decided to conclude so he could go out for something to eat. Allan freshened up and went for a drive.

'Nothing much to see here', he thought. 'Just cows, dung, and tractors'. So, back to the B&B he went. At the B&B, Allan went through to the lounge to join the other guests, with the smell of the countryside still clinging to his nostrils. 'Oh, you don't see many inglenook fireplaces these days', he said to a fellow guest. The fireplace had many old-fashioned artefacts around it, such as a copper bed warmer, poker in a brass coal bucket, and one of those boot scrapers for getting farmyard mud off which Allan thought should have been left at the door outside. In the corner, there was an old bearded man enveloped in a thick cloud of pipe smoke; the smell of which Allan found very tempting, but he did manage to resist. It turned out this man was a retired shepherd; a relation of some sort to the owner. He intended to spend the rest of his days here. Allan smiled when he saw the old man's black and white collie lying restfully at the shepherd's feet, who had one hand on a closed newspaper and the other on his pipe. He looked dangerously close, as usual, to falling asleep and dropping the pipe, but he never did. The rest of the guests were a few holidaymakers and a number of refinery workers. Allan watched television for a short while and sometimes chatted with some guests , then went off to bed after hearing the news at ten.

The next morning, he wakened to the smell of a nicely cooked breakfast being prepared. So, he jumped out of bed, had a quick wash, and got dressed. He told Leanne that he would see her that evening, and headed off for his rendezvous at the sports centre, hoping to meet his contact from work this time.

Stepping outside, he shivered. Although it was a bright sunny morning, there was a crisp nip in the air which reminded him of an old uncle who used to like the cold mornings. He liked a dram or two as well.

As he drove into Strathmanor, he was immediately hit by the same fumes which he thought he would have to get used to eventually and hopefully not notice before too long and drove straight to the sports centre, which he found easily as it was in the centre of Strathmanor. It was a relief to Allan, as he still didn't know the town very well.

'Great!' he thought. 'That must be him', as he looked at the tall and slim, curly-haired man in an old crumpled suit, standing next to the parked car that was already there.

Shaking hands, he was greeted by, 'Hi, you must be Allan. I'm Ivan Dapper. I've been sent to meet you, and take you back to the office. I hope you worked out, that yesterday was a public holiday, and you didn't turn up waiting to meet me?'

'No, no, I realised that. Don't worry, I'm not that daft', he lied. They both went back to their cars, and Allan followed Ivan closely to the refinery where their office was situated.

They stopped off at the checkpoint gate, with Ivan speaking to the smiling, moustachioed, sweaty gatekeeper, who wrote out a temporary entrance pass, and said to Ivan, 'Give this to your mate and tell him to keep it on his dashboard. He won't get in without it'. Ivan did as he was asked, and told Allan to follow him as they drove the short distance to the offices.

They went into the office, and Allan was introduced to everybody: there were two David's; a Tommy; a Curtis; a Gregor, sometimes called Andy for a laugh, as his second name was McAndrews; a Wilson; a Derek; an Ivan; and a Geophrey and some others out on site,but most pleasingly was a blonde typist, Gemma, about his age who he immediately thought made this whole job even more appetising.

Allan was told exactly what his company was doing, and what he was expected to handle (job description). 'This all seems quite straightforward', he thought, 'and everyone is friendly'. As luck would have it, it seemed he would be sharing an office with Ivan and Geophrey.

Ivan said, 'I'll take you out, and show you the site after lunch where all the buildings are, and where all the engineers will be. It's a large site; wherever you may be; within this vicinity, you'll see the flare stacks, which would serve as your bearings in case you get lost'.

When asked if he smoked, Allan said, 'Yes, I was told you must only smoke outside, and not in the office'. Then Allan added, 'Well, actually, I've just stopped, so that shouldn't be a problem'.

'Good', said Ivan, 'we'll have a coffee while you get your desk sorted, then we'll go round the site'.

Over the coffee, Allan, looking at the TV times, said, 'Oh good, *Charlie's Angels* is on tonight. I like that blonde one. Well, actually, they're all nice'.

To which Ivan agreed, 'Especially the one with big hair'.

'Right, that's us then', said Ivan. 'I'll take you around the main building and show you where things are. Especially the typing pool – there are eight typists', he said dreamily. 'I'll probably take you there the first time myself'.

Allan smiled knowingly, and asked, 'Who's that Gemma in our office, though? She seemed nice'.

Ivan nodded and agreed, but said, 'She's only a temp. We don't know how long she'll be here. Besides, you don't shit on your doorstep'.

The two got up and went out to Ivan's car. On the way, Allan stuck his head in Gemma's room, and said, 'Hi, I'm Allan, the new start. I'm just off out with Ivan. I'll say hello properly when I get back'.

Giving her a wave which she returned, Allan hurried out to the car, when Ivan said, 'Come on, Allan – let's get going'. As they drove over to the main building, Ivan told Allan, 'They are very fussy about adherence to the prescribed speed limits on this site, so be careful, always'. Ivan spent some time with Allan just driving around the site, pointing out the various offices, and finally pulled up outside a large building near the gate. 'This is the main building where all the engineers are, and there are many girls in the typing pool.

You'll be in and out here as much as you are in our own office'.

After some time, Ivan looked at his watch, and said, 'I best go back to our office now, and I'll leave you with the Boss for the two of you to decide a few things'.

They both went back in, and the Boss said, 'I'm sorry I couldn't be with you, but I had a great deal of calls to make which couldn't be helped. My diary is clear now, so we'll all go to lunch and when we come back, the two of us can have a pow-wow about the operations here, and how we'll organise things'. At that, everyone in their rooms traipsed out to the cars.

With two full carloads, they set off to the canteen which, being so well subsidised, Allan made a pig of himself in thinking, 'If I eat enough here, I won't need much tea when I go home tonight'.

Everyone had their lunch over small talk; Allan, as the new boy, being the centre of attention, asking loads of questions, and answering just as many as they all got to know each other.

Just as everyone was leaving to go back to the office, Allan looked back, surveyed the canteen girls, and said, "Well, this place should satisfy anyone's appetite'.

Back in the office, the Boss told Ivan to take Allan around the site tomorrow: 'Show him where the engineers are, introduce him to a few people that he will be working with, and generally, let him get a feel for the place. This afternoon, introduce him to the people at this side of the site', he requested.

Ivan said, 'I've already done half of that, so it shouldn't take long tomorrow. You should enjoy it here, Allan. Lots of girls, plenty of cheap food, and some great guys to work with – especially the Boss'. Smiling with approval, they both went to the adjoining building to meet with the others from this side of the site.

'Hi girls, this is Allan, our recruit. I'm just showing him around this block, Ivan said to the girls. 'Allan, meet Tracey and Anna'.

'Pleased to meet you', said Allan with a broad smile, and shaking both their hands with a firm grip. They left the secretaries and went through to the big adjoining office.

'This is *Derek Tate'*, Ivan said. 'He works for us, but in this big office. All the rest in here are refinery engineers'. Allan looked around the large open-plan office, and the disappointment at seeing it was all males, was very visible on his face.

Ivan nodded in agreement, and said, 'I know. Not very interesting in here really, but them's the breaks'.

Shrugging his shoulders, and with a sad look on his face, Allan said that he couldn't agree more. Feeling somehow cheated, he followed Ivan back to their own office.

In their own office, they met Gregor McAndrews, who asked, 'Have you told Allan about our nights out and other things?' Ivan said, 'Give me a chance, Andy. We're going to have a pub crawl in Edinburgh on the not-so-distant horizon'.

They usually took turns to be the designated driver using the Bosses eight-seater. Another thing he was told to look forward to was what they called the 'Super-rats' competition. This was based on television's Superstars. Everyone chose two sports or games.

These games were played over lunchtimes during the summer. Dominoes was a substitute for the Bosses, 'Who Can Whisper the Loudest' which, although causing much mirth and merriment from the others, was decreed to be not sports-like enough, and was overruled. Then, Ivan went on to agree on the complicated sports scoring system.

Gregor McAndrews said, 'Slow down, I have not yet quite ascertained that' to which you are alluding'. And Curtis responded, " 'Really? I just haven't got a clue'.

Allan put his name down for the tennis, the penalty shoot-out, and the one-mile race. This would all be done in the sports stadium.

The rest of that afternoon was spent drinking coffee, chatting to the rest, and briefly discussing how socially active together the office was. Allan was especially excited to hear that the Boss was a real ale fan, very enthusiastic, and took great pride in his own home-brew, and loved when anyone came to his house to sample it.

When he saw the Boss put down shove, ha'penny, and dominoes as his chosen games, he thought to himself, 'This could be good. I'm obviously a lot younger and hopefully fitter than these guys.' He jumped in, and said, 'I have lots of room in my house. We could all just crash out there after the pub crawl'. Ivan said, 'That would be good, as they all stayed at my house last time'.

When Allan said. 'I just stay along the road. Just opposite the police station'. When he made this offer, Ivan and Andy just stared at each other blankly. 'Well,' one of them said, 'It's time to go home. See you in the morning'.

They all went and cleared their desktops for the night, and Allan headed out to buy a fish supper for his tea which he ate in the car, while listening to the radio. 'After all, I will go back on Friday to tell everyone about my week'.

CHAPTER THREE

Home for the Weekend

Friday morning Allan awoke bright and breezy. Again, it was to the smells and sounds of sizzling sausages, bacon, and eggs being prepared for all the guests. 'Time for a quick shower before I go down for breakfast'.

He dried himself down, got dressed, splashing the last of his Christmas aftershave on, then he looked into the mirror making sure he was presentable, down he went to the dining room.

As he passed the payphone, he decided to phone Celia,

'Hi, it's me', he said to her mother. 'Just a quick call to Celia as I am in a rush, its just to say it's breaking my heart down here without her'.

'Well, I'll stop you there then', said her mother, 'Cecilia is not in. She wanted to get to work early so she could leave sharp to get to the pictures with a friend'. 'Oh right' said Allan, 'That'll be nice. Who is she off with and what's the film?'

After a long pause to think, her mother said 'It's a romantic comedy but I don't think she said, It's whom'. As he hung up, he stared at the telephone for a few seconds thinking before continuing to the dining room.

As he sat down to his breakfast, he asked the waitresses what they were up to this weekend, told them he was going back home to Dundee, and blethered some small talk to other guests.

Taking an interest in the inglenook fireplace again, he mentioned to the landlady that it was rare to see those these days, except in big old houses like this. Allan paid the landlady in cash, which pleased her, as she said, 'I prefer cash, it's a lot handier. Thanks'.

Glancing at his watch, he said laughing, 'Well, I best make tracks for the office, as I'll have to go to the bank for more money now since you've just cleaned me out'.

She smiled kindly as she put the money in her handbag, patted it, and said, 'Well, thanks very much, and if you need to come back at short notice again just give me a call. If I don't answer, one of the other girls will see you're alright'.

'That sounds great. Thanks very much. I'll call you if anything goes wrong with my house. Here's my number and address. Give this to the girls, and tell them to pop in anytime if they're in the area'.

She looked at the piece of paper, and looking quizzically into Allan's eyes, said, 'Oh, right... I'll do that', and put it in her apron pocket.

Thinking that she was trying to protect her daughters from him, as soon as she had turned her back, Allan tapped one of the girls on the shoulder, and said, 'Thanks, I'm off now. I may be back here, I'm not sure, but it would be great to meet you for a drink either way. Here's my office number. Please phone me during the week'.

Angela looked at the phone number which he had just given her, and said eagerly, 'Right, you're on. That's a definite'. Smug with himself, he bade them all farewell, picked up his suitcase to put in the boot, and put his jacket on the back seat so it wouldn't get crushed.

'Can't let anyone see me in a crumpled suit'. Allan then looked at the cigarette packet, and said to himself, 'Soon as I get there, they're in the bin'.

Fifteen minutes after leaving, the familiar smell which he was beginning to get half-used to by now, announced his arrival into Strathmanor. Looking up at the flare stacks, he wondered whether or not one of the girls would actually phone him. 'Hope so', he said to himself.

He stopped at the barrier, and handed his entrance pass to the gatekeeper, who nodded and said thanks, and waving him on, opened the barrier.

A few cars were already parked outside the office, and a quick look at the clock on the dashboard showed him he wasn't late. Reaching into the back seat of his car to get his jacket, he smiled and said hello to Gemma as she pulled her blue escort next to him. Jokingly, he said to her as they walked in together, 'Well, that's another week over. Have you any plans for this weekend?'

She smiled back, and said, 'No, not really. Probably just stay in the house and watch TV or maybe go and visit my gran. What about you?'

'Out with a few mates, around the pubs, and visit my Gran as well, and get my washing done while am home', Allan said with a smile.

'I hope you will be taking some flowers back home for your Mum if she's doing your washing?'

'Of course,', said Allan. 'Women always like flowers, don't they?'

'Yes, well, I know I do', smiled Gemma. 'When do you move into your new house?' she asked, 'You must pop around some evening'. said Allan 'When I get more settled, I'll tell you the address'.

'No, it's okay, I know the address. I heard the lads talk about it'.

He opened the entrance door to the office, waved Gemma in, and said, 'That's good. We'll do that soon then because I'll get lonely to start with, in this new town'. Following her into the offices, he said good morning to everyone as he went straight to his room, then joined the Boss.

'Well, that's your first week nearly finished. What do you think? Do you think you will enjoy it?' he asked.

'Yes, it's been great!' said Allan. 'You have a great team working here; all very friendly, and I can many possibilities here', he said with a grin. 'I'll go now and finish that paperwork you gave me yesterday'.

'Yes, that's great', the Boss said. 'Then, we can all go to The Drovers Arms Hotel for lunch. Could you drop Ron off at the airport after that, and just carry-on home for the weekend, and I will see you on Monday?'

'Yes, I have my suitcase in the car anyway, so I won't need to come back to pick it up'.

'That's what I like to see – you're well organised', said the Boss.

I'll fill up my tank with petrol on the way to lunch so that afterwards we can just get straight on the road to the airport'.

Allan finished off his paperwork, made a few phone calls, and lunchtime was upon them. They all went in a few cars over to the canteen. All except Allan; he took his own car, as he was to get off immediately after lunch.

There was a beautiful selection as usual in the canteen, with everyone making full use of the subsidised prices. Allan offered to carry Gemma's tray over to the table where everyone else was sitting at and asked her on the way what she watched on television last night. 'I didn't, I was at my Gran's. What TV shows do you watch?'

'Well, I find things like Mastermind, Panorama, Man Alive to be interesting. You know, things that make you think'.

Amongst the dull noise of idle chatter, one voice was heard over them all. 'Who is that loudmouth guy?' asked Allan.

'Oh, that's one of the engineers. A perfect know-it-all, he is. I don't think he likes us very much'.

At the mention of engineers, a discussion started up about how nice some of the other ones were. The engineers seem to keep themselves to themselves more than the lads in Allan's office, who were obviously much more socially active together, as he had been told. Allan took this opportunity to ask Gemma how she got on with the engineers.

'Well, they're all very polite, especially the good-looking one in the main building'.

Hearing this, Allan immediately felt pangs of jealousy, and asked, 'Do you fancy him then or do you have a lad anyway?' This was a subtle way of prying to find her availability for when the moment arose.

Allan didn't take the dessert of peaches, ice cream and jelly, saying to Ron, 'Just take your time, and I'll pick you up in a few minutes, as I have a small errand to run. I'll meet you back at the office in 20 minutes'.

He immediately ran out to his car, and drove to the precinct and bought two bouquets, then hurrying all the way, he got back to the office just before the rest arrived giving him just enough time to leave one of the bouquets on Gemma's desk.

He went back outside and met Ron, saying, 'Right then, we can shoot off now. See you all on Monday morning, guys', as he set off for the airport, then home.

The road was quiet with few hold-ups, and they were at the airport in plenty of time. Ron was dropped off, and Allan headed back to Dundee to see his family. He tooted his horn to Davie Brenson as he saw him coming off the bus, indicating with his left hand that he would give him a call. Just as he was pulling up outside the house, his Mum appeared, coming out of a neighbour's house. 'Oh, that's good timing', she said, giving him a bag of messages to carry in. 'Come in and tell us all how your week was. I'll just start the tea'. As Allan took his dirty laundry out of the suitcase, the phone rang, and as luck would have it, it was Davie phoning. 'Fancy going to Squeezers tonight?' 'Yes, that sounds great. I've never been to that club. Let's try our luck there for a change'. Allan hung up, and as everybody else came in, shouted to his Mum, 'I'll have a quick shower, Mum, and get ready for going out/nip over to see Gran before going to thepub! So, I'll just eat, then make a quick get-away!''Okay', said Mum 'We are not waiting for Tilda, she is seeing someone about a new job'. 'You'd think that she would get a new job quickly with all her qualifications, what does she have again?' ' An "O" grade' laughed dad. 'Well, she did her best', said Mum. 'Hmm, what is it in though?' said Allan. 'Woodwork' answered dad bluntly.When Alistair sat down at the table, he said to Allan, 'I see you're all poofed up for a night out. If you lend me a tenner I'll drop you off in town so you can have a drink'. 'Sounds good', he said. 'Pick up Davie, and drop us off in the town'. 'What about that thing you were seeing?' butted in Ronald. After a long pause, Allan said that she'd phoned him in the afternoon to say she wasn't well, so she was staying in.

Mum gave him a dirty look and said, 'She's a lovely girl and her name is Cecilia, not a thing', and then turningto Allan, she said 'And you, why are you not going over to see her?' Allan took a sip of tea to give himself some thinking time and then said ' Ehh, I think, hmm, it might be the mumps that she has got. It was very difficult to understand her, so I won't bother her with a call just now and it's probably best if you don't either'. Allan gave his brother the car keys, and saying cheerio to everybody else. He asked Ronald what he was up to that night. 'Well, I'm off doing a disco with Ally Fagg, so could you drop me off on the way?'

'Okay, but hurry up. I don't want to be late'.

Alistair quickly put his jacket on, and seeing the look on Ronald's face, said, 'I didn't think you'd mind if I wore your jacket. At least it will smell of decent aftershave; not that crappy stuff you've pinched off Dad'.

'Who stole what from me?' came a booming voice from another room.
'Oh, nothing at all, Dad', was unanimously chorused back.
'We're off now'.
'Cheerio now, and you all be careful out there', called Mum from the kitchen sink. 'I'll do your washing tonight and iron it first thing tomorrow before you are ready to go back, I'll be up early anyway, and thanks for the flowers'.
'Thanks, Mum. I'll see that you are alright in my will', said Allan.
'That's me off to see my grands, I'll probably be home late from the pub', said Allan as he was closing the front door, 'so don't wait up, then added with a laugh, I may be gone for some time'.

Halfway down the pathway he heard Ronald calling
'could you drop us off in the town?'
by the time he had reached his car both of his brothers had caught him up and asked to be dropped off.

On the way, Alistair said exactly where they were going to that night and told Allan not to go there and cramp their style. After dropping them off outside Fat Tuesday's night club, he headed off to see his first gran.

As he drove into her car park he could see her outline through the kitchen window and her cheery pleasant face. Gran opened the door and said smiling 'oh hi Allan, I didn't expect you', she said excitedly, 'come in and tell me all about your new job'. After wiping his feet and giving his gran a hug he followed her to the living room, 'I can only offer you biscuits with a cuppa as I can't bake like your other gran can', Allan took a ginger nut and assured her that it didn't matter, as it was just a fleeting visit to say hello, and he was meeting friends later, he told her about some of the characters he was working with and how he missed back home .

'That reminds me', said his gran 'I have an electric blanket for you in case your cold during the long lonely nights'.

Another two ginger snaps, later gran asked 'what will we do with Tilda?' I hear she's been fired again' when Allan feigned a surprised look, gran told him that, apparently, she had been sacked from a hotel where she had been working as a chamber maid.

She had been trying to squeeze a double duvet into a single cover and put a single cover in the double, when the manager came in and said "I've been watching you from the corridor, you are making a right hash of that. She was very flustered by now and said "but you could help me instead of just standing there criticising'. When he pointed out that he was the general manager. Tilda just said 'Yes, and am the General Dog's body, so If you don't help me , you'll end up in a duvet cover yourself'. That was when the general manager lost his temper and said, 'any more and you'll be sacked. She just looked at him with a stern face and said. 'No, any more from you and I'll just walk out', and he said 'that will be a shame because you are a hard worker and turn your hand to anything we ask of you'. Instead of listening to him, she gave the ultimatum of, 'well, treat me with a bit of respect instead of just looking down your snotty nose at me'. 'I take it that's when she got the sack'. 'Sounds just like her gran, but I'll need to love you and leave you now, I have to drop this off at my other grans'. The two walked over to the door where gran pecked him on the cheek and he ran down stairs to his car and drove over to his other gran.

Allan saw his gran peering through the curtains when he pulled up outside the chip shop that was across the road, waving to his gran's neighbours, he rang her doorbell.

'Hi Allan, come in your mum just phoned to say you were on your way, I've got some new bed socks here for you, I've heard your house is very cold'. He took the bed socks and put them in beside his electric blanket.

'I was just about to have a cup of tea, so stay and have one with me. I was baking this afternoon, so have a scone and a chat'.

As Allan spread some butter on one, he shouted through to the kitchen, 'can you bring through some of your own strawberry jam please?'

Gran brought through a tray with pan cakes, and the jam, and a fruit loaf which was rapped in a tea towel in a tin.

'You could take these home to Strathmanor with you, I've put some jam and marmalade with it, we all worry in case you don't eat enough when you're through there'.

Allan switched off the television to which gran said 'That's better, its only a distraction anyway'. The settee had two or three tins on it, which gran told him were for some other members of the family.

'The big one in the middle is for Celia. How is she now anyway, over the mumps I hope?' Allan looked to the ceiling for a few seconds, 'she doesn't speak very much about it, I may pop over to see her tonight', and looked at his watch.

'Are you in a hurry dear?' asked his gran, he assured his gran he wasn't, but that he was meeting some friends later so couldn't stay for too long, 'that's okay' said gran. 'We'll just have another cup of tea then you could drop me off at Phil and Jess'. Phil was grans younger brother who lived just round the corner. So when they finished up, they put their coats on and left with the tins.

He dropped his gran off and declining there invitations to come in for a drink, he left them and set off to meet his friends.

As he pulled into the car park of the hotel, he muttered an obscenity under his breath when he realised it was full. He decided just to park the car on the double yellows at the entrance of the hotel and chance his luck. 'No one should mind', he thought at this time of night.

'Is that you back for the weekend Allan?' said the receptionist as he walked quickly to the bar door. 'Most of the usual crowd are in already, its filling up quite nicely'.

As he opened the door to go down the few steps he felt good already, back into his old familiar haunt. 'Hi Allan' called the bar maid, as she started pouring him a pint in a jug with a handle as usual. By the time he had got to his seat at the far end his beer was ready, so he took up his seat.

'Thanks' he said and started to sip his beer. 'What about me Allan'? Said a solitary figure from the game machine 'Oh yes and one for Jim as well then'. Jim was an old regular who'd been drinking here for years, he was more of a pain to everybody else than a friend to be embraced. 'If you can lend me a tenner Allan I'll buy you one back before I go'. Allan handed over the money and looked round for someone else to speak to. When he saw Harry he lifted his pint and went over to join him.

Harry was with a group of others who all sat together every Friday night in Churchill's. "'Bet you're glad to get away from him', said Steve, pointing in the direction of Jim. 'Yes he's better off over there with the bear and holding on the game machine. Apparently he's been in here all day as usual'.

Steve looked up and saw Freddie coming over with a tray of beer. 'Hi Allan', he said, 'I'm glad to get away from that waster what will we do tonight?'. After thinking for a while, Allan said that he was easy and happy just to stay here. The others looked at each other and then agreed that could be a good idea. Andy started drinking his pint and said 'Why don't we try out Fat Tuesdays, that's usually quite good'. Allan shook his head, and said, 'no, anywhere but there, that's where my brothers are going, I don't want to see them tonight'.

The bar maid shouted over all most on queue, 'Your brothers were in earlier and they left quite drunk, so don't go to Fat Tuesday's, that's where they're off too'.

Some of the others suggested maybe they should go there just to annoy them. "No, they're the last folk I wanna see tonight". Most of the others agreed, they decided just to go along with Freddie's suggestion to stay here all night.

'There's not much life in here though lads, no girls or any talent'. Everyone looked around and agreed. 'Lets have a bet to see how long Jim lasts before he's thrown out', said Steve. Allan stood up and said 'Someone distract him while I get another round'.

Harry went over to distract Jim while Allan bought the next round.

When he sat back at the table, Steve said that the guys at the next table had said that they were going to a party and they were welcome to come with them. It was up at the nurses flats near the hospital but they decided just to wait and see.

'Did I hear a party being mentioned', shouted Jim from the far end. 'I'm right in the mood for a party'. 'No, we were talking about the Conservatives', said Freddie and Jim looked away.

'No Jim' shouted April behind the bar, 'you cant have another pint on your tab'. 'We don't do tabs in here you know that'. Jim put on a fake hurt look and said 'well I'll just go home then', 'If I collect some empty glasses for you will you give me a free pint'. 'No Jim, just go home' said April.

As the dejected Jim trudged slowly to the exit, April rang the last bell. 'Times up lads, that's your lot' she shouted, then turning to Allan's table said quietly, 'You lads are okay to stay behind, I've not seen Freddie and Allan for a while, we'll have a lock-in tonight'. When the bar had emptied, all except Allan's table, April came over to join them and bought the first round. One by one they each bought a round and they lost track of time and continued drinking the early hours when a duty manager came in and furiously shouted: 'You lot should have been out of here hours ago, we could lose our license'. They all went to the reception to get taxis home, with Allan telling the receptionist that he would be back to collect his car in the morning.

Despite the frequent request from his mother to get up he just stayed in bed all day nursing his hangover until eventually he went down for some tea.

'I think I will stay in tonight mum and have an early night, I am going out with Davie Brenson tommorow night'. After tea, he called Celia then went back to bed.

CHAPTER FOUR

Setting Up

The next day he just lounged around the house until it was time to meet Davie. Turning to his brothers he asked Alistair if he would drop him and Davie off in the town centre. Ronald chipped in asking if he could come for the drive. At that, they went to the car and drove around for Davie.

Davie was ready and waiting, and ran out to the car as soon as it pulled up. 'Let's go to the Epsom for a quickie, then take it from there', he said.

When they got to the Epsom, Allan said, 'Be careful with my car and don't do anything he would do', pointing to Ronald.

The Epsom was an old-fashioned pub, so they had one pint and decided to go somewhere more lively. Allan said, 'I had hoped there might have been some student nurses in there tonight. So, let's check out Churchill's, then onto the disco. I noticed you eyeing up that girl next to me, so I hope you're on form tonight'.

'So do I', said Davie, as they emptied their glasses then quickly went across the road to Churchill's.

Once inside, a quick look around proved this could be more fruitful, so they ordered a couple of drinks and nodded to a regular at the end of the bar who looked a bit the worse for wear. There was no response from him as he rested his head on his arms on the bar.

'He has been sitting there all afternoon, I can't get him to go home', said the barmaid. They looked at him perched precariously on his barstool and laughed; when he lifted his head to look all around the bar to see who it was they were talking about but did not see anyone who fitted the description. |He was about to go back into the resting pose when Allan said, 'Is that you out for a session Jim?' Jim blew out his cheeks then shaking his head, said, 'No, I'd be glad when I've had enough. I'd be off soon, so I'll just have another couple then go off home'.

Davie said hello to two guys they both knew, and told them they were off to Squeezers which drew a dirty look from Allan, as he felt these two may prove to be unwanted competition. Nevertheless, he ignored the others and spent some time chatting up two girls in the corner. Making sure that they knew what disco Allan was going to, he bought them both a drink, then spoke to some other girls at the bar, and as soon as he thought his possible competition wasn't looking, he agreed with Davie to slink off for a drink at the Directors on the way.

They hurried quickly across the road to The Directors, pleased to get in out of the wind. This was a newly refurbished pub, and many youngsters used this as the final watering hole before a disco or a club. Spotting a couple of girls in the corner, Davie said, 'They'll be going to Squeezers as well. Let's just finish these and go in'.

Allan finished his drink, and put the two glasses on the bar, and smiled inwardly because he was pleased to see the girls had noticed his helpfulness.

'Come on, Davie. Are we going to Squeezers, or are you happy just to stay here and speak to them?'

'No, right – I'm coming. Might see you there, girls'.

They both looked in a shop window on the way, commenting at the mannequins: 'Well, I wouldn't be seen dead in that', laughed Davie.

At the next window, they laughed, and said, 'Who would go out wearing that? That's the kind of thing you'd expect teachers to wear'.

At the next window, full of chef outfits, Allan laughed, and said, 'That's just like a mate of mine Hutty – only that those looks less vacant'.

Reaching the shop doorway where two policemen were watching the revellers, Allan said, 'And that's just plainly ridiculous'. After a few minutes of apologising and trying to convince the very angry policemen that it was only a joke, Davie tugged Allan away, and they moved on to Squeezers.

When they got into the nightclub, they smiled and said hello to the check-out girl at the entrance, who had been at the same school as them. 'Can't keep you guys away from here, can we? Is that you being home for the weekend?'

Nodding in affirmation, Allan handed in his jacket and climbed the stairs to the disco. It was nearly full and they bought a drink, sat at the only empty table, then decided to go for a dance. Nonchalantly, they walked over to two girls dancing in a group around their handbags and tapped them on the shoulder. Davie gave them a nod, which was the customary signal for the girls to interpret this gesture as, 'Would you care to honour me with the next dance, ma'am?' The girls agreed, and so Davie continued to give his impersonation of a man with a very sore leg trying to do the jitterbug, or at least that's what Allan would say.

Halfway through the first dance, Allan turned to Davie, and said, with a smile and a wink to the girls, 'Have you got a groin strain?' The girls just raised their eyebrows and continued dancing.

'No', said Davie with a frown.

'Then why are you dancing like that?'

Quick as a flash, Davie replied with; 'Just to make you look good'.

'We have a table over there, girls. Would you like to come over for a seat?' Allan asked.

'No, no, don't bother. There's a nice slow song coming on. Can we dance to that?'

Two or three slow dances later, and they appeared to have clicked. Davie laughed out loud, and gestured to everyone at some older lady, 'Mutton dressed as lamb', Allan called her, that was all dressed up to the nines carrying a tray full of drinks along by a row of tables on the far side.

She was looking at her reflection, in the full-length mirror and obviously didn't realise it was herself stepping from side-to-side, to avoid what she thought was an oncoming patron.

With one eye watching carefully the mirror and the other on her tray, she tottered on her platforms further along the passage, until smack!

She was stopped in her tracks. Not realising she had just walked into the mirror, she looked around with a dazed expression, got her bearings, then hobbled off out of sight.

'As I was saying', said Allan, 'Would you like to join us at the table?' They all went over and sat down. Allan was relieved to get a seat, as he was now quite breathless, and making a mental note to try to get himself fitter, he asked Davie to grab some drinks, as it was his round.

As the night went on, they all got friendly, and at the end of the night, they took the girls home. It transpired the girls shared a flat, and after a long hard drinking session, they all fell asleep in the living room.

When they woke up in the morning, Allan, disappointed that they had squandered a golden opportunity, tried to make amends by saying, 'We had a great night. Could we do it again sometime when I'm back in Dundee?' Exchanging phone numbers, they all agreed to phone each other soon, even if it was just for a chat.

'Right, Woogie we best make a move', Allan said.

'Why do you call him Woogie?' asked one girl.

'Ah, that's a long story', said Allan. 'At school, the Music teacher asked what animal does this signify in *Saint Saens Carnival of the Animals* and he stuck his hand up first and said it's the Boogie Woogie.

When all the laughter in the classroom died down, she then said "ok Brenson, come out and draw this creature the Boogie Woogie on the board, does it look like a curdlie wuddlie by any chance or even a Scarey Weary?"

He was actually the only one smart enough to know what a Boogie Woogie was in the first place, none of us had ever even heard of it before, so for evermore his nickname has been Woogie, "Thank you letting out that little secret Dopey" Why did he call you Dopey asked one of the girls, "Well it's a long story but very briefly in English class at school the teacher asked me which happened to be the part did I enjoy the most in Treasure Island?' 'That's right', said Allan. 'Then he said the end when it all was finished". When all the laughter settled down in the classroom, the teacher said, "Why do you always have to act so dopey" . "You only got to this school because you are smart. You have a very powerful brain, so use it"

Allan went on "we all called him dopey as a laugh for the rest of the day and when we got fed up with that, it had registered in our brains and it has been that ever since"'

'Well, thanks for keeping my secret', glared Davie, 'but I'll still keep yours a secret', he said, hurrying Allan out. Outside, Allan asked, 'What secret?'

'Oh, let me see. Could it be Gemma or Anna or any of the others at Strathmanor that you've talked about, or some you haven't even mentioned, any of the different girls you haven't told me about, or more importantly Celia? I don't know what she sees in you'.

In a good mood and still feeling flush, they decided just to get a taxi and head for home. In the cab, they sat quietly, and listened to the taxi driver asking the usual questions they ask: 'Have you guys anything planned for tonight?'

'No, nothing yet, but I'm sure someone will be having a party somewhere. We'll maybe just go there', said Davie. 'That girl you went out with two weeks ago; she's having a party. Let's turn up there and see what happens'.

'No, Davie. I'm not going. I need to leave for Strathmanor tonight. Let's go to Frankie's ice-cream shop for something to eat before we get home'.

'No, I don't feel like eating anything', said Davie. 'Maybe just an ice cream to take home for pudding tonight. That should make up for being out all night, eh?'

Since the shop was quite busy, they decided just to go in for a coffee. The seating area was spartan, but very clean and comfortable, nevertheless. Most of the other customers were in for the morning rolls and newspapers, so they just sat quietly waiting for some service.

An older lady who was serving came over with a notepad, and said, 'You lads look like you could do with a good breakfast. What will it be?' They sighed at the thought of eating and gave their order.

Turning to Davie, Allan said, 'I once went out with a girl that worked here. I remember her well. We used to come in because of her great squashers, lovely raspberry ripples, and she used to make my coke float. Very refreshing, with a cherry and two straws.

Woogie asked: "What are squashers?". 'They are marshmallow snowballs with ice cream', said Allan. 'Aye, the ice cream isn't as good in Strathmanor. And I remember you as well; your name's Bella, isn't it?'.

'Yes', said Bella. 'You're talking about my niece, and you were just as cheeky then as now. She sometimes reminds me whenever she mentions you. You and your mates used to sit all afternoon with one cup of coffee until you eventually got bored'. With that, she said, 'I'll tell her you were in today, and I'll give you a top-up here'.

They finished up, and went over to pay, saying goodbye to Bella, and leaving her a tip.

'Well, you're in a good mood, aren't you? You don't normally leave tips', said Davie.

'Yes, but let's get this ice cream home. Not a word to anyone about last night; I'm still partially seeing that girl from school'.

'Oh, you're not?' asked Davie.

'Well yes, you've got to keep your options open'. Adding, 'If no one knows, no one gets hurt'.

"Well, be careful, didn't your mum tell you not to snack between meals?"

'Oh quick, here's the bus. Let's get on fast'.

The bus was full of people going to work, going to do shopping, or visiting friends, and even some other stragglers making their way home. There was no one on the bus they knew, so they just got off at their stop, and walked the short distances to their houses.

50

Most members of the family were already up when Allan entered the house via the back door. 'Some girl phoned for you early this morning, so I just said you were out', said Alistair.

'That's fine, thanks', said Allan. 'I'll just pack my suitcase and head back to Strathmanor. That's the rain pelting down'.

Ten minutes later, he reappeared downstairs, and shouted, 'Well, that's me off, Mum! Thanks for the washing!'

'Okay, be careful. That's the rain on'.

The weather hadn't lightened up very much by the time Allan got to Strathmanor, but at least he knew exactly where the house was, so no chance of getting lost this time.

As he approached the house, Allan mulled over whether or not to have a drive around town, but it was late, so he decided just to grab a bag of chips from the chippy in the shopping precinct across the road.

Holding the chips close to him for the warmth, and to try and keep them dry, he ran back at full pelt to the car and drove the short distance back to his house. Luckily, the block of four houses of which one was his, was set back off the road, so a parking space was no problem.

Parking outside his house, he braved the weather, and took his suitcase and supper straight in, expecting some kind of refuge from the elements, and warmth in the shelter.

On opening the door, he found he was sadly disappointed; the damp, and stale coldness engulfed him. Shivering, although indoors, he put his suitcase down, and ran with his chips to the kitchen to put the kettle on for a hot drink. 'Ah, this is the life. I'll make a hot chocolate, and leave out my clothes for tomorrow'.

When he opened his suitcase to take out his clothes, on the top was a hot water bottle sneaked in by his Mum. Shivering, he said to himself, 'There must be a window open in here. I will have a quick look round'. Seeing the window was indeed closed, he pulled the curtains, and ran back downstairs for his chips, and to fill his unexpected hot water bottle.

The chips had hardly gone down when he swallowed his cup of hot chocolate, almost in one go. There was a warm sense of satisfaction within him knowing that on his own he could eat what and when he chose, without his Mum always harping on about one thing or another, his brothers or sister annoying him and getting in his road, and his Dad – well, just being a Dad.

This was definitely a cracking job. As he ran up the stairs with his hot water bottle to put in bed, he held it to his chest and thought the smell and warmth was a comforting reminder of home.

Putting his jacket on, he ran back downstairs and nipped across the road to have a quick pint, and to check out what he thought could be his local hostelry. Looking around the bare old-fashioned pub, he went to the bar and bought himself a beer.

Although he said good evening to a number of old regulars and the bar-tender, he was disappointed that no one responded, and felt really out of place. Allan tried to tease some conversation out of the bar-tender who seemed to be spending more time reading his paper than serving any of the others.

He offered the barman a drink which was refused and tried to strike up a conversation by saying, 'Well, I've just moved into the house across the road, and I don't really know many people, so I'll probably come in here quite often. My name's Allan by the way', offering his hand, but receiving only a limp handshake.

'Is that the house next to the doctors?' asked the barman.

'Yes, that's the one', said Allan, looking around, hoping this would maybe encourage some conversation, but the only response was a slow, 'Oh, right'.

Allan could sense that he wasn't very welcome here, and so he thought the place was just missing some sawdust and a spittoon; it seemed so unwelcoming. So, he just finished his pint, and put the empty tumbler on the bar, deciding to brave the elements and go home.

As he left the shelter of the pub, he put up his jacket collar, and tightened his scarf, remembering the weather wasn't nice. He ran quickly across the road, thinking the house he was going into looked more welcoming than where he had just left. With all the house lights on across the road, including his vestibule, he went smartly across the road through the busy traffic, and felt happy and safe that he was back home.

When he opened the door and walked in, he felt a bit warmer, but only because it had been raining outside, and the wind was picking up. It was certainly not because the house was warm, as it still felt freezing. 'Think I'll have myself a quick cocoa, and go to bed with a scotch'.

After checking that all the doors were locked, he stared out of the kitchen window at the rain pelting down. The clouds were being blown wildly across the sky as he stood mesmerised by the different shapes and sizes, trying to make pictures from them. 'Enough,' he thought. 'I Think I'll just go to bed with my bottle, and listen to the radio. I must try to make a point of speaking to that girl from Squeezers.'

Right away, he leaped back out. 'What on earth', cried Allan. 'This bottle is stone cold. Well, I'm not sleeping with a cold water bottle', and gritting his teeth, he went down to refill the bottle with piping hot water.

'This will do nicely', he said to himself. With his professional magazine in one hand and the bottle in the other, he ran upstairs to get into bed quickly, only stopping on the way to check again the front door was locked, just to make sure he was safe maybe a touch of OCD too.

Upstairs in the bedroom, he jumped into bed and opened his magazine. This was full of financial news, progress reports on various projects in his field up and down the country, economic growth reports, and some other extremely boring articles that he was supposed to take time reading and digesting. He hardly ever opened the magazine, but this one caught his interest because on the front cover there was a prototype sports car surrounded by some pretty models. Skimming through the pages, and finding nothing else of

54

very much interest, he just took a final swig of his scotch (purely for medicinal purposes), and drifted off to sleep.

Allan kept wakening; because he was feeling too hot throughout the night. He found that if he kept one arm out of the covers that would keep him cooler. After five minutes, he felt it was too cold, so covered back up. Another five minutes had pasts, and he was too hot again. 'What a palaver', he thought, so he took a swig from his bottle which he left at a convenient distance besides his pillow next to his shoulder, and tried getting some more sleep, while leaving his arm out.

A loud bang at the window woke Allan again. Lying there quietly, and wondering what the noise was, he stared at a shadow on the wall which was like a head looking into the bedroom window. As he was upstairs, and it was highly unlikely that someone would climb a ladder to peer at him in bed, he just ignored it.

He eventually plucked up the courage to turn around to face this apparition, or whatever it was. Slowly, he turned his head, until suddenly, there was a tap on his shoulder. He froze, and listened, but all he could hear was his breathing and pounding heartbeat. Out of the corner of his eye, he noticed the head's shadow was now moving slowly as well. Beginning to work his fear up into a frenzy, he turned to face the wall again in order to jump out of the bed and run downstairs. This time, as he sat there, the shadow was gone; it was simply his arm, and the head was now his clenched fist.

But what about the tap on his shoulder? Once he had worked out it was his bottle sliding down on the pillow, he cursed his stupidity, then finished the remainder of the bottle. But not before checking the window was securely shut and the curtains drawn, blocking out the reflection of the full moon.

Getting back into bed, Allan tucked himself up and tried to drain the last few drops from the bottle. After several hours just lying there and thinking, he finally fell asleep.

CHAPTER FIVE

Setting Up

The sound of someone trying and trying in vain to start a car wakened Allan just before his alarm was due to go off. 'Well now am awake' he thought 'I might as well make a start to the day', knowing that there would be coffee already waiting for him in the office, he just showered and dressed. 'I'll maybe come back at lunchtime and see if there is any mail', thought Allan. Hoping to be in the office sharply, he jumped in the car and set off down the drive way to join the long line of slowly moving traffic on its way to work.

The office was filled with the pleasing smell of filtered coffee that the first of his colleagues had made. The rule was: first in makes the coffee, and whoever finishes it makes the new batch. Simple, straightforward stuff. While he was pouring himself a cup, Gemma came in, smiled at him, and went straight to her office. 'Think I'll play it cool', he said to himself. 'I'll finish this, and wander in and see how her weekend was'. Allan finished his coffee and went into Gemma's office.

'Hi, Gemma, hope you had a good weekend. Did you do anything in particular?'

She smiled, and answered, 'Quite quiet, really. Spent some time with my gran, and just watched television. You?'

'No, not much. I don't know anyone down here yet. I was hoping your boyfriend might have taken you to the pictures, then you could have told me if it was worth going to see'.

'No, I've told you – I don't have a boyfriend just now, but there are a few good films on. I might go with a girlfriend', she said, sipping from a tin of coke.

'Well', said Allan, raising a hand, 'if you are free sometime maybe I could take you?'

'Well, I can't this week, but definitely sometime next week'.

'Great, then. I'll hold you to that, but keep it from the rest for now. I'm going back home again this weekend, so I'll have something to look forward to when returning here next week'. Allan then went around everyone in the office, and said to them, 'I'm off over to the main building with some reports. Does anyone want anything dropped off?'

Taking some things to drop off, he just got in the car when Anna, one of the typists from the adjacent offices, asked him, 'Could you take me over to the main building with you? I have some things to hand in to my father'.

'Yes, sure, jump in', he said to her, pleased at getting this opportunity to chat to the pretty young girl, especially when he discovered her father was in charge of the whole refinery.

'You don't mind me hitching a ride do ya'. 'No, of course not', he said 'It's a pleasure'. 'If you drop me here', she said, 'I could meet you back here in ten minutes once I've got a few filled rolls from the machine'.

The machine was free, so Allan took two for himself for the evening, and said, 'Just because they're free don't eat too many and ruin your fantastic figure'.

'Oh, thanks very much for the compliment', Anna said, smiling with embarrassment.

'Well, it's true', and he moved on to deliver the reports.

After delivering the reports, Anna was still nowhere to be seen, so he took the opportunity to nip into a room full of girls busily typing, and photocopying lots of paperwork and plans. 'Just popped in to see if you've anything for my lot I could take back over?'

'No, nothing', one of them said.

He was just about to sit down and chat for a bit, when Anna appeared, saying, 'Oh, there you are. Can we go now?'

Not showing his annoyance at being interrupted, he said, 'Sure, your wish is my command. Let's get going', and with a reassuring touch on her elbow, he ushered her to the door.

They both made sure they had the files and paperwork which they had come to collect, and put everything in the back seat of the car. Anna said that it was a nice car, and asked, 'How long have you had it?' Pleased that she liked the car, he told her he had only had it for a weeks, as it was a company car, hoping that this might impress her and make her think he was important.

'Any other time you want a lift, or even a drive after work, just come over and ask."

'I might take you up on that', she said.

'Well, that's good, and talking about after work – I haven't made any friends here yet, so how about the pictures one of these nights? Just let me know.'

'Well, that sounds good', she said, 'But I'm seeing someone at the moment, so don't let on to anyone'. With a smile on his face, he went back to his office.

'Allan', called his Boss. He went through to the other office, where the Boss said, 'You know when we all go out for a beer we tend to stick to real ale, as I'm a member of CAMRA, so I've brought in half a dozen bottles of my home-brew for you. It will give you something to savour on your long, lonely nights on your own'. And, smiling with a nod, he handed them over, adding, 'It's a new type of hops I'm using'.

Never having made home-brew himself, Allan took the bottles, saying, 'I might try this lark myself some time'.

As lunchtime approached, Allan got ready to leave swiftly to go to the shopping precinct to have a look around the home-brew shop.

After lunch, Anna called out to him as he was going into his office, 'Oh Allan, glad I caught you. If you are going over to the main office again can you take me over, as I have to see someone?'

Deciding just to go straight away, hoping no one else saw them, Allan reached over to put a cassette on, but no sooner had the music started than the tape suddenly stopped. He reached over to turn the tape to the other side thinking it had come to the end of the side but was a bit embarrassed when the tape which had got stuck, unravelled to the extent that he was left holding an empty cassette with yards of tape strewn between him and the dashboard. Anna laughed, and a very embarrassed Allan smiled back, even though it was his favourite tape.

As she got out of the car, Allan decided not to sit idle, just to wait in the car, but to have a wander around with her, just to acquaint himself with any possible targets needing his attention. Single girls of course. Unfortunately for him, there was no time to wander around, as she only had to hand in an envelope to a very stern, but an important-looking man on the top floor.

Five o'clock arrived, and Allan, deciding he would just pick up a takeaway for his meal, said goodnight to the rest, and went home. Settling down for the night, he thought to himself, 'This beer is not half-bad at all. I'll go over tomorrow to buy all the gear, and give this home-brew a real go'.

As soon as he was finished eating his takeaway, and after dumping the empty cartons in the bin, he settled down, and phoned home. 'Hi, Mum. How's everything back home?'

'Everything is fine here. Hope you're well. Your brothers are right here. They're looking very smart in their kilts and jackets. They're going to a wedding at the weekend, and they're wearing kilts. Here's one to say hello'. She gave the phone to one of his brothers, and they talked about the coming wedding.

'Mum said you are wearing kilts. Very smart and patriotic. I can't wait to see a photograph of the two of you. You'll bring the house down when folk sees your legs. What's the tartan anyway?'

'Oh, she'll be wearing white probably', said his brother with a laugh. Handing the phone back to his Mum, he added, 'I remember now why we're glad he's down there'.

Mum took the phone, and said, 'That was nice of you to say hello to your brother' and then asked, 'What did you have for your tea tonight? I hope you're eating properly, and not just junk?'

'Of course not, Mum. I cooked myself a meal from a recipe a girl at work gave me. Not as good as yours, but good enough. Even if I do say so myself.' 'Well just before you go, Tilda got a job as storekeeper in a builders yard', Allan shook his head and paused before he said that 'He hoped that one lasted'.

'Ah well, that's the thing, she's left after one day, it was the bad language apparently'. Allan laughed and said that 'he wouldn't have thought that will bother her', mum said 'But it was her bad language they complained about', 'right, I'll leave you now mum, I'll phone soon'

Putting the phone back and checking his watch, Allan went through to settle down in front of the television to watch the ten o'clock news. The news appeared to be all doom and gloom, and there was nothing very good on television that took his fancy.

After finishing his last bottle of ale, and enthusing as to how good it was, he sat bolt up-right, and slapping his thighs, he said out loud, 'That's it! It's late-night opening at the precinct. I'll nip over to that shop that sells all the home-brew kit'. Switching the TV off, he put his jacket on, and quickly ran over to the precinct.

The shops were quite busy, and approaching the one he was looking for, he sighed with relief on seeing it was open with no customers in it. A bell tinkled as he opened the door, and the assistant stood up and put her newspaper down. 'Hello there', she said, greeting him with a smile.

'I've just decided to make some home-brew of my own. I don't know anybody in Strathmanor and have no clue what to buy or how to go about it. Can you help me?'

'Yes', she said. 'I will help as much as I can'. She then set about pointing out all the equipment required. After a while, she said, 'That's about everything you'll need'.

Allan looked at the large display, 'That's a hefty amount', and looking at the bill, said, 'Oh! That's a lot more expensive than I thought'.

'That's everything, and you'll need it all. It's not too dear for you, is it?'

'Oh no! Not at all. With that smile, I know you're not out to do me', and smiling, he added, 'Unfortunately'. She looked at him quizzingly, wondering what exactly he meant by that.

'Now, if you need any more help or advice don't hesitate to come and ask'.

'Well, thanks very much. Maybe you could give me a hand to make it sometime, as I don't know what I'm doing?'

'Yes, sure that would be okay, as long as I can help you to drink it when it's made'. And with that, they exchanged telephone numbers, and Allan left with his multitude of gear.

Inside his house, Allan looked at the girl's name and phone number, and thought, 'Alice. Who the heck is called Alice these days?' and put her number on top of his phone book by the phone to remind him to call her the next day.

Just before his lunchtime at the office, Allan thought of phoning Alice to make arrangements for her to come around later to help. After making sure the rest had left for lunch, especially Gemma because he didn't want her to know what he was up to, he picked up the phone and called Alice at her work. 'Hi, it's me, Allan, If you're still up for helping me make the home-brew tonight I'll pick you up at six, and we'll do it'. She was quite conducive to this offer, and so, feeling very pleased with himself, Allan hurried over to the canteen to met the rest for lunch.

Most of the afternoon, Allan's mind drifted between his work and thinking of Alice. Wondering whether or not to go home for a quick shower, he looked at his watch, and seeing it was 5 P.M., decided there was no time, so he just left to go for her.

When he parked his car in his driveway, he ran in to put the hall light on; the house always looked more inviting that way. A smart BMW pulled up next door, and his next-door neighbours came out. They smiled and said hello. Allan commented on the recent changeable weather,and said 'You must have had some fun in bed the other night judging by the noise and laughter I heard through the wall, it must be paper-thin'. His neighbour shook his head and said 'You must be mistaken, we've been away for a few days and this is us just arriving now'. Allan smiled dryly and said, 'Alright I'll believe you, thousands wouldn't'. 'Well to change the subject, my brothers may come through on their own to visit me some time, I hope they behave and don't bother you'. The neighbours assured him they would not.

Alice was just locking up as he got there, so taking her by the arm, they walked to the Indian takeaway, and bought some curries for an easy tea. 'I live just over here, next to the doctors'.

Stopping in her tracks, Alice looked intrigued, and said, 'That house lay empty for a number of years'.

Nodding, Allan said, 'Yes, I know. That's probably why I got it so cheap'.

'Well, perhaps', said Alice, 'But let's get moving, and eat this before it goes cold'.

The pair hurried into the house, and as soon as Allan opened the door, they were hit by the usual coldness in the hall. 'It's okay; it's always cold as soon as I get in. You get the plates. I'll get the electric fire on'.

They sat down in the living room to eat their curries, Allan watching every move on her face, and picking up on the frequent eye contact. With a smile, Alice tapped Allan on the elbow, and said, 'Right, let's get down to it. Are you ready?'

'For what?' asked Allan, suggestively.

'Well, the home-brew. How, what did you have in mind?'

They spent the next few hours making the beer, with Allan saying, 'I won't be very good at it. I've never done anything like this before'. She assured him that she'd done it plenty of times before, so she would keep him right.

They decided to leave the preparation in a corner in the large kitchen, and she reminded him that when it was all ready, he needed to get her back to sample it. 'I won't be able to drink too much of it, though. I get drunk quite easily, and sometimes lose control', she said.

'Yes, we'll do that then', he said. 'I'll tell you when we need to do the next stage, but in the meantime let's have some of my Bosses stuff'.

'Yes, that seems a plan. I see you have a piano out there. Do you play?'

'No, but I think I might take lessons because I have plenty of free time'.

'Well, my cousin's a piano teacher. I'll bring her contact details the next time I'm here', Alice offered. 'She sometimes prefers to go to clients houses instead of her own'.

After much more flirting, and suggestive conversation between the two, Alice said, 'I feel quite light-headed already, so next time could we make a night of it, and I'll just sleep on the couch to save driving while being tipsy'.

'Yes!' Allan thought to himself. 'This could be the start of something good'.

By the time they finished their beer they had both become very friendly and tactile, and what turned out to be a quick departure peck on the cheek, turned into a good five-minute snog. Allan ran his hands down her back gently as they became even more closely entwined. Smiling inwardly to himself, as he realised she wasn't wearing a bra, he gradually and stealthily drew his hand down and to the front. Slowly, he was bringing his hand up to her pert bosom, and as he looked into her eager big blue eyes, he felt his passion rising.

Just as Allan was to lead her upstairs, the telephone rang. Instinctively, Alice picked up the phone, and curtly said, 'Hello? Yes, he's here'. Then, thrusting the handset over to Allan, she said, 'It's some girl for you'.

Allan took the receiver, and said, 'Well, I'm a bit tied up just now, but half an hour is okay. Bye'.

He looked up at Alice, saying, 'Bike', and put the phone back in the cradle.

Alice stepped back, and indignantly said, 'Well, I'll be off. I'll leave you to it', and stormed out, slamming the door.

Twenty minutes later, a girl arrived at the front door, and Allan brought in the racing bicycle he had ordered. Slightly disappointed that the delivery had interrupted what might have been,

Allan asked the delivery girl if she would like to come in for a cup of tea before she left. "No, I have a workmate in the car and we may go on to a night club". Allan looked into the car and saw someone with long dark hair in the passenger seat facing the other way reading a paper. Unperturbed Allan said just to bring her workmate in,"the more the merrier". Adrian shouted to the delivery girl. "Come in here for a quick drink before we go". Then Allan went to get some drinks leaving the door open for the workmate just to come in, he was absolutely horrified when her workmate a tall man with a ginger beard entered his house. So, Allan just gave the pair a cup of tea and quickly ushered them away saying that he didn't want to hold them up.

As soon as they had goneAllan finished the last two bottles, watched the news, and decided to give the pub over the road another chance.

Once again, there was a deathly hush as Allan opened the pub door and went in, ignoring the locals muttering under their breath. On his entrance, he just marched straight over to the bar Area. 'Oh, you are a new face around here', said the young attractive bar assistant. 'What would you like?'

With a smile and a glint in his eye, he asked for a pint of heavy.

As she poured his pint, Allan said, 'I'm new here. It's nice to see a pretty face behind the bar, instead of that greeting-faced bloke the last time. At least you've got a friendly face'.

Her smile broadened, as she laughed, and said, 'That greeting-faced old man is my Dad. I'm just helping out for the night, so stay awhile to keep me company; it's extremely boring with all these old codgers', as she nodded to the corner. Allan perched himself on a barstool near the till so he could speak to her more.

As the night wore on, Allan asked all his usual questions to find out more about her. She was great company and poured herself a drink along with Allan's next pint. 'It's fairly quiet now', she said. 'I'll come round the front and join you'.

He was captivated by her chat, and after a few more pints, he said, 'I'll be back in a flash. I'm just off to the loo'.

'Well, I don't suppose you'll be long', she said cheekily. Allan smiled and nodded, then eased himself off his stool. As he tried to stand up, he realised the position he had been sitting in had caused pins and needles, and his leg completely gave way. As he leaned forward to grab the wall on the way down to the toilet, he glanced at the girl, and missed a step, tumbling ungraciously down the full length of the stairs.

Immediately, Karen put her drink back down and rushed to Allan's assistance. 'Oh, that looked sore. Are you okay?' she asked, smoothing over his hair.

'No, I'm okay – just out of breath, and a little embarrassed'. 'Think I'll just head home now'.

Karen looked towards the door just as someone came in, and said, 'Ohh, that's my brother. He'll take over the bar while I take you home'.

'Yes', thought Allan. 'Things have turned out okay', and as she helped him up to his feet, she told her brother why she had to leave. She put her arm around Allan to keep him steady, and a very happy Allan left full of hope with Karen, for home.

As they both crossed the road, he tried to repair the damage he had done to his image, and they walked up to the front door, with Karen still lavishing the attention. At the front door, Allan's neighbour, who was just going past, called out, 'Evening, you been drinking too much again, Allan?'

He was about to explain things, when Karen said, 'Let's get you inside and sorted'. When they opened the door and got inside, an expectant Allan was disappointed to hear Karen say, 'That's you home safe and sound. I'll maybe see you over the road again, soon', and as Allan leaned forward to try and peck her on the cheek, she turned and ran back to the pub.

Pride damaged and body a little sore Allan decided just to go up to bed. Neatly tucked up in bed he was pleased to see his bottle within arms reach. As he unscrewed the lid and placed the bottle at his mouth he heard quiet muttering from downstairs 'Damn' he thought 'I must have left the television on all the while I was out' when he got back downstairs he was confused to see that the television wasn't on at all. Bewildered, he shook his head and turned to go back upstairs.

From the bottom of the stairs he could hear quiet giggling and with great trepidation slowly climbed the staircase, the giggling stopped as soon as he reached the landing and after looking in the spare bedroom door and seeing no one, went to his own bedroom which was also empty.

This is all very strange and spooky, thought Allan as he got back into bed. He had one last large swig and tried to drift off to   sleep   keeping   one   eye   open.

CHAPTER SIX

The Visitors

A shaft of early morning daylight was an unwelcome visitor as it found a way to penetrate a slit in the bedroom blinds. Rubbing his eyes and stretching, Allan woke up and looked out of the window to check the weather. Noticing dark clouds in the distance, he thought to himself, 'I hope the family gets down here safely'. His Mum, his Gran, and his brothers were coming down to spend the weekend with him in Strathmanor.

The telephone rang; it was his mother saying that they probably would be slightly later than they had arranged, as they were still about to pick up Gran as Tilda would be unable to manage because she is starting a new job in a baker's shop. He spent the next hour or so making arrangements and tidying up to the best he could, knowing that his Mum would move everything into, 'A more suitable position'. Still, he could always change it the minute they left.

Thinking that they would probably bring lunch with them, he just had a plate of porridge and did his last night's dishes. When the kitchen was suitably tidied up, he looked around hoping that would suffice, and went through to watch some television in disguise of waiting. He then sat up with a jolt, thinking, 'I suppose I better bring the washing in that; I left out all night in the rain'.

After bringing in the washing, and hanging it on an airer in the large kitchen, he sat back down to continue watching tv; until about two hours later, he jumped up again to answer the phone. 'Hi, it's me', said his Mum. 'We are in Strathmanor now, but we can't find your house, so we've just gone over to a cafe in the precinct. Maybe you could come over for us?'

'Yes, okay', said Allan. 'I'll leave the vestibule door open in case we miss each other'. Doing so, he ran across to the precinct, but could not find anyone; his brothers had found an arcade, and Mum and Gran were looking in a shop that had a sale on to keep out of the rain. After about ten minutes of looking everywhere but the correct place, he decided to go back home and wait for them to call again.

When he got to the edge of the precinct he saw across the road they were huddled in the vestibule. It looked quite inviting and warming, as he had left the hall light on, but it was still cold and windy. Ronald shouted at the top of his voice when he saw Allan, 'At last! I thought you had forgotten about us! Let's get in!'

Running across the road to open the door for them, Allan said, 'Well, it seems to be raining ever since I've been here. I put the kettle on before I came to look for you, so it shouldn't take long for you to make us a hot drink.

'You two – bring the cases in', Allan said to his brothers.

'We've just gotten here and he's bossing us already', said Alistair.

'Stop squabbling', said Gran. 'Just get inside and get warm'. They all went in and took off their coats, Allan put the fire on, Alistair and Ronald watched the television, and Mum joined Gran in the kitchen for a coffee. 'Mum, it's high time you phoned home to say you've arrived safely', said Allan.

'Oh, did you remember the Marmite, Gran?' Allan asked.

'Yes, here it is'.

'Okay, great, thanks. I love that eaten between two pieces of Ryvita. You go upstairs with Mum for a look round, and I'll go get those two to come up as well'.

When they were all upstairs, Gran said, 'Lovely big rooms you've got, Allan'.

'Yes', said Alistair, 'But it's freezing away from that heater downstairs, so I'm going back'. In agreement, they all went back downstairs to the fire, and gran asked if they had phoned Tilda, 'I did', said Alistair. Mum looked up from the dining table she was polishing and said ' Well, I hope you were nice to her', he screwed up his face and said 'I was, but when I told her we got lost and that the weather down here is atrocious, she just laughed and said: thank you for another piece of useless information and hung up'. Gran looked up and said 'Well she was probably busy and in a hurry to get to work' and then continued her discussion with the others about what they would do over the weekend.

Mum said 'You could show us around Strathmanor'.

Looking at the window, 'Not in that weather' said Ronald 'And am not spending my time here just sitting in the house'.

Gran said that she would take them all to the Pictures 'That would at least past the afternoon,' said Ronald. So they sat down to watch TV until time for the Pictures while Mum did some ironing and Gran hoovered.

When they eventually found the picture house, after Mum and Gran had spent a great deal of time looking at every shop window, they rushed in and Gran paid for everyone then Mum said 'I hate the smell of the onions on the hamburgers and Hotdogs'. The boys immediately looked over and said 'Oh yes please! can we have one more'. Mum frowned and shook her head saying 'No, it would only put you off your Lunch'. By this time Gran was already opening her purse to pay for the ice cream Alaister had ordered and then the burger and hotdog the other two had ordered. Mum looked over and raising her hands said 'That's enough food now, into the Film before it starts'.

After much jostling and arguing, amongst the boys for the best seats, they settled down to watch the film.

When it ended, Alister said 'You sent us into the wrong film Mum, that was a sad love story, and look at Gran she is in tears now', Mum looked at Gran and said ' Yes, but it's probably with all the money she spent on you too',

After the Pictures, with Mum still complaining about the price, even though, Gran had paid for it, it was still raining so Mum said she would treat them to lunch.

After lunch, they all wandered aimlessly around the museum until the boys' continual moaning about being bored made Mum decide to go back to the house for some tea as it was almost tea time. After tea, Mum and gran said that the day hadn't turned out too badly at all. Douglas and Ronald disagreed vehemently. They settled down to watch TV and eat the cakes gran had brought, then discuss what they would do tomorrow.

Just as Allan mentioned Callander Park and that they may go there tomorrow, all the lights went out and the fire went off. 'Oh, don't say it's a power cut', said Ronald. 'Where do you keep your candles?' They all rummaged about in cupboards and drawers in the dark looking for candles that may have been left from the previous occupants.

Not finding any, Allan said, 'I'll nip across to the police station, and ask where I can buy them at this time of night. I'll do that, and you two go to the precinct to see if there's anything over there. And don't get lost'.

Across at the police station, he explained their plight, and was told by the policeman that there'll be nothing at this time of the night. 'But I knock off in about half an hour, and my wife comes to pick me up, so I'll call her, and ask her to bring some of ours for you to borrow. Did you say you were next to the doctor's surgery across the road?' Allan nodded in affirmation and was told, 'Leave me your telephone number, and I'll phone you when they're here, and you just come over for them'.

'Thanks very much', said Allan, and went back to the house to wait.

His brothers were already back at the house, and one had gone upstairs to the loo and had replaced all Allan's toilet paper with some shiny, medicated stuff they had found in the precinct, hoping nobody would notice until after they had left. He felt very uneasy and uncomfortable in the loo; continually looking behind him, as he felt someone was watching him.

Downstairs, he told everyone of his experience upstairs, and how having no lights made it worse, to which everyone else sniggered and laughed. The two then explained how they had not found any candles, and that they wished they had stayed at home instead.

'Now, now,' said Gran. 'We could just play some games we played during the war or even I spy'.

'Well done, mother', said their Mum. 'It's pitch black'.

The telephone then just rang. 'That's probably the police saying he has some candles. He could have quite easily brought them over', Allan grumbled.

'Just be thankful he's got some, and go and get them', his Mum demanded.

Allan went over the road to collect them, and said to the policeman, "These will see us through the night. We'll replace them tomorrow, and I'll hand them in personally'.

'Great, there's no rush. Just drop them off. I've taken the liberty of telephoning the electric board who said it seems you're the only one out, but they'll try have you fixed by the morning'. With that, Allan took the candles and headed back across the road.

Sure enough, his was the only house with no lighting. As he got back to the house, the door opened to let him in, and he went straight in, closing the door quickly to keep the night out. 'Here's the candles. Does anyone have a light?' They were all non-smokers, so Alistair and Ronald were delegated to go to the pub to buy some.

'No Gran, I'll nip over. They know me there anyway', Allan said.

'Aw, we'll just come with you all the same', the other two piped up.

As they all left, Gran said, 'Well, don't spend too much time in there in the warmth, as we need the light'.

'Sure, Gran – straight over and right back', said Ronald.

As soon as they got into the pub, a hush descended over the room, and again everyone turned to see the incomers. Ignoring the looks, Allan marched up to the bar, saying, 'We've only come over for a box of matches. Our electricity is all out. But can we have three pints, please?'

They each downed their pints quickly, gave hurried thanks, and left to go home. 'Mind and close that door', said one fierce-looking drinker sitting on his own in the corner.

'And dinnae hurry back', muttered another under his breath.

'Well, they weren't very friendly', said Alistair as they left, and made a point of banging the door closed.

'Well, if that's your local', said Ronald, 'I think you're best being TEE total'.

'Yes', agreed Allan, 'But I've just got here. Once I get my feet on the ground I should find lots to do'.

All three ran back with the matches, and Gran said, 'The battery in the transistor is fading now, so it's probably best if we stay up for an hour or so, and I'll tell you some ghost stories as we used to when you were kids'.

'What, only an hour?' said someone sarcastically.

'Yes', said Mum. 'Early to bed, and then Callander Park in the morning. We'll just go home after lunch if that's okay with you all'.

'Waaaay', cheered the brothers.

'Will you be making us a nice little picnic?' asked Alastair with a big smile.

'Good idea', said Mum. 'I'll take two candles and start making sandwiches, and we'll just buy drinks there'.

Mum and Gran made the sandwiches, while the other three just talked and grumbled, and then as the candlelight dwindled and flickered into darkness, Gran clapped her hands. 'Right! Bed, everyone', and they all trudged wearily upstairs.

'Oh', said Alistair, 'We'll have no light to get undressed'.

'Surely to God, at your age, you're not scared to get undressed in the dark?' laughed Allan.

'Goodnight, everyone', called Mum. Everyone said their good nights and went to bed.

Gran, who was up first, went to waken the boys: 'Come away, come away, it's time to get up, get dressed quickly, and we'll move out sharply'.

'Ohh, there's no hot water', cried Alistair.

'Well, there won't be if the emersion isn't on', said Gran. 'We'll just make do. We never had hot water in the old days'.

'Yes, we know', chorused four voices in unison.

They decided it would be more fun if all five of them were in one car. 'Let's go in Mum's', said Allan. 'It's more exciting when she is driving'. The look on his mother's face made him wish he had left that remark for one of the others to make.

'I hope you know the way to go, Megan', said Gran.

'Probably not', said Ronald, 'But it's only a few miles, so we should get there before dark', he added, not daring to make eye contact in the mirror with his Mum.

With their mother insisting that she knew the road and everyone else having to be quiet, they all shut up and left their Gran to do any talking required to their Mum.

It was just a short journey and the weather had brightened up surprisingly, and although the boys were desperate to start eating, they just waited and listened to Gran's commentary on the scenery. She passed some comments on every road they turned into, until very soon, they arrived at the park.

'Oh, that's good', said Alistair. 'There's a fayre with all sorts of stalls and rides. I'll have a go on the dodgems first'.

Ronald agreed, and suggested they all do that, then go on the big wheel.

'Well, that's all very well, but remember you all wanted to go home at lunchtime', said Mum.

The rest of the morning was spent going on as many rides as they could afford, with their Gran constantly supplying them with money for all the snacks.

'One last thing before we go, Mum', asked Alistair. 'Could we have a go on that crane thing to see if we can win a prize?'

'No', said Mum, sharply. 'We don't have time, and you know damn well that it's a fix and you can never win'.

At that, Gran opened her handbag, saying, 'Let them have a go. I will pay for it'.

'Thanks, Gran', said Ronald, and taking the money before Alistair could get his share, ran over to the machine. Carefully positioning the crane over a bar of chocolate, he tried to grasp it, but it wouldn't take grip.

'Right, my turn', said Alistair, and pushed Ronald out the road. Concentrating intensely, he also manoeuvred the crane into position, but this time he succeeded in getting a firm grip. Very slowly, he raised a bar of chocolate and glided it over to the drop-zone. Just as he was about to release it safely, it slipped and dropped back in with the rest.

'Right, my turn', said Allan, and hearing his Mum saying, 'Be quick because we have to leave soon', replied with, 'Yes, I will, but let me concentrate!' After a few unsuccessful attempts, he got a good grip and deposited it into the drop-zone. 'Success! he cried, but his smile soon faded as Alistair grabbed it.

Opening it, Alistair said, 'Well, it's real chocolate, not cardboard like you said it would be, Mum', and breaking it in two, he shared it with Ronald.

'I'm glad you came with us, Allan, and thanks for the chocolate. That's made up for not getting the phone numbers off those two girls we spoke to'.

'That's okay, I did', said Ronald.

Looking at her watch, and with a shocked tone in her voice, their Mum said, 'Well, we best get heading back now. It looks like you two didn't have as bad a time as you thought you would' Reluctantly admitting it had been good fun that day, the younger two said it was good up to a point, apart from last night.

At that, Mum ushered everyone into the car, with Allan mentioning there was a really good chip shop in the precinct if they fancied getting something to eat before they went home. 'That would be nice, but maybe another time. We really ought to get home before it gets too dark'. said Mum.

They drove straight to Allan's house, stopping only to get their cases which Allan nipped in the house for. After the second journey with cases, he said, 'Well, you two could've helped you know, instead of leaving me to do all the work'.

Alistair replied with, No, you're okay. It's warmer out here than your house, anyway'. With all the cases in the car, Allan closed the boot, patted the top of the car, and waved them all off.

Although it wasn't too warm, he decided to take a walk further along the road to see what it held. Coming to The Drovers Arms Hotel, he went in for a swift half or three and a whiskey, just to get warmth inside. In the corner stood some girls, so Allan went over and introduced himself, saying he was new to the area. The tallest of the girls smiled, and said, 'We're in here most weekends', and introducing her friends, asked, 'Where around do you stay?'

'Well, I'm just staying along there, next to the doctors. If any of you are ever at a loose end, pop in to see me'.

Looking at the others, she said, 'Okay, we might do that sometime, but we're off for now. See you soon'. Allan didn't fancy staying in the pub on his own, so he hurriedly finished up his drinks and headed home.

All the lights were on in the neighbouring houses, but when he got inside his house Allan found that his electricity was still off. The hallway felt draughty, so he picked up the phone and called home. 'Hi, Mum, it's just me checking to see if you got home safely.

'No, my electricity haven't gone on yet. I'll just go to bed and read a book, and deal with it in the morning.

'Oh no, I don't even have a torch, so I won't be able to read after all. I'll just go to bed. It was a tiring day, but good though'.

'Okay, then, bye for now. I'll phone you soon'.

Putting the phone back in the cradle, he looked at his watch, and thought to himself, 'I'll nip back over for another couple of '.. . He decided against going to the pub across the road that he'd been to with his brothers, but instead went back to The Drovers Arms. When he got there, he was greeted with a warm smile from the barmaid, who said, 'Back again so soon. You must've missed me too much'.

'Yes',

he nodded, 'Something like that. Anyway, could I have a large scotch and a pint? And that's me for the night'.

Standing at the bar, the barmaid said, 'I heard you tell my friends who were here just now that you're new in the area. Do you live nearby?'

'Yes, I'm just across the road. Pop in some time if you're free. I'm in the house next door to the doctors'.

'Yes, that would be nice. Can I bring my boyfriend?' With a non-committal grunt, Allan took his drinks and wandered over to a table near the door.

As the last orders bell approached, he finished up and headed to the door, and was peeved to have the door opened for him by an incoming punter, who came in and gave the barmaid a peck on the cheek. Putting his coat on, Allan quickly looked over his shoulder at this quaint old tavern, and thought, 'She is wasted on him. Still, it may not last, and she's got some nice friends. I'll come back in a day or two. I like it in here'.

When he crossed the road and got inside, a quick look at his watch prompted him to go straight to bed, as he didn't want to be late for tomorrow. 'So many people to meet and things to do'. Switching the bedroom light on, more by force of habit than expectancy, he was surprised and relieved to see the light go on. 'Oh, that's great. They must've got the electricity back on. I'll get a good night's sleep now with that happy thought in my head'.

Monday morning saw him up with a lark, and one of the first in the office. Popping his head around Gemma's office door, he said, 'Morning, I saw you getting here just before me.

We're quite early. Can I get you a coffee as well, and you can tell me what you did this weekend?'

Bringing the two coffees in, he said, 'We'll have a few minutes before the rest get here. So, what did you do over the weekend?'

'Nothing much. I have a very boring life just now'.

'Well, I've had a good weekend with my family coming through, but it's back to the grind for another week. I love my job, but I still don't know many folks. That's why I spend so much time here speaking to you. I hope you don't mind?'

'Oh no', she said. 'I quite enjoy it'.

'That's good. I must go and do some work now'.

Hesitating as he turned to leave the room, Allan said, 'Well, I have an idea. It's a really good idea. No, it's even better than that. Well, actually – it's the best idea I've had all morning. Oh, the others are turning up now. I'd best go. See you in a bit'.

'Yes, but what's your idea though?' Gemma asked, expectantly.

'I'll need to go – that's them. Will tell you at lunch'.

That day was to be the start of Super-rats. All morning, Allan and Geophrey bantered with each other over the impending tennis match they were to have at lunchtime; Allan frequently mentioning that he had been playing most Sundays at home with his friend Ewen, so that Geoph should probably start worrying. Geoph just sat there, smiling and nodding quietly.

As everyone else set off for the canteen, Allan and Geoph went out together to Geoph's car, then off to the sports centre for their long-awaited duel. All the way to the sports centre the jovial banter continued, carrying on into the changing room. Then, together they went out to the court, and recapped the rules. As agreed beforehand, it was just the one set, with Allan full of confidence, as he was dressed in an old football strip, and had borrowed his brother's racket.

A few gentle lobs and warm-up strokes got him and Geoph loosened up. Then, Allan raised the ball and racket for the first service of the game. After a few short bounces of the ball and a hard powerful serve, the ball whizzed over the net, and Geoph just managed to reach it, but didn't fully return. 15-love.

The next service was an ace. 30-love.

Geoph managed a weak return of service on the next two serves, with Allan winning both points. Allan returned each of Geoph's services and won the second game himself quite easily. 'This should be a doddle', Allan thought, and cockily reminded Geoph of the score. Moving swiftly over to the centre line for his next service game, he won the next game... three-love.

Perhaps he was being a bit too serious about the whole thing, but Geoph managed to win the first point of the fourth game. Allan watched Geoph wipe some sweat off his brow, and said to himself, 'Now's the time to crank up the pressure'.Hoping to go for a quick win, Allan thundered the ball at his opponent's court, but unfortunately hit the net.

Really annoyed with himself, he returned Geoph's service, and turning quickly to chase the ball, twisted his ankle slightly.

For the rest of the game, Geoph cashed in on this, winning the remainder of the games, and ultimately the set. As he limped over to the net, Allan said to Geoph, 'Well done, but when the ball hit the net that time you might have at least acknowledged the good luck that gave you the point'.

Geoph, who was a quiet and unassuming man, and extremely modest, felt guilty inside and a little responsible for Allan's ankle which had been damaged already in some stupid drunken antic when he was much younger. Geoph had never told anyone that in his youth he had been an excellent tennis player, and his deft and skilful spins and crafty strokes were the main reason Allan had turned so sharply and went over his ankle. Geoph just smiled and replied, 'Well, that's the name of the game – Super-rats!'

Back in the office, Geoph played down his victory, being the proper gentleman that he was. And the results in the league table so far were displayed. Allan was at the bottom.

*   *   *

CHAPTER SEVEN

Saturday Night At The Movies

Whenhen Allan got to the office early the next morning he tried to accentuate the limp so as to glean as much sympathy from the others as possible. "Morning Gemma," he said, hoping to get some empathy from the typist.

"I see you were well and truly beaten in your first game."

"Yeah, it was a fluke, but my next match is a pool. That should be quite easy. Oh, the really good idea I had – I don't remember if I've told you?"

'No'.

'I wanted to ask you if you fancied going to the pictures one of these nights? If you find a good film you fancy, let me know, and we'll go'.

Remembering that he had told her, she said, 'I remember now. How about this one?' pointing to the newspaper. 'And, how about this weekend? My friends have seen it, and I've been told it's very scary'.

Allan looked at the paper, and said, 'Yes, that sounds great! Where will I pick you up?'

When she told him her address, he said he was looking forward to it, and deliberately didn't admit to telling her he'd already seen this back home. 'We could have a drink beforehand if you like?'

Gemma agreed, and asked, 'Can I bring my friend and her new boyfriend?'

'Yes, that sounds good! The more, the merrier'.

As he went into his office and said morning to the other two, Ivan said 'Morning Alan, am just off to the main building, see you later' and left. Just then Wilson came into the office looking quite excited and flustered 'Ooh listen to this guys', Geophrey and Allan looked at each other then turned to face Wilson who was standing at the door with a coffee. 'I'll need a seat for this', he said and sat down.

Sipping his coffee, he looked up and said 'Ow it was terrible, you will never believe what's just happened to me'. 'We are all ears', said Geophrey 'Go on but we are quite busy'. Wilson wiped his brow and blew out his cheeks 'Well?' said Allan. 'Give me a chance to get my breath then, it was awful'. 'So you said' Geophrey quickly responded.

'Well' said Wilson standing up 'I was in Stoopchurch looking for a new calculator and just as I left the shop the security guard called me back. According to them I had taken an apple from the food counter and not paid for it, but when I denied this and told them I had no apple, he said that I must have eaten it already.

When I argued with him he asked me to accompany him to the manager's office as it wasn't good for business arguing in full view of the public. 'The store detective explained to the manager why I was there'. Allan and Geophrey looked at each other surprised 'What happened then?' asked Allan. 'Give me a chance', said Wilson 'I'll tell you'.

After a brief pause, Wilson continued 'Well, the manager said that since it was theft even though it was only an apple, the company takes a very dim view of thieves so, he would have to phone the police' . Geophrey said 'And did he?' Wilson shrugged his shoulders and said 'Well they left me in the room alone while they went to the phone, by this time, I was sweating and very worried, the room I was, was on the ground floor so I thought I would just do a runner out the window.

Unfortunately, I was only halfway out when they came back, the security guard grabbed my leg and started pulling It.' Wilson turned and left the room saying 'Just like am doing to the two of You'. Geophrey and Allan just looked at each other for a few seconds with Geophrey breaking the silence saying 'I was believing every word of That'. 'Yes so was I', said Allan 'The Swine'. 'Well that's him all over, you can never take him seriously'. 'Yes', said Allan. 'He's a laugh a minute *that* guy. Always joking. Mind you I was happy already that I am going to the pictures this weekend. It makes a change from just reading all this stuff at home. Geophrey looked down and said, 'Yes let's crack On'.

Allan looked at his desk and picked up the phone to call home, ' Hi mum, it's me, just a quick call to say hello before Iget busy here', as he moved his calculator closer to the plans on his desk, his mum said, ' Well, everything is okay here except for Tilda' . Allan drew a deep breath and asked what was wrong. "In the baker's shop, she had promoted herself without permission to what she called 'Quality Control

Supervisor' and was constantly sampling everything in full view of the customers when the manager told her not to do that, she furiously put it down and said, "Nobody talks to me like that" and stormed out. But then, she had to eat humble pie when the manager came after her, saying 'Don't forget the cream cakes you bought for your mum and the old folks Home'. Apparently she just grabbed the cakes and told him to put the change in the charity box. Allan shook his head and told Geophrey about Tilda and said 'But that's her usual problem anyway. Generous to a fault but taking no prisoners. 'Well, I don't care am off to the pictures this weekend' before starting back to work.

On Saturday night, Allan got dressed in the smartest of the small array of clothes he had in his wardrobe and made a mental note that these were all old clothes he has had for ages. Some were even his brothers', so he would need to buy some new clothes in the mall next week. 'There're always nice sales girls in these Boutiques', he thought.

Looking at his watch for the millionth time, at last, it was time to set off. As he drew up outside Gemma's house, the door opened and she came out with four others. 'This is my friend and her boyfriend', she said, 'and his mate and his girlfriend'.

'Well, as long as I remember your name, that'll do because I'll probably forget everyone else's. So, let's get going so we don't miss the start'.

In the foyer at the cinema, the others spoke briefly with some people they knew, while Allan bought lots of goodies to eat, and they all headed up to the balcony. They were all slightly miffed that there were no seats left in the no-smoking area, so they had to sit in amongst all the smokers, with Allan constantly complaining about having to peer through a haze of second-hand smoke, and frequently accentuating a cough.

On the way up, Allan complimented Gemma's friend on her really nice jersey. 'And so is yours,' he said to the third girl, cutting short any further chat when he got the evil eye from her boyfriend.

They shuffled along the row, and just got seated when another couple shuffled along, so they all had to stand to let them past. When they took their seats on the balcony, Allan opened his box of Smarties only to discover he'd opened them at the wrong end. Not wanting to look a fool, he teased the little packet out of the box, shaking the Smarties out of the paper bag into the box.

Just as all got quiet for the start of the film, the bottom of the box opened, and the contents showered onto the floor between his legs. 'Well, that's me, making a right fool of myself to start with'. As he tucked into his hot dog, the others started to eat all the goodies they had brought as well, and at last the opening scene started. No sooner had the first actor spoken, they all had to stand up to let another couple through. As they edged along the row one of them stood on a discarded ice-cream tub, and kicked it further along towards Allan, much to his disgust, as it hit him on his sore ankle.

Everyone was enthralled with the film by now, and the theatre was in absolute silence as it got more and more gruesome and scary. As the end of the movie approached, Allan leaned closer to Gemma and dared to put his arm around her shoulder, as he knew a scary bit was coming up. Everyone in the audience sat with bated breath hoping the monster wouldn't break the door down, and they waited and waited, expecting the door to burst open at any moment. Just at that precise time, Allan succeeded in getting his arm right around Gemma's shoulder, but accidently touched her friend's shoulder. Her friend, who was waiting for something terrible to happen in the film, gave a loud scream when Allan's hand touched her, and the whole theatre screamed with her, as they were excepting the monster to come in the door.

They realised it was a false alarm and settled down, only for the door to burst open to loads of screams, and then much laughter when they realised it was only the dog that had gone missing earlier.

Everyone settled down, except the boyfriend to Gemma's friend's who had got Gemma's drink in his lap when his girlfriend screamed because Allan touched her. Everyone sighed a sigh of relief, and just as they stood to leave when all the tension had subsided, the monster dived through the window to howls of fear and surprise which gradually subsided into laughter.

As they hurried out of the cinema discussing what had happened and how much fun it had been, with Allan commenting on the wet trousers, they decided to nip across the road for a few drinks, with Gemma saying, 'Your car will smell for weeks of our clothes'. Allan agreed, hoping that there were no remnants or clues of his smoking days left in the car that may serve as evidence.

As everyone was in high spirits and had *had* a hard-working week, they drank quite a lot, quite quickly, as it was late. Allan refused any drinks (alcohol) because he was to drive, but did take blackcurrant and lemonade that left a purple stain on his lips, which brought a few tears of laughter from Wet Pants.

As they were driving home, Allan said, 'Would you like a towel or something to sit on, so you don't get my seats wet?' He then interrupted the laughter, by saying, 'There's a police car behind us, so behave in the back'.

At this, they all immediately turned and stared at the oncoming car. This of course aroused suspicion for the police, and they immediately signalled for the car to be pulled over. When Allan wound down the window he was asked all the usual questions, and said, 'No, I have not been drinking'.

'Well, the inside of your car smells like a brewery, so we'll breathe-test you anyway'.

He passed the breath test of course, and when he gave his address, the older policeman chipped in, 'Oh, I know that house. When I was a raw recruit many years ago, I was called to an incident at that house. Looking at Allan strangely, he said, 'Well, that's my trip down memory lane over. On your way, and keep that crowd in the car under control. Drive carefully !'

Closing the door, Allan drove on to drop everyone off. 'I have an idea. It's not too late – how about I treat you all for some coffee, and then I can drop you all off later?'

'Yes', said Gemma, 'as long as it's not too late'.

They turned the car around and went back to Allan's. One of the boys said, pointing across the road 'There's a pub. We could nip in there for one'.

'No, no', said Allan. 'They're really unfriendly in there. We'll stick to the coffee'.

As they sat in the living room drinking their coffee and chatting, one of the boyfriends said he had noticed a bookcase full of books through the window of the other room. 'Do you read much? There's a piano I saw as well. You must be really cultured'.

'No', said Allan. 'They were included in the house. I will start reading more though, since they're there, and maybe even learn to play the piano'.

'Well, my sister-in-law gives piano lessons', said Gemma's friend. 'I'll write down her number for you, if you like'?

'Well thanks',said Allan, 'but Gemma has given me one already'. 'And we had best go; it's getting late, and I'm getting a bit chilly now',said Gemma's friend.

'Yes, said Allan, it's a cold house. I've been struggling to find someone to come and deal with that'. As the girls started to put their coats back on, he went on saying: 'I won't give up trying though, I'll get it sorted if it's the last thing I do'.

One of the boyfriends laughed and said: 'Good for you, It would have been the first thing, I would have done though'.

Allan saw his guests to the front door, and shaking hands with the boys, he pecked the girls on the cheek with a special lingering kiss for Gemma, whispering, 'See you on Monday, Gemma', and went inside with a broad smile.

'Well, that was a fun night', Allan said to himself. 'It's quite late now, so I'll just have a large scotch, and go to bed'. As he did every night before bed, at the foot of the stairs he picked up the phone to call home "Hi mom, just a quick call before i go to bed" his mother sighed and said, "well you have just woken the whole household up, we were in bed, i was all for rolling over and forgettimng it, but your father said that it must be very important or you wouldn't have called so late" Allan looked at his watch and said "sorry, i didn't realise it was too late, i am just back from the pictures with some friends" his mom went silent for a few seconds then said "well it's great to hear from you again but maybe do it a little bit earlier next time but your friend Ewen phoned about an hour ago, why don't you go and annoy him at this time of the night, he looked at his watch and said "he will still be up i will go call him now, bye for now". He replaced the handset and looked at his watch, it wasn't too late he thought so he called Ewen.

The Telephone rang afew times before a breathless   Ewen said "Hello, who is calling at this time of the night"?, "It's me Allan sorry it's late but i have been out with some friends. I am having a ball down here in Strathmanor, you want to come down here for a weekend and I will try to get a few other friends here as well". Ewen sighed and said "Well, I

will come down but try to phone a little earlier next time "
Alan looked at his watch again and apologised for calling so
late then said "Goodbye".

He checked both doors were locked, everything was switched
off downstairs then ran up to the bedroom. Allan laid out all
his clothes for the morning, saving time, which would give
him a few more minutes in bed. Picking up a book from the
bookshelf downstairs, he thought, 'I've tried to get into this
book a few times; I think I'll give this a skip and read
Method instead'.This was from his professional society
which he read from time-to-time, and invariably sent him off
to sleep. Scanning through the magazine, there were no
pictures of sexy girls modelling, fast cars or funny anecdotes.
Not even a quiz! So he decided just to forget reading,finish
his bottle and then go to sleep.

CHAPTER EIGHT

Monday morning blues

Waking up nice and early to the radio alarm, he had a quick stretch, and headed in for a shower. The exhilarating feeling of the warm water cascading over him and the stimulating sports shower gel, all succeeded in hurrying him up. Just as he got the last of the soap off, the electricity cut off once more. 'Damn, I'll need to see to this at work. I'm lucky I finished my shower'.

Quickly drying off, and dressing in the cold bedroom which he was, by now used to, he began to set off to work. Then, checking the phone on the way out to make sure nothing else untoward had happened, and with the dialling tone intact, off he went.

Driving up the main road, Allan honked his horn and waved when he saw the barmaid come out of a nearby house. The pleasure at seeing her smile and wave back dissolved when her boyfriend followed her out. 'Well, at least I know for sure now', he thought. 'Not a very nice start to a Monday', he said to himself, as he continued to drive to work.

In the office, the first few minutes were spent telling everyone of his exciting electricity problems again. He telephoned the electricity company straight away, and they assured him they would send someone out as soon as they could.

At lunchtime, he nipped back to the house to see if everything was back working yet, but no luck! He phoned the electricity company from his house phone, and they apologised profusely, and said, 'We couldn't get anyone to come out, but we're trying our best to sort something out for you this afternoon'. Slamming the phone down in disgust, he left for work again and spoke to an electrical repairman who had just pulled up.

'Sorry, we've not got to the bottom of it yet', he said as he scrathed his head and wrote something in his notebook. 'I'm a supervisor, so you're in good hands now. You'll be up and running in a jiffy'.

'Well, as long as it's working before I come home', said Allan, and drove away quickly back to work.

He waved to the gatekeeper who had already started opening the barrier as soon as he saw Allan's car. 'That's me back', said Allan, as he got into the office. They've still not figured it out, but the main man's there, just now, so it should definitely be sorted before tea'.

'Thank God'! came from a few offices.

In his room, he looked at the Super-rats league table to see if any other games had been played, and discovered he had a game of pool the next day against Wilson Stewart...

When the pool tournament started three matches were being played. Allan's opponent, Wilson, maintained he had never played a game of pool in his life, so needed to be told the rules.

Rules explained and apparently understood, Wilson had won the tours so chalked his cue after Allan explained that this would give better contact with the ball , he broke off by smashing the cue ball into the pack as hard as he could. It ricocheted, back off a cushion, and accidently nudged the black into a pocket.

'Well, hard luck! That's you lost. You've potted the black ball out of sequence. That means you lose. The game's over'.

Wilson protested vehemently, 'I never knew that. This is the first time I've ever played this! Be a sportsman and let's start again'.

'Okay then',said Allan, 'but just this once'.

His second break was a bit more subdued, with a few pots going down by each player, until eventually, Wilson hit a winning streak and cleared the table. 'Game over, I believe!' said Wilson, with a cocky grin, and a wiggle of his glasses.

'Oh, surely we could play that frame again since I was very lenient letting you start again, when really you should have lost'.

'Well, I'd love to', said Wilson, 'but remember, we are playing Super-rats'. Then, with a grin, said, 'I'll order, then you pay for them, but I'll be gentlemanly, and update the league table for you while you're away'.

Back at the office, Allan sat glumly, muttering, 'Specky git'.

Right on cue, Wilson came in Allan's room, marched over to the league table on the wall, and said, 'I just came in for another look at the positions. Oh, look… you're bottom still'. As he turned to go out, he put on a really cheesy smile and a deliberately accentuated vacant grin, and said to Allan, 'Maybe it's you who needs specs'. Then, wiggling them again, he marched out chortling to himself.

'It is funny though', said Allan, 'but wait till the race. I'll put something in his beer next time! What's the next event anyway?'

That night in the canteen, Allan had the three-course tea that he had pre-ordered at lunchtime of course. The canteen girl said he would get it free if he was a night worker. While eating his tea, he mentioned to the man next to him, 'I must try to get fitter'. He said this in a stage whisper to try to impress the canteen girl.

On the way home, he was passed by a jogger who he had seen a couple of times before, so Allan thought, 'That's a good way to start my fitness campaign, and tomorrow night I will join the sports centre. I'll join the Gym at the Sports Centre that bloke was talking about'.

On Monday morning, Allan, who was in first, left his car parked just around from the office, so as to leave room for the other cars, as he was often in and out all day. All the other cars stayed parked, and he parked his at the end after he had been out on his first trip.

When he saw Gemma's car arriving, he had a quick look in the mirror, straightened his tie, fixed his hair, and then went into her office to say good morning. 'Well, I enjoyed myself at the pictures with you and your friends. Maybe we could do that again sometime? I take your point about my house being freezing. Everyone says so. I'll try to get central heating put in soon. Even though it's the middle of summer the house is cold, but central heating engineers might need the work'.

He saw Ivan take a cup of coffee into the office, so he asked him to get him one as well. The first part of the morning he spent looking up adverts for plumbers and made a shortlist. Everyone he contacted either said that they were too busy or were out of their offices, and their answering machine promised to get back. Beginning to get a bit disheartened, Allan said, 'No wonder I don't like Mondays; no one answers their phone'.

Not wanting to give up easily, he tried one last call, and the jovial plumber said he would send someone around tomorrow. Pleased to have made some headway, he thought it might be expedient to do some work now.

Finishing off the contract he was working on and then contacting some outside contractors, Allan thought he deserved something more entertaining. After all, as much as he loved his work, he had zipped through it in record time, so perhaps a jaunt to the main building just to see who he could see would be in order. He looked to Ivan and said, 'if you are about to eat that orange here am off out to the other side'.

He called through to the other offices, 'Anyone wants anything delivered over to the main building?' A few voices shouted through that they would welcome this, so he picked up his briefcase, and collected what needed to be delivered. 'I'll be back shortly', he said and went to his car.

Opening the door, he met Anna, who said, 'Can you give me a lift over to the main building next time you're going?' Telling her he was on his way over there now, he opened the front door, and let her in.

'You're turning me into a personal slave. Not that I'm complaining though'.

With her face blushing slightly, she said, 'That might be quite fun'.

'What's that?' queried Allan.

'Nothing', she answered with a cheeky smile.

On the way over, Allan reminded her that as he was new in the area, and didn't know anyone, 'Maybe we could meet up sometime after work?'

'Yes, we will do that, but don't tell anyone. My dad, the general manager, would have a fit'. Relieved at the thought that this dalliance was to be kept secret, he thought this offered him more scope with others (prospective mate).

On the short drive over to the main building, Allan asked her, 'If we do go out what would you want to do? Drinks, pictures?'

'Oh, anything you want, really. You can come back to my house, and listen to some records'.

'No, probably not a good idea. Your dad will be in'.

'Oh yes, I forgot about him. Let's just go for a drive then take it from there'.

They agreed to make a firmer arrangement on the time, with Allan suddenly coming up with, 'I have an idea. How about a meal somewhere, and a drink? There's a good restaurant across from my house'.

'That sounds good, but if we have a drink, I'll probably have to stay over. Do you have a spare room?'

'Yes', said Allan, watching her every move out the corner of his eye as she straightened her hair for the umpteenth time. As they reached the main building, Allan felt an inward glow of, 'An almost result'.

They got out the car together, with Allan not quite getting around quickly enough to open the door for her which he thought would put him in good favour. Allan walked behind Anna for a while, watching her and catching up to her, opened the doors, and said that he would meet her there in half an hour. 'This should give me plenty of time', he thought. Not stopping to talk to many folks on the way around, he handed in the necessaries, then made a bee-line for the typing pool.

From a few yards away, the click-click-click of the typewriters, and the chit-chat from the typists were heard. Going straight to the office supervisor, he handed in the documents he'd brought over and was a little less than pleased when the typists continued their chatting to each other, ignored him, and continued their chattering about someone's impending wedding. He tried to muscle in on the conversation and asked who the bride-to-be was. 'Well, god help the bridegroom', Allan thought when he saw the bride, but still congratulated her. 'Oh, I do like a good wedding. Full of happy people having a good time',

Looking at his watch, the bride asked him, 'Are you in a hurry?' Allan shook his head. 'Well, sit and have a coffee with us before you go back'.

'Yes, please'. And when asked how he took it, he said, 'I normally just take it any way I get it'.

A tall dark-haired girl poured him a cup, and said, 'Come and sit here, then. Your friend will probably know where to find you'.

Allan quickly corrected her by saying, 'She's not my friend. I was just giving her a lift from the office. I'm new here, so don't know many folks'.

He made his coffee last for fifteen minutes before Anna came in to collect him. 'Well, I'm off now. Thanks for the coffee. What's your name by the way? I'm Linda'.

'Linda', she said with a smile, pointing to her name badge.

'I'll see you all again, soon'. Turning to leave with Anna, he pointed to the rolls, reminding her he usually took two home for his supper.

As they left the typing pool, he decided to pick up a few more filled rolls, and then went back over to their office. In the car, Anna asked, 'Was that you trying to hit on that girl Linda?'

'No', replied Allan, 'I was just being sociable, I'm waiting and saving myself for you anyway'.

'Oh, you're a right smooth talker, you'. Anna said, pointing at Allan.

As Anna got out of the car she handed him his rolls, and said, 'You will need to watch all those rolls you eat. You're developing a bit of a paunch there'. Sucking in his belly, he nodded in agreement.

'Bye for now. If you need a lift again, just give me a shout, and let me know what you want to do for going out'.

Anna looked quickly at their offices, and with a finger to her lips, said, 'Shoooosh'.

'Of course', said Allan, and strode into his office.

Popping his head in Gemma's office, he said that's a nice perfume you are wearing. What's it called? A blusaing Gemma said " Thanks" then looked away. Then Allan asked if she wanted a coffee.

'No, thanks. I've just had one'.

He got a coffee for himself anyway, and called out on the way to his own office.   'That's everything delivered, lads!' On hearing this, someone called out, 'About time – where have you been? Your mother phoned and she said you are to call her back for a quick chat. It sounded important. Thanks said Allan as he went back to his own room and rearranged the desk after downing one coffee he poured another one for himself then sat at his desk ready to call his mum. " That's right said Godfrey you go on the phone now to your mum she has called here twice while you are out. It must be important Allan offered Godfrey a roll which was declined Then he tutted when he only heard the engaged tune "serves you right" said Godfrey laughing . " She is probably trying to phone here again." He said.

Turning his head to the side he asked Godfrey "Apparently i am putting on weight so much for my health kick. I'll need to buy some more equipment. Godfrey laughed and swivelled round quickly. Looking straight at Allan he froned and said sharply " perhaps if you actually did something instread of just talking about it and continually thinking that new equipment would do it all for you".

Allan looked at Godfrey and said "yes you probably are right, i would definitly go out for a jog tonight".

Well, I'll just have this coffee, and head off as well. See you all in the morning', Allan said to them. One-by-one they drifted out, and Allan tidied his desk, drank his coffee, then drove over to the canteen for his dinner. The canteen was empty apart from two early night shift workers grombling about having to work over time at this time of the night when it all sounded spooky. He couldn't wait to finish eating and leave the gromblers to their moans. Picking up his empty plates and putting them back on the counter he set off for home.

Tooting his horn and waving to a neighbour he parked outside his house and ran inside quickly. He headed upstais quickly, Allan changed into some more comfortable clothes then went back downstairs to make some phone calls. The first person he called was his mum as usual who never really listened much but always had a lenghty diatribe about the happenings back home. When it seemed like she was running out of puff she ended up by saying:" Well I will have to love you and leave you now, those scallywags have left me with all the dishes to do. Supposedly taking Tilda to see about a new job. Oh wait a minute, wait a minute". She added just before Allan put the receiver down. " Yes what is it mum", "i bumped into your friend Ewen in the town centre. He wanted your phone number, best give him a call"." I will do that mum he said and hung up".

Allan picked up and dialled through to Ewen. Ewen's Mum answered the phone, asked how Allan was enjoying his job then shouted for Ewen.

" Hi Allan, I was about to call you. You said earlier that you might have a reunion sometime with your collage mates could I come through as well? Most of them were a good laugh all those years ago". Allan smiled to himself and said: " am glad you have reminded me. I must get on to that soon."

They spent a few more minutes with just some idle chitchat. Both highly exagerating their different versions of course." Well I have to go now Ewen, I have to continue with my strict keep fit regime". " Oh said Ewen you did tell me about all the cheap food and the rolls you had. You will need some extra keep fit to make sure the pounds stay off. What does your routine involve? Allan paused then quick as a flash he said " Oh the usal stuff, a bit of swimming much jogging and I go on the weight as much as possible. Ewen thought for a minute then said: " If you do all that, as often as you say, then you will end up like Lou Ferringo."

Not knowing that Lou Ferrigno was the name of the actor who played the Incredible Hawk on T.V. he just said: " Well am half way there already."

Ewen, laughed quietly and said: "well keep up the good work and let me know when you are all meeting up." " Sure thanks" said Allan. Then he went to look up the telephone book to call the gymn.

After calling the gymn to be reminded of the opening times and prices, he ran upstairs to change into a t-shirt and some shorts.

He could see out of the bedroom window that all the trees were blowing in the wind. So decided instead just to watch televison and have an early night instead of exercise and start his regime properly the next day.

During the advert the televison set just went off on its own accord without any intervention from Allan. So he opened a tin of beer drank it quickly then laid out his clothes for tomorrow. On his Pillow, he saw the book he had got from the library entitled "Learn to play the piano quickly and easily", " right" thought Allan, " Lets give this a go", and armed with the book he went downstairs to the piano. He lifted up the lid and pressed three or four keys and after atleast forty seconds with his attention sparn exhausted, he decide to give up for tonight and restart proper lesson.

With no televison to watch now, and no piano skills he trutged slowly upstairs to bed to listen to his transister and put a fairly non productive evening to an end. Half a dozen swigs from his trusty bottle was enough to send him off to sleep with few cares to worry about.

bullet points

looked for a gym
swimming pool
scary things happening at home
change Geofree to Godfree
find the bit from the 8th of August and put it in position.
find copyright for front cover.
Extend chapter seven,
(Goes to sunbed, to dear, does'nt know how long i could do that, free trial, phone call, chapter up , gets burnt

CHAPTER NINE

Dirty Dog

Allan woke up at his usual early time, even though it was the weekend. He was not one for lying in bed at the weekend like some, he didn't want to waste any of his free time, so he jumped out of bed, and ran down to put the kettle on.

'Ah, there's nothing like the smell of a nice cup of coffee in the morning to wake you up,' and after taking one sip, immediately spat it out saying 'And that's nothing like a nice cup of coffee!' The milk had gone off overnight. 'That's really annoying. I just bought that milk on the way home last night'.

After drinking a cup of black coffee, he ran upstairs for a quick shower. His plan that day was to start a regime, whereby he could start reducing the belly he had developed which Anna had so delicately pointed out. 'Well, it's all bought and paid for from many lonely nights in the pub', he had told her. 'I'll get dressed quickly, then maybe go to that gym'.

At the gym, he filled in all the necessary details and was trying to find out as much as possible about the receptionist, like boyfriends, where she goes after work, etc. When looking at the form he was filling out, she butted in, and asked, 'Is that where you live, just opposite the police station?'

Nodding in affirmation, he said, 'Yes, I just moved in there recently'.

'Is it nice? It was up for sale for quite some time. I hope you got it for a good price'.

'Well, as a matter of fact, I didn't care too much about the price, although I did get a good deal. I just wanted to get a house next to my new job quickly, and that fitted the bill'.

When the receptionist told him that he could use the gym after his details had been processed, and that would take two days, Allan said

'No problem but could i pay extra and use the sun beds just now?'

The assistant slowly looked allan up and down then said

'well i have some paperwork to do in the office if you keep quiet about it you can use the sunbed until i am finished and then ill come back for you in ten minutes'

A delighted Allan imediatley went through to the room the assistant was pointing to and started the sunbed.

The assistant sat down at her desk to complete some forms including Allan's before filing them away, as she closed the fiiling cabinet the telephone rang, siting back down at her desk she said

'Ohh hi Kirsty i've not spoken to you in ages, how did that party go?, opening a soft drink can and eating some crisps she became immersed in conversation and completely forgot about Allan who was still on the sunbed

'Ohh sorry i need to go ill call you back later'

She said and slammed the phone down then ran frantically over to where Allan lay completely oblivious as to the length of time he had been lying there alone.

'Ohh quick Allan youll need to come off now you'll get me shot if my supervisor see's you there, Allan replied with

'Ohh that was really relaxing i hope i have a nice tan now' ushering Allan out and hurrying him up to get dressed, she said

'you'll best be going before i get into trouble'

Allan said goodbye to her then decided since he had all his kit with him he would just jog all the way home.

Pleased with the fact he had made some progress in his fitness campaign, he went straight out to the shopping mall to buy a tracksuit and the rest of the designer poser gear and decided it would be good to check out all the other shops. 'Oh, and the assistants as well!'

In the first shop he went to, he struck up some good banter with the girl behind the counter, and said, 'I was going to look round the other shops, but you seem very friendly, so I'll just buy the stuff from you, and I'll maybe see you again sometime'.

'Well, thank you very much. At least you know where to get me'. Seizing this opportunity, he said that he was new in the area, and as he lived alone he was trying to find a cleaner and didn't suppose she knew of anyone.

'Well, it's funny of you to say that', she said. 'My mother is called Evelyn as well as me, and she is looking for something, She might do it'.

'Yes, please. Give her my details, and I'll hope she's as pretty as you are'.

'Well, you can make up your mind about that, but she's very nice'.

Allan picked up a pint of milk from the adjacent shop and was about to go home for a quick cup of coffee when the girl said 'We have a special offer ongoing just now" Allan turned back to face her and saw she was pointing to a notice on the wall behind her.

Hoping to see some items that would interest him, such as whiskey or beer, he read the notice.

Unfortunately, the special offers were only for fresh fruit and veg, he was less than impressed when she told him that they had made a mistake in the quantities they ordered, the apples and bananas were very cheap and the oranges were at a ridiculously low price 'They are almost free so try to buy a lot" Allan didn't want to upset her by saying he didn't like oranges, even though she continually looked away when he tried to make eye contact with her, so he just said ' Thanks, but I have got loads of fruits already'

But when the girl said she had hoped Allan would have taken some of her hands, he thought he might still be in with the shout here, so he said since it's you I will take half a dozen.

As he turned to leave the shop he looked outside at the weather and said I hope it stays fair I want to go out for a quick jog. She came over to open the door for him and said 'With all that fruit and veg you must be trying to look after your body well'as Alan was about to pass by her, he said

'Yes, I just started trying to get really fit but it's quite a chore, you look very fit though what do you do?' 'Thank you,' she said coyly, but I have my special regime.

I don't go out running or to the gym, I have my workout in bed. Allan found out by now she was making some eye contact with him and so said 'That sounds very interesting, maybe you could come over and show me one of these night'. They swapped phone numbers and as Allan left to cross the road she said "But I work really hard at it and I guarantee you will be exhausted by the time I'm finished with you'.

'Oh Charlie,' said mum to dad at the dinner table back in Dundee, he didn't hear her as he was engrossed in a war movie on the portable TV.

'Charlie' she repeated slightly louder, still he was oblivious.

'Charlton!' she shouted to gain his attention, he looked up sharply and said, 'what's up, you sounded just like my mother there'. Nodding, she said, 'that was the intention, you listen to her'.

'I know am sorry, go on'. She sat at her place at the table and said 'if you are going to look at a new car take Alistair with you' he looked at Alistair and said, in his best Barney Rubble voice with his finger in his mouth 'Oh yea, to make sure its got four wheels and that the engine works. Well, we need to go now cause am going to the legion later'.

As they grabbed their jackets Alistair told Ronald to come as well; as he didn't want to take all the blame on his own.

'Good idea', said dad 'you know she won't be happy with whatever we buy anyway'.

'That must be him over there', said Ronald, pointing to a tall man standing next to a car with its bonnet open as they drew up. They all got out and Dad went over to the man while Alistair walked round the car and Ronald eyed up with interest a tall brunette who was in the garden.

'Hi, I am Charlie, I phoned earlier about the car,' said dad. 'I see you are wearing an R.A.F tie, I served as well, I spent most of my time in Germany, where were you billeted?'

'Ow, we were based all over, we saw more countries in the Regiment than most people have been to on holiday in a lifetime.

'If you two would stop reminiscing over how you won the war, would you come over to the car, after all, that's why we are here?' as he looked at the engine.

Dad shook his head, looked at the seller and the two went down to the car 'I hadn't the time to clean the boot properly' dad was told. 'That's okay, the wife will do that later', he said while pressing various buttons on the dashboard 'she will do the inside as well, I like a nice clean car'.

Dad got out and walked around the car rubbing a hand over the smooth, highly polished wing and gently kicking all the wheels, he looked up and saw Ronald going inside with the girl, 'Oi' he shouted, 'where are you going?' as they both walked through the door, 'it's okay Dad, we're just going in to listen to some records', said Ronald.

115

The girl explained to her own father that Ronald had been the DJ at the disco she was at, the night before.

'Well don't be long we haven't got all day, am meeting my friends tonight at the Legion,' Charlie called back. Dad patted his trouser pocket and fumbled in his jacket for some cigarettes then asked Alistair for a fag.

'Sorry dad I can't help you, I've given up'.

'Since when', asked a surprised Dad, and was told;

'Since Allan did, if it's good enough for him, it's good enough for me'.

The disgruntled and clearly annoyed father discussed the car with Alistair then agreed to meet the asking price. When Alistair asked why he hadn't even haggled the price down, dad said 'Oh I know a good car when I see one, after all, I worked in a garage'.

Alistair said ' Yes, but that was in the office though dad'and Dad replied 'Yea, whatever, get your brother, let's get going, am driving the new car'.

In the kitchen, mum looked up from the sink and said 'I thought you three had lost your way, I need to catch the bus soon am going over to my mum's'.

'Don't worry darling,' said Dad 'I'll drop you off, there is no way you are going on a bus, not when I've got two cars parked outside anyway. In fact, if I teach you how to drive you could have the old one'.

Just then, Tilda came through and said 'Am just off to see someone about a new job', then she looked at what Dad was holding in his hand.

'What's that horrible evil-looking thing you are holding,' Dad looked up and said 'your mother', after a quick laugh to himself, he explained it was a Gonk that had been attached to the mirror of the new car, he had brought it in as he thought it might obscure his vision while driving.

'Could be a child running across the road or just someone not paying attention. They should never be allowed, get rid of it'.

'No,' said Tilda 'give it to me, I'll give it to Celia'. Alistair protested pointing out that dad had said to throw it out. With a stern look on her face, Tilda held out her hand and said fiercely, 'Just do it!' Ronald thrust the gonk back in Tilda's hand and gave her a Nazi salute then watchful of a venomous backlash, the two brothers laughed and goose-stepped away to join their father.

Alistair could smell some aftershave from behind him and turned to see his parents putting on their coats.

'That's us off now', said mum, 'I expect to see this place as neat and tidy as it currently is when I come back, and be nice to your sister'. When mum and dad drove off, Ronald looked out the window and said 'Great, what can we do now?' The two decided just to watch television.

As dad drew up outside grand's house, he said 'I won't come in, just say hi to your mum for me' and seeing the net curtain pulled back slightly and a nose peering out, waved to the nose and said, 'I won't come in am late as it is, so phone me when you want to be picked up'. He gave her a peck on the cheek, tooted the horn and set off.

After a mile or so, he picked up three people. They were all wearing camel coats and one put a carrier bag on the back seat.

'That's your coat Charlie, if you want any more just give me a shout, you don't get a receipt though'. 'No, I think it will be a bit obvious, so many of us wearing the same coat'

Unperturbed, Walker went on 'Well, I can get them in different colours and I've lots of videos you might like' . 'I don't have a video', said a voice from the back seat. 'I can get you one of them as well' 'No thanks', answered back Martin 'My girfriend will get suspicious'.

'You all are under the thumb anyway, just as well, we've arrived so I can talk with people with more life in them'.

As they signed themselves in at the front door, McDougal looked at the book and asked why they called him Walker as it wasn't his real name.

'After the spiv in an old comedy', said Martin

They climbed the long staircase and said hello to many of the other regulars as they walked over to the bar to meet Walker who had already ordered up the drinks. The large smokey room stank of cigarettes, sweat, beer and a hundred different aftershaves, the walls were bedecked with pictures of fighter aeroplanes throughout the years and the blue carpet had the R.A.F. ensign above the motto *'Par Ardua Ad Astra'*.

'Come on lads' shouted Walker from the dartboard. They each took their turn in throwing the dart with their weaker hand, this was to determine each players number. The others then had to throw with their stronger hand and try to knock off each of the ten lives they had been allocated by hitting anyone else's number.

When Charlie said he couldn't drink as he was driving, Walker just smiled and said 'Well, I'll have yours' then ordered a coke for Charlie and drank the extra pint.

'What is your wife up to anyway?' he asked. ' Oh, I dropped her off at her mother's, I'll pick her up later'.

Megan and her mother were very close, and whenever Charlie went to The Legion, out with the family, or golfing, which were his only real interest, , they spent their time with each other.

They spent their time reminiscing about the old days and putting the world to right, tonight was no exception. Mr Snatcher, the Prime Minister was usually high on the agenda. Hours could be spent with the two crucifying him and leaving him without a name.

After they were finished with him and other famous people of his like, they would turn their attention to more important things, things like; the hideous dress, Mrs Green upstairs had bought, the price of washing up liquid, the new hairstyle of one Elizabeth down the road, and anything else they could do better.

'How is Allen doing in his new job?' asked Isabella. Megan poured another cup of tea and said that 'He seem to be doing very well. He eats well in the canteen and he is about to start going to a gym at the sports centre'.

'I still worry about him though', said Isabella. 'Mr Bell over the road says that it's very dangerous where he is'. Topping up their cups, Isabella continued 'There is a prison in nearby Stoop Church and that nosey neighbour kept saying that it was full of murderers and other low life's'.

Mr Bell was a very jealous man whose own children had never amounted to anything even though they had been educated at a costly public school which he continually reminded folk of. He took every opportunity to decry everyone else's relatives.

'He is just envious because Allan is doing so well', said Megan.

While Isabella went through to refill the teapot and brought some more cakes. Megan asked, 'when will you be getting this room done? It all looking quite shabby'. Her mother nodded and said 'soon and I will be needing some new furniture as well'.

Megan looked around the room at the very classy and expensive, though dated, furniture and decided to go with her to help her choose. Helping herself to some ginger biscuits. Megan said, 'I suppose I better phone Charlie for a lift and go back home'.

'Well, you phone later when we finish talking, it's still quite early', said Isabella, 'He'll only keep me talking' then she put some biscuits and the spare cake in a tin for Megan to take home. She added that its a pity she didn't drive. If she did then she wouldn't have to rely upon lifts from others.

'Its funny of you to have mentioned that but Charlie has said he will teach me to drive and give me his old car'. Then Megan said that she thought she was maybe a bit too old.

'No you are not', said her mum, you will manage fine. You have never failed in anything before.

They closed the curtains and put the small lights on 'We'll just finish this last bit of cake and watch TV till I phone Charlie, he doesn't mind how late I phone.

'Ah, you landed on your feet when you married him, he is one in a million. Am glad he is out enjoying himself playing games with his old mate'

'Let's have a game of snooker now', said Walker, 'I take it you all remember how to play snooker though''yes', they all said slowly with black looks'. 'Different partners from last week though', said McDougal

Walker went first and broke with his usual powerful opening cue action and handed the cue to Martin with his usual conceited, and self-assured smile. Martin viewed the positions on the table and potted two balls, then McDougal potted one more before handing it over to Charlie. Charlie walked slowly round the table bending down frequently, checking positions and angles. 'Get on with it man', impatient Walker said to Charlie.

Ignoring this, Charlie continued walking round, checking distances and angles, then sensing Walker's growing annoyance, very slowly and pronounced, started to chalk his cue. Eventfully, bent down and lined up the white ball, very slowly the cue ball hit the first red ball, Charlie sank, then the pink, then a red.

'Fluke' said Walker as he went to light a cigarette.

'The notice behind you says: No Smoking at the Table' said Charlie, then proceeded to clear the table. As the last ball went down, Charlie handed the cue to Walker and said 'Your turn, now I believe'.

As they sat down for a break, the bar-tender shouted over 'don't get too comfy Charlie, your wife phoned earlier, to say when to remind you to collect her and its time now'.

'Right, okay lads, am going now to collect her'.

Walker looked at the others and said 'She's got you right where she wants you, hasn't she?' 'Yup', said Charlie 'Right by her side….always'.

"See you next week Charlie," said McDougal 'Same time, same place', 'Tell your wife, mine will phone her during the week'.

'Why have you never married' asked the listening bar-tender, when Walker came up for more drinks. 'I prefer to spread myself around and after this drink, I'am off to a club to give the girls a treat'.

Charlie arrived back at Bella's house and waited for a while until his frequent ringing of the doorbell proofed to be of no avail. Charlie nodded his head and with a resigned, as usual look on his face, smiled and went to the back garden to find the spare key which was secretly hidden under a flower pot. Despite been told many times by Charlie that this was the first place a burglar would look, Bella still put it there. Saying her brother used it.

Charlie rang the bell once, then just entered, the very loud TV was one of the reasons they never heard the bell the other being they were both fast asleep.

Charlie turned down the television and took a half full cups through to the kitchen then cleared the rest of the table. He put a tea cosy on each of their heads then left them for a minute or two while he phoned home. There was no answer so while he looked for a camera to photograph the two sleeping beauties Bella started to waken up. He shook Megan and told her that they should get back quickly as there was no one in at home and it was late, so they said their goodbyes and left with the extra cakes.

As they drew up outside their own house, Charlie grumbled.

'If they had to pay the electric bill, they wouldn't have every light in the house on', Megan just looked up and said, 'they are only young'.

Inside the house, Charlie said that he hoped when they are older they learn how to keep the place tidy as he looked at the empty crisp packet, beer cans and various videos scattered across the floor

'Arc well, boys will be boys, you were young once', then she started tidying the house again and put the kettle on for a cup of tea.

As Charlie switched the television on the front door opened and in came Tilda.

'How did you get on?' asked Megan 'Rotten' she replied 'I thought I was in the canteen but she put me on swimming watch and tried to get me to wear this horrible swimming suit, I told her am not doing that so she told me to go on the bar'.

Charlie laughed as he had heard this all before and when Megan asked "But what will she do, you promised to work to the weekend. Tilda shook her head and said, "I handed in my notice but I have to work till the end of the month she's put me on the bar out of spite'.

Charlie laughed again and said 'But you detest alcohol and people getting drunk'.

Tilda then said that she will only sell soft drinks until she can leave and without another word stormed off to her bed just as the boys came in. Megan started to tell them all about Tilda's night until Alistair butted in saying 'Am off to have a bath'. 'Not before I have a shower, you won't', then the two raced off to see who would get to the bathroom first.

'Well, am off to bed now'. 'I'll be right behind you' said Megan 'Once I've tidied up these first'. Then with a smile on her face finished her cup of tea.

Earlier, at the start of the evening, when Charlie had dropped Megan at Gran's, the smell of baking filled the entrance to Gran's house and the door opened and more warm baking smells filled the close.

'Hi dear, I've just been baking so we can have some fresh cakes while having our tea. They walked together up the hallway and Isabella took her daughter's coat and hung it.

124

They sat down at the coffee table which was all set up neatly with napkins, a two tier cake stand and good, quality china. She always insisted on the best.

'This cake's lovely',said Megan as she cut another piece, 'it seems like a new recipe?' Pleased, Isabella said that it was one she had read in a magazine and she handed over the magazine to Megan.

'Tear it out and give it to either Tilda or Celia, I know they often bake for the old folks'. Megan laughed and said, ' Mum, you are one of the old folks yourself'.

As she came back from the kitchen with another fresh pot of tea, Isabella brought with her another large cake and fruit loaf that she said was for Charlie's brother-in-law.

CHAPTER TEN

A Capitol Night Out

Allan checked the newspaper again to see if there was anything worth watching. There was absolutely nothing that took his interest, so instead, he thought: this would be the day he would start his fitness campaign.

He checked the time on his watch before he left, believing the more time he ran the fitter and leaner he'd get.

Twenty minutes of gentle jogging, and taking in all the sights and new surroundings, left him feeling a bit out of breath. When he saw a pretty girl on the other side of the road, he looked both ways, then quickly ran over to ask her what the time was.

Jogging on the spot, and with one eye on two oncoming girls, he asked if she could tell him the correct time. Laughing and pointing at his watch, she said, 'I thought you could've come up with a better chat-up line than that. Why don't you just look at your watch?'

Slightly red-faced, Allan looked at his watch, and said, 'Oh yeah, I forgot that one! I got distracted when I saw you. I must be off, then'. On the other side of the road, Allan saw the fellow jogger he often saw, so he crossed over to join him.

'Hi', said Allan. 'Right, let's see what you're made of. You tend to beat me every night'.

"Right. Let's go then. It would probably help you if you didn't just give up after 50 yards when I pull away, the Jogger said.

Puffing and panting, Allan struggled to keep up, but drew forward to the same level when the fellow jogger slowed down quickly to avoid something a dog had left behind. Allan laughed when the other stumbled, and as he drew level, quickly sidestepped the obstacle, and stood on a leaf that was covering some more concealed dog poo. 'Oh, my good new trainers. I've had enough. I'm going home'.

As Allan approached his house and slowed down, four youths disembarked from a bus at a nearby stop. The first one banged into him, and shouted, 'Watch where you're going!' Allan quickly replied, 'You barged into me in your haste!'

'No, I didn't!' said the Youth, and swung a punch. As Allan tried to defend himself the others joined in and set about him. Punch after punch reined in, with the occasional kick.

Somehow Allan got to his feet, and shouted to the bus driver, 'Help!' as he tried to jump on the bus to escape. The youths pulled him off the bus and continued on their attack.

'There's no one here to help you', said one laughing assailant.

Allan managed to get to his feet and ran as fast as he could towards home. He was a lot further from his house than he had thought, and ran at full speed all the way, not daring to look behind in case this slowed him down and they caught him.

As he got to his front gate, one of his neighbours who was just getting out of his car, said to him, 'Well, that's what I call a fast jog. You'll be exhausted now. Have you been in the wars? Your face is all scratched and bruised.'

'Yes, I bumped into some young nutters who set about me, but they picked on the wrong chap here – I soon saw them off. They won't do that again in a hurry, and they won't stop me jogging'.

Allan's neighbour agreed, saying, 'There are some dodgy folk round here... Best see to that face. I'll leave you to it'.

'Yes, maybe see you at The Drovers, said John'.

'Oh, by the way, Allan, when you're out jogging or coming back from the pub, could you make less noise coming in the front door? It's not me; it's the old man next to me. He reckons the noise you make with the door upsets the chickens he has in the back garden, and it upsets their laying routine. Oh, and he is moaning about your dog making a noise'.

"Okay," said Allan, with a puzzled look on his face, 'But I don't have a dog'.

'Yes, laughed the neighbour, 'Butthat's Daft Duggie all over. He is old and a bit wondered. He thinks that your house still belongs to the previous owner who had a big black lab. Maybe you should get one for yourself for protection and some company. Yes, that would really annoy him. I've never liked that crabby old man, anyway'.

'But no, I wouldn't even have time to look after a goldfish really, what with my exercise regime and all that', Allan said.

He then quickly went inside his gate, moaning to himself, 'That neighbour was never very talkative before now'.

Realising the chasers must have given up, and still slightly panting, Allan hurried up his path. Looking at his tired, shabby front door, he fumbled for his keys, and thought, 'Must at least get this house looking a bit more inviting'. The first task will be to paint this door'. He unlocked the door, and looked up the street to make sure his attackers weren't anywhere nearby so they wouldn't find out where he lived. After scraping his shoe, and leaving it outside beside the bin, he ran upstairs. 'Oh, that shoe. I will need to clean it properly as soon as I've done my face'.

In his stocking soles, he ran upstairs to see to his face. With a facecloth, he dabbed off as much blood as he could. Since it was quite tender to touch, he just filled the wash basin and tried to do the rest of the job with soap and water. Opening the bathroom cabinet to see if there was anything there he could use, he realised there would be nothing as he hadn't bought anything that may prove useful to his current circumstance, not having expected anything like this to happen.

As he was closing the door of the cabinet, a small container with disinfectant hand gel caught his eye. 'Gran must have left that here when she visited, I never noticed that before'. He found the writing on the label difficult to read when he screwed up his bruised and painful eyes. He opened the gel and sniffed it, this stuff is bound to do the trick he thought as he squeezed some into his palm. "Eyeyabassa!!!" he shouted at the top of his voice 'That stuff stings like heck, still in for a penny in for a pound' and bracing himself, rubbed more gel into the other side of his head. This time it was even more stingy and by the time he had finished, two big red marks had replaced the slight grazing.

Once he had attended to his face, he went back downstairs to have a coffee, while watching the news. He took one sip of the coffee and spat it back out. 'Oh, that's disgusting. That new milk's off as well'. Allan poured the coffee out, and ran across to the shop to complain, and buy another pint.

Luckily, the shop was still open, and the same assistant smiled and was surprised to hear that the milk was sour. 'Well, sorry about that. Take this as a replacement'.

'Thanks', said Allan. 'I'll just take a slug to make sure it's not off as wel'.

'No, that's fine. Thanks very much. I'll see you again, soon'.

He left the shop and ran home to make another coffee.

On the way through to the living room, he put the coffee down and ran upstairs to run a bath. A good long soak in the bath to ease the aches and pains seemed a really good idea to him; the smell of his Gran's foamy bubble-bath seemed to make all the troubles of the last few minutes evaporate from his mind.

Allan ran downstairs to catch the tail end of the news, carefully taking the coffee back in. There was nothing of any interest on the news, and nothing much better afterwards, so he downed his coffee and went upstairs to soak in the bath.

Just as he was about to get in he remembered when he was very young and had to share a bath with his brothers; his father used to run the bath so hot that he and his brothers had to stand in it for ages to acclimatise to the hot water, and they would see who would be the first to brave the heat.

With this thought in mind, he got into the bath, and immediately jumped straight back out, shouting obscenities a paratrooper would be proud of, and stared in disbelief at the bath. The water was stone cold! He was sure he had put the immersion on that morning. 'Ah, damn all this. I'm just going to bed now'.

CHAPTER ELEVEN

Pound and Lost

As usual, Allan had woken early, it was Monday morning, but this time, Allan had difficulty dragging his battered aching body through to the bathroom. Still feeling sorry for himself, he decided that, although he was running a bit behind his normal schedule, he would try again to have a quick bath. While having the bath, he realised that his ankle had swollen up again slightly due to last night's frantic run, so he would still play on it for a while.

When he arrived at the office, seeing that everyone else had clocked in already, he braced himself for the jibes and comments he was expecting. Everyone except Gemma that was. But he did get some sympathy from them after, he had explained to anybody who would listen to the weekend's events. 'It looks really sore, I hope you will see to it with something; to avoid infection', said Gemma. 'Oh yes' said Allan. 'I rubbed some of that disinfectant hand gel all over it'.

'Oh that would really sting' she said. 'Really? I never noticed', said Allan.

Gemma showed extra concern over his wounds, and suggested maybe he should get a dog to take with him jogging, as much for some company as for protection.

He agreed with her, and she said, 'You could get a good one from the pound'.

'Wow! Great minds think alike! I was just thinking that myself, thanks for helping me decide', and pecked her on the cheek. 'That's just what I'll do. Will you come with me to help me choose?'

'I'd love to, but I'm very busy with my Gran. Why not ask Anna in the next office? She lives next door to the pound'.

'Maybe you would like to come round and see it once I have it though?'

Satisfied with this turn of events, he made arrangements to go up to the pound with Anna straight from work. She agreed, on the condition that he took her for a few drinks beforehand.

As soon as work finished, Allan went to meet Anna, and said goodnight to the rest of the office, amidst calls of, 'Make sure you get a fierce-looking yorkie', and, 'I'll bring you in some dog food tomorrow for your man-eating Pekingese'. Someone even called out, 'My granny's cat has just had kittens – will I save the biggest one for you? And finally, 'My wife's granny's got a parrot – do you want to borrow it, and train it to bark?' Ignoring the comments, he got into his car, while Anna drove in her's behind him. With Anna following him, left his car outside his house, and then got into Anna's car.

'Thanks for coming up with me, Anna'.

'That's no problem, Allan'. Turning the radio on, she said, 'Anything for a few free drinks. Maybe we could make a night of it?'

'Interesting', he thought, but said, 'we can't be too late because I have to collect the dog and run home with it, and the weather isn't looking too clever at the moment. We must do it another time, soon. I will look forward to that'.

'Right, you're on', she said enthusiastically. 'And you're right about the weather; those black clouds are looking very ominous'.

As they pulled up near the pound, Anna said, 'You can take me for a drink in this pub, here. I often come here'.

'Suits me', said Allan, as he opened the door and followed her in. Allan and Anna walked over to the jukebox, and Allan asked her, 'What was that tune on the radio in the car? I've never heard it before, but I really liked it'.

'The Black Heart Procession, It was; *A Cry For Love*. It's a weird song, but I'll put it on anyway since it's you', she said.

'And would you get me a vodka and ice, please?' he said to the barmaid. 'I'll sit at the table'.

The large, fierce-looking barmaid shouted, 'In a minute! There's a queue!'

After a few others were served first, she slammed down their drinks, took the money, and slapped the change on the counter beside the drinks.

Anna said to Allan, 'I wanted ice. Will you ask her for some?'

Nodding, he turned to the barmaid at the far end. Joy appeared to be her name, and a most inappropriate choice if ever there was one; every time someone called it she seemed to just shout, 'Wait your turn! I'm busy!'

They discussed the oak panelling in the old fashioned bar and the fake gas lights on the wall. 'It was really quaint', thought Allan. 'Like something from the last century', she said, 'I've been coming here ever since I was seventeen. I suppose it's my local. All my friends come in at the weekend'.

Looking at her glass, she said, 'I really could do with some ice in this'.

Allan, peering into the empty ice bucket, was about to ask Joy, who looked like she had just eaten a raw lemon and washed it down her throat with a shot of vinegar. But he changed his mind when he heard her shout to some young lads at the other end of the bar, 'Look! I've only got one pair of hands! I'm busy. You'll just need to wait your turn!' before turning to carry on her conversation with her friends at the hatch.

'Don't tell me you're afraid of her. Will I need to ask her myself?'

'No, I'll ask her', looking at the empty ice bucket, as though some ice would miraculously appear.

'Look, you!' she snapped. 'Can't you see I'm busy here!'

'Yes, but we only want some ice, and we've been waiting for a while'.

'Well, if there is none in the ice bucket there won't be any, will there? And I'm far too busy to go and get some', she spat.

"'Well',said Allan, 'just stick your finger in it, you frosty-faced, frigid, auld cow'.

'What did you say!' screeched the furious barmaid, as she stormed from behind the bar, pushing her friends aside, running straight up to Allan, and said, 'If it wasn't because Anna comes in here every weekend with her friends you would be out on your ear, so finish your drinks, and get him out of here. I'm off for a break and a fag to calm down'.

'I'm really sorry. Can we just listen to our tunes, and then go?' said Anna

Mm, said Joy, as she pushed past them, and went on her break.

Anna looked out the window when the music came on, hoping that maybe no one would realise she had chosen it, and as Allan came over, she said, 'That song really is awful.

'Well, I like it,' he said.

'Cheers!' said Anna.

Enjoying the ambience and the warmth in the bar, Allan rose from his seat and asked Anna what she would like put on next. She gave him a few choices, which he then went over to the jukebox to select. On his way, he acknowledged the many nods of approval and taps on the arm from other patrons over his encounter with the menacing barmaid and put on his newly found favourite as well.

Looking at the clock behind the bar, they both agreed that they had better finished up their drinks, and make a move for the pound. Making sure they were well wrapped up before leaving the bar, Allan said, 'It's got quite dark now. I hope I get home before it rains'. He opened the door, and they both went to the dog pound next door.

It was a grim-looking, cold, and loveless place. Anna introduced Allan to the kennel-maid who, as it turned out, knew Anna. Allan was already looking at the fiercer dogs. 'I would like a big dog, good-natured, maybe fierce-looking so it could scare off any attackers'.

'This one could do you', the kennel-maid answered, looking up at Allan, as she pointed to a large black and white dog. 'This one has been with us for a fortnight. Nobody wants him because he's boisterous, and needs a lot of exercising all in one go. He's happy to lie in the house all day, as long as he gets out for a long run in the evening'.

Knowing he would be at work most days, this seemed ideal to Allan. 'I'm at work all day anyway, and in the evening I like to go for long jogs, and if he's as well-mannered as you say, I can leave him unattended when I go to the gym'.

'Okay then', she said. 'Come over here, and fill out the necessary forms'. From behind the desk, she called out the questions and filled the answers with Allan's replies.

'Well, all seems to be in order now, He's all yours then. Any problems, you know where I am'.

Waving to the girl as they left, Anna said to Allan, 'I live over there', pointing over the road, 'So I'll leave you here.

Unless you want to grab another drink?' 'I need to get off home quickly in case it rains'.

'No thanks. I'll give that a rain check, and looking up at the sky, a rain check is the operative word; that sky looks like it's getting worse. Thanks for coming with me. I'll see you in the morning."

Allan played with the dog for a minute or two, with it jumping up and licking his face repeatedly, the two seems to have hit it off quite well. Then, feeling the first hint of drizzle, they both took off for home, and a gentle canter. 'Those creeps from last night won't come near me again,' he thought.

After a few minutes, the drizzle turned into heavy rain, and although the dog tried to get Allan to make a detour into the park for more play, a sharp call soon got the dog chasing Allan again.

Soon, the pair were running at full pelt as they tried to get home, before the sudden downpour completely soaked them. 'I must remember to get this dog to dry and shake itself in the vestibule, and not the rest of the house.'

They ran past many people struggling with their brollies, and pulling up their hoods. It seemed everyone was prepared for this sudden deluge, all except Allan. As he passed a few girls coming out of a car, he just said, 'Hello, rotten weather!' and continued running.

One girl said to the other, 'He normally speaks to me every time we see each other. I'll probably see him tomorrow'. Then, opening her own front door, both girls went inside, firmly closing and locking the door to the elements. They were very glad to be able to lock the night out, and one said to the other, 'I wonder how far he's got to go. He's not really dressed for this weather'.

As Allan and the dog went past the closed refinery gates, he looked in, and wondered why the lights were still on. 'Someone must be doing overtime. I wonder if I could get some. The extra money would be nice.' A flash of lightning, followed by a crash of thunder jolted him into remembering the task at hand: 'Getting home as soon as possible, out of this weather'. Nearing his own house, an ongoing vehicle splashed into a puddle, the contents of which ended up on the dog and Allan.

'Right, that's us home now', he said to the dog. As he turned to go up the path, with his hand in his pocket raking for the key, the dog stopped in its tracks at the gate, looked at Allan, refused to come up the path, and took off in the opposite direction. Despite Allan's constant calling and shouting, the dog didn't slow down and didn't even look back as it ran as fast as he could back from where he had just come. 'Well, I'm not going chasing for it right now. That daft dog wants to stay out, he knows where I am. I best go in before I get my death of cold, and get a raincoat'.

Allan made himself a hot drink, took a large swig of whiskey to warm himself up, and got ready to go back out and brave the elements to look for the dog. With his overcoat on, a scarf, and a brolly, out he went into the dreadful rain. I must try to get that dog back. He'll be scared and lonely, and cold and wet, like I will be, thanks to him. But the sooner I find him, the sooner we can get back inside'. Then off he went, searching up every alley and street he could see.

There weren't many people outdoors by now, and everyone he saw, said, 'No, sorry. Good luck, though', in reply to him asking if they had seen his dog.

Well and truly soaked by now, the wind and rain being assisted by every vehicle that went by splashing more water on him as they mercilessly drove through the puddles, he decided just to head home. Hurriedly opening the door, in hanging his coat up, Allan felt guilty at having to give up on his search. But it was late at night, he was tired and wet so he decided just to go straight to bed, and hoped someone had found the dog.

Allan poured himself a large scotch, got dried off, and went straight to bed. Feeling warm and content in bed, but still feeling worried about his dog, he lay in bed and listened to the wind and the rain. Just as Allan was about to doze off, there was another flash of lightning which jolted him out of his dose.

Trying to get back to sleep again, another flash of lightning was followed by the sound of a large dog howling. 'That's him', cried Allan . 'Must find him'. Putting on some clothes and wrapping up against the elements, he ran out back into the storm.

Just as he went out the front door, a dog howled again in the distance. There was nobody out now, but some people were peering out their bedroom windows, looking at the storm. As he braved the weather and ran quickly back the way he had previously searched, he heard the dog howl from yet another direction. 'He's over there now', he thought, and ran towards where he thought the dog was.

After he had ran a quarter of a mile, the dog howled again from yet another direction. Allan checked his watch; it was late, very late, but he still ran towards where the noise came from. Again, a howl came from still another direction; behind some houses this time, but again he couldn't find the dog.

As he looked up at the lit bedroom windows with people looking at him, he said to himself, 'I know what they're thinking: "What's that damn fool doing out there at this time of night?' Shaking his head in quiet disbelief of his predicament, he decided that he was quite jealous of the people in their warm rooms, and so he would just head for home and give up for the night.

As soon as Allan got back into his house, he made a cup of tea to warm himself up. Then, drinking it quickly, picked up his telephone, and phoned the dog pound to let them know that he had lost the dog. After letting it ring and ring, he gave up, and phoned another number; the out-of-hours emergency number. No answer here, and just as he was about to hang up in frustration, a voice came on, saying, 'District Council Dog Pound Emergency Services'. He quickly started to explain what had happened, but the voice just continued, saying, 'I'm sorry there is no one available, please leave your number –'

When he heard this recorded message he slammed the phone down in disgust. Thinking that maybe he had been a bit hasty there, he picked the phone up and dialled straight back. 'After all, they may pick the phone up at intervals during the night.' This time, he left a message explaining what had happened, and his telephone number, in case they needed to contact him. 'No doubt they'll find this very funny back at work, but I'm definitely off to bed now'.

As he climbed the stairs, he listened to the outside weather, and took a swig from his bottle of scotch which he decided just to take and leave in the bedroom anyway. He lay in bed, and thought to himself, 'At least I'll get to see that kennel-maid again'. He intended to go up tomorrow to explain in person what had happened, and depending on how it went, he might ask her out. She might say yes out of sympathy. 'That's okay'. Or think he's an idiot. 'That's still not okay'.

'A well, as Scarlet says, "Tomorrow is another day",' and picked up his magazine, then put it down immediately when he heard his mother's words ring through his head: 'Now, you make sure to phone that nice wee lassie'.

Although it was late, he decided to call her right away, as he knew she liked spontaneity. 'No, on second thoughts, I'll do it tomorrow, and just lie here and watch Miss World on TV.' Allan had bought three sweepstake tickets from the engineers' office, and not his own office, as he had told everybody there that shows like Miss World just demean and belittle women, and just portrays men as lecherous and sleazy.

Allan must have dosed off for a while, and was awakened by the sound of the fanfare and the announcer saying, 'The winners are, and in reverse order…' There was a puff of smoke and a spark, and the TV went dead. 'Drat!' said a shocked and surprised Allan as he went over to unplug the still-smoking TV, then got back into bed with his bottle.

As he lay in bed, he wondered whether the office guys would own up, and tell the truth about the winner. His mind temporarily drifted to the sound of the wind outside. At the top of a particularly loud gust of wind, he convinced himself it was someone moaning, 'Go hooooooooommmmmeeeee! Go hooooooooommmmmeeeee!' He listened quietly and motionless until eventually, he drifted off to sleep.

CHAPTER TWELVE

Edinburgh Night out

After having a fairly restless night, Allan wakened before his alarm went off. He hadn't slept very well at all; wakening up frequently, with his dreams being gate-crashed by constant reminders of last night's occurrences. Thoughts like: 'Where oh where was the dog?' steamrollered over any other peaceful thoughts that he might have had, that were normally given to him by the comforts afforded by his bedtime pal. He was always gifted a half-bottle at Christmas from the pub back home.

Although his head was pounding, he still jumped out of bed, and ran into the shower, hoping that this, coupled with an Aspirin, would make him feel better. Dressing as quickly as he could, Allan ran expectantly downstairs when the doorbell rang, hoping against all hope that somebody had found his dog and was returning it home.

No such luck, unfortunately. Instead, he was greeted by a smiling, cheery, older lady, well-built with ample proportions, who introduced herself as Evelyn. 'Hello, Allan', she said. 'My daughter sent me round. She said that you are looking for a cleaner, and I am looking for a job'.

'Well, come inside, and I'll explain things quickly. I'm actually just off to work in a minute, but how much do you charge?'

All the time Allan was speaking, she was plumping up cushions and tidying some of the last night's clutter. Very impressed by this, Allan gave her the job on the spot. When she gave him her hourly rate, feeling he was onto a winner here; an obvious hard worker and very conscientious, he decided she was probably worth more per hour so offered her a slightly higher rate.

When she gave him a cake she had made the night before and some fresh fruit, Allan told her, 'You can help yourself to tea, coffee, biscuits and the like, while you are here'.

'Well, thanks very much, I brought my oranges though. I'll have tea, I detest coffee, even the smell seems awful to me'.

'Well, whatever, it's all there if you want it. I must go to work now. When can you start?' He had a feeling within himself that this would work out well.

I can start anytime at all'.

'Well, here's a key so you can let yourself in when I'm at work. I'll leave you now. You just carry on. Oh, and your money. I will leave it in an envelope on the mantelpiece. I'm off now'.

At work, Allan picked up the phone and phoned the dog pound. The receptionist answered the phone, and said that she remembered him, and that, 'Yes, the dog had found its way back'. He sighed heavily with relief on hearing this, then took a sharp intake of breath when the girl continued telling him how it was not all good news; the dog had been knocked down late last night, and although alive, was recuperating at the vets and was heavily sedated, but it would be very helpful if he could pop in at lunchtime.

Allan replaced the handset, and with mixed emotions, started to work. Everyone had already arrived at the office by the time Allan got there. Pouring himself a coffee, he told everybody who would listen of last night. The Boss said to him, 'That's quite sad. Nip off early before lunch, and go to the pound. We'll meet you in the canteen when you get back'.

Pleased at the thought of some progress being made, and sympathy being offered, he went down towards Gemma's room, as he knew she would be all ears and would try to console him. Halfway down the corridor, a loud cheer and a roar from the bottom office aroused his enquiring nature. 'What's all the noise, lads?' he said.

'There's been a few flies in this office for days, and I've just killed one against the window'. He watched intently as Wilson 'Loaded up' for another go at yet another unsuspecting fly. The idea here was to stretch an elastic band over the plastic scale ruler they used for measuring the drawings. Stretching the elastic band almost to breaking point, before releasing it in the direction of their quarry, was the idea of the game. Aiming... then splat! Success. Another one squashed and plastered against the window. Allan turned and left them to argue over who was in the lead.

The Boss shouted, 'See you at lunch, Allan! Just you, head off to the pound now. We'll meet you in the canteen, hopefully with some good news'.

As he opened the door to leave, Gemma said, 'I heard about the dog. I'm off for lunch as well. Can I come with you?' At that, they both left and set off for the pound.

Allan turned to Gemma as they entered the pound, and asked her, 'Is Anna's friend likely to be furious with me for losing that dog? I don't want to look an utter fool'.

Laughing, she said, 'No, she'll be fine. She's a very easy person to get on with. Mind you, she doesn't look too happy just now at that desk'.

The assistant looked up, and said, 'Hi, I'm sorry I've got some very bad news for you'. Allan looked at Gemma, and heard the assistant Sarah say, 'The dog was too badly hurt; he had to be put down. We kept him comfortable for as long as possible, but unfortunately, we couldn't help him anymore. We'll take care of the body this afternoon. There are others you could have a look at'.

'The body?' he said in a very irate voice. That was my dog! You murdered it, and now you're offering me another one?' He was about to continue his onslaught when the look on Gemma's face silenced him completely, and they decided to go back to the office.

Gemma patted Allan on the shoulder, and said, 'I'm sorry, but don't take it out on Sarah'.

Allan replied, 'Yes, you're right. You just go to the car, and I'll go back and apologise'.

As Allan opened the heavy glass doors to allow some girls out, obviously off for lunch, he smartened up his tie and jacket, and went straight over to Sarah's desk. She looked up when he cleared his throat. 'Yes? Oh… it's you.'

'Yes,' said Allan, looking very embarrassed. 'I've just come in to say how really sorry I am for being a complete ass by being so rude to you earlier. I know it wasn't the fault of anyone here. I was just very upset. I'm not really as nasty as that'.

She accepted his apology, and said, 'I know Gemma. She did say you were a nice person, and anyone who wears a tie like that must have a sense of humour'.

'Well yes, thanks. I've just had an idea; a really good idea. No, it's even better than that, actually. How about me taking you out for a drink or to a club some time, to say sorry properly? I hear there is a good one in Stoopchurch. What do you think?'

'Well, normally I would say yes and jump at the chance, but I've just started seeing a new boyfriend, so could we do it, and not let on to Gemma?'

'That's fine by me', agreed Allan, pleased that Gemma need never know.

Back in the car, Allan said to Gemma, 'Well, we've got lots of time. How would you like to just go back to The Drovers for a drink and some lunch, instead of the canteen?'

'Well, I suppose we could since you've had some bad news', she replied.

As they sat down to eat their meal, Gemma shrieked with laughter. 'What's so funny?'

'You'll find out when we get back to the office'.

'Okay', said Allan, not realising that the blackcurrant and lemonade, his favourite driver's drink, had left a purple ring around his top lip again. He went to settle up the bill, making sure Gemma saw him leave a decent tip, and said to the waitress, 'We both really enjoyed that. We may be back again. Thank you'.

'Glad it's still not raining. I'm fed up with this rain coming off and on', said Gemma, as they got back into the car.

'Very true!' said Allan. 'I get a bit fed up with this temperamental weather as well, but we best get back quickly'.

Heading back, Gemma said, 'I told you Sarah was a nice girl, and she would be very understanding. What did you think?'

'Oh, I never really paid much attention to her, not with you around', said Allan quickly.

It didn't take long before they reached the security gates at the refinery, and with the security man smiling and winking to Gemma, he lifted the barrier for the car to enter.

They just got their car parked, and back into the office when the rest all filed in, with comments of, 'Where have you two been?' and, 'What have you been up to, eh?' They both ignored these comments and went into Gemma's office so Allan could fish for more info about Sarah. Gemma sat down at her typewriter to continue her work, and Allan headed back into his office.

On the way, he heard, 'Got it! That's one side completed. Let's see how I get on with the next corners'.

Allan went into the room where the noise had come from, and watched quietly, as Wilson's office mate Bobby said, 'Yes, well done! How long did that take you? Let me have a go!' As Allan looked over to see what the commotion was, he was surprised to see they were still not pouring over some drawings or contracts, but instead had merely succeeded in completing one face of a Rubik's cube. These were all the rage with many of the upwardly mobile types..... and children. He of course never got involved, pretending he thought it childish. Truth was, in reality, he just couldn't do it. Wilson handed the cube to his office mate Bobby and said 'You give it a go now. See if you can be any quicker'.

He heard the Boss call him in, who asked, 'How did you get on with the dog? We never saw you in the canteen'.

Shaking his head and looking down, 'No, unfortunately, the dog had to be put down, so we just went to The Drovers for lunch. I wasn't really in the mood to join everyone else'. Turning slowly to go back to his room, Allan wondered why the normally sensitive Boss was smiling, then he heard another cry of delight from the far office.

In his room, he sat down to do some work, but his mind kept drifting, not to the dog, but to Sarah. While he was wondering whether or not to make a date, the Boss called him back into his office. 'I have an idea, Allan, that might perk you up somewhat. I told you earlier that we sometimes have an office pub crawl in Edinburgh, so if your work is quite up to date, take an hour or two to start planning it'.

This cheered Allan up to no end, thinking, 'They're a great bunch of lads here, so I'll get to know them all even more'. At his desk, he studied 'The C.A.M.R.A. (Campaign For Real Ale) Guide to Good Beer' the Boss had handed him. It seemed everyone here had been converted by him to enjoy drinking real ale, as opposed to the normal stuff that had been dubbed fizz by the rest.

Soon, Allan had arranged an itinerary of what pubs to go to, and in what order. He also compiled a list of various ales on offer, including price, strength, and marks out of ten. With this done, he gave the list to Gemma, who typed it up for Allan to photocopy and distribute. 'Well, that's a job well done, and to a complete high and professional standard',he thought to himself. 'Lucky we're quite ahead of schedule with the workload'.

When he went back to his own office, one of the others, David Plain, popped his head around the door, and said with a grin, 'Hey smiler. Put me down for the designated driver. I'll take the Bosses car. He's got a bigseven or eight-seater. He says it's okay. We discussed it over lunch'.

'That's good', said Allan. 'Suppose I best do some work now and earn my keep'.

After some phone calls and reading, it was time for everyone to head home. A joking attempt to emulate the Waltons saying goodnight echoed throughout the offices as they all drifted away.

By this time, Allan had discovered the blackcurrant marks and why everyone was smiling at him; when Allan got home and went to the bathroom to freshened up and get changed, he saw the purple marks. Laughing to himself, he made sure there were no traces left, and then ate some filled rolls he had brought home. He decided to go out for a walk to work off the rolls, and when he saw no one of any interest, returned home quite early, watched some TV, and went to bed, looking forward to the impending pub crawl.

Thursday morning, the day of the pub crawl, everyone came in with their holdalls with a change of clothes for Edinburgh. These clothes were to forever be known as the honking gear, for obvious reasons. They also contained fresh work clothes for the next day. Thursday night was the preferred night so that they would all suffer in unison on Friday, and it was fun spending the day recounting the night's exploits.

After much debate and discussion, it had been agreed earlier in the week that they would all just stay at Allan's house that night, with Allan being a bit peeved that no one seemed particularly pleased with this idea, and got the distinct impression that they had all just agreed to his suggestion out of politeness. However, a few days later his thoughts had been proven to be correct, when the others told him that they had decided just to stay at Tommy's instead as they had done that a few times before.

At last, it was time to set off. Not all of them from the office were to attend, and some were to meet up later in Edinburgh, so there was just enough room. Everyone jostled for a good seat in the big seven-seater; every one that is except David

Plain who was designated driver, and the Boss, whose car it was, in the front passenger seat.

As they waited at the junction to go on to join the dual carriageway, David asked for everyone to keep their eyes peeled and tell him in advance where there is a gap. Gregor, who was sitting in the second row at the window, said 'Hold on, not yet, not yet, just wait, right, quick, go now.....after this furniture van'. By the time David had said 'furniture van', the car was halfway into the dual carriageway. As soon as he heard the word van, he rammed on the brakes causing all the passengers to fall forward abruptly. 'When will you grow up and stop doing this?' asked Allan. 'Yes?' asked Ivan. Tommy readjusted his seatbelt and turning to Gregor, said 'You did that the last time as well'. 'And the time before that' said the Boss. 'And the one before that' added Wilson. Gregor continued his laughing then pretended to bury his head in the itinerary.

A loud blast from a horn behind them prompted David to look in his mirror and say 'Well the driver behind seems to think that was the second time. At least that's what he is signalling with his hand'.

As they drove towards Edinburgh they made good speed, as most of the traffic was in the opposite direction. While most of them talked about the previous pub crawls, and argued about who had drank the most and made the biggest fools of themselves, someone piped up with the rules of engagement for the evening: 'Now everyone, look at your lists of pubs and ales. We've all chipped in £10 – a fiver of that goes as prize money to the first person who throws up, and the other half goes to the last person to go to the loo'. They all nodded and gave their approval to the rules. Looking forward to a really fun night, some continued talking whilst others started singing some songs just to get in the mood, and the rest read over Gemma's itinerary.

As the car slowed down, everyone, realising this was the first pub, raced out of the car and straight to the bar. Allan, who had been nominated to carry the kitty, ordered up all the beers. By the time the last one was poured and he got his, most of the others had finished theirs, and were ready to move onto the next pub. No time for another round in here, he was told to drink up and hurry up, and follow them to the next pub. Allan had to drink his almost in one go as he followed the rest in quickly, not wanting to lag and get lost, even though he did have the kitty, and they couldn't get any more drinks without him. 'Hope every beer isn't to be as quick as this', he thought to himself. 'There are lots of girls out tonight. I won't even get the chance to say hello to any of them'.

Following the rest into a pub next door, he was immediately called to the bar to pay for the drinks that someone had already ordered up, but this time he made sure he grabbed his first. Thankfully for Allan, the pace had slowed down somewhat, and he and Ivan talked to a few girls in the corner. By now, each of them were beginning to feel the discomfort of an extended bladder, and Ivan suggested that he and Allan sneaked to the loo when no one was looking. Secretly, they hurried over into the loo, and were surprised to see the Boss and Curtis already in. The Boss looked rather sheepish, and said, 'It was his idea. We didn't think anyone would notice'. Agreeing not to say a word to the others, they all had a quick wee, and just as they were drying their hands and about to leave, in sneaked two of the others. While they argued amongst themselves as to who was first in, the rest all came in through another door, and one said, 'There you all are, you cheats'. As no one admitted to being the first to give in, they decided to make this game void.

By now, everyone had suitably emptied their glasses, and been to the loo, so they trooped out after Allan to the next pub on the agenda. The Cannon it was called, apparently after an armoury that had been on this site many years ago. A swift beer in here was followed by a quick trip to the bar across the road.

The Fossers. In there, they saw two actors who were obviously playing at the Fringe which was on at the same time. The Boss spotted them first, and unsure what one of them was called, said to Allan, 'That one's Ronald Fraser, so go and ask the other one for his autograph. We'll find out that way'. So, Allan went over and asked both actors for their autographs.

'Certainly', they said, 'but tell me, why do you want them?'

Not wanting to say, 'Because my Boss can't remember your name, Allan could only say on the spot, 'Well, why does anybody ask for an autograph?' Feeling embarrassed at this answer, he thanked them both, and went back to join his crowd.

'The guys want to go for something to eat now', said the Boss. 'There's a nice Indian restaurant next door that we booked earlier, so we'll go in there, have a meal, and call it a day'.

'Oh, by the way', said Ivan, 'somebody has thrown up in the toilets here, and it looks like we're the only people in here right now'. With nobody owning up and admitting to this, yet another of their games was decreed void, and they made an exit to the Indian next door.

The smell of all the Indian cuisine hit them as soon as they got out of the pub. They hadn't noticed it when they arrived, as they were concentrating more on getting served at the bar first. When everyone was in, they all sat salivating as they perused the menus given to them by a young Indian girl, to who Allan immediately took a shine. As everyone gave their order, Allan read down quickly trying to figure out what all the different curries were. He had never really been one for curries, as at home his mother used to make them so hot that everyone cooled them down with beetroot, and as he hated beetroot, he just avoided curry and never got a taste for them. Everyone turned to see a familiar face entering the restaurant and waving over to everyone, before hanging his coat up and joining them all. "This is Willy Short, Allan. He used to work with us before you came', Ivan said, 'and as he lives in Edinburgh, he always joins us'.

'Well, what's everyone ordering?' said Willy. 'I see you've got me a beer as well. Thanks'.

'Well, we've already had an up-chucker next door, but no admission', said Ivan. 'But, I'll have this one here', pointing to his favourite curry.

'Well, I'll go for the hottest one they've got', said Gregor McAndrew, pointing to a Vindaloo.

'No, that's not the hottest – this one here's much stronger. I'll go for that', said Willy.

The waitress went around the table getting everyone's order, and stopped at Allan, who said, 'Could I go for a korma (an Indian meal consisting of meat and vegetables), please? I believe that's quite sweet and mild. That's what I fancy tonight, and smiled with a twinkle in his eye, causing the waitress to look down.

'What a woose (a weak choice). Be a man and try something stronger', said Ivan.

'No, just let him have what he prefers', said the waitress. 'He's probably a bit more discerning than the rest of you'.

Pleased with this backhanded vote of confidence from her, he said, 'You guys have probably dulled and scorched your taste buds with all the hot curries. I want to appreciate the flavour'.

As the evening wore on, and the ale got tastier and tastier, and the lads got thirstier and thirstier, one of the guys spied a large watermelon in the middle of a fruit display at the cash desk. When it was time to leave, they all went over to the cash desk to settle up, while Tommy Davidson grabbed the watermelon, and put it up to his jersey, impersonating a pregnant lady. 'Does anyone of the girls you've been seeing recently look like this yet, Allan?' he said, deliberately making sure the waitress heard him so as to embarrass him fully.

Before he could make any answer, or give a suitable off-the-cuff rejoinder, the owner of the restaurant came rushing from behind his desk. 'That's not a toy!' he shouted. 'Put that back now!'

Tommy, feeling silly now, retrieved it from under his jersey, and trying to put it back with an air of nonchalance, dropped it. It splattered all over the floor, rolling over to the owner, and stopped at his feet, leaving a big mess on the carpet. With the restaurant owner now about to fulminate in anger.

Before he could say anything, the Boss stepped in immediately, apologised to the owner, and said to Allan, 'You've got the kitty. Pay the man for all the damage, round it up, and let's get out of here quickly. I think it's time for us to head back now'.

When everyone was back in the car in their seats, the driver, David Plain, said, 'Well, you guys will have some hangover tomorrow, and I bet Geophrey's glad he saw sense and stayed sober to keep a clear head because he knows he'll probably need to hold the fort tomorrow and cover for the rest of you. I'm glad I'm driving. Let's get back to Tommy's'.

Tommy Davidson sat very quietly in his seat, and urged everyone not to tell his wife about his antics, and to behave when they got back to his house. This, they all agreed to, and soon the car was hurtling along the motorway.

As they entered his house, Tommy said, putting his finger to his lips, 'Try to be as quiet as you can, lads. You are all downstairs in the living room. The wife's left out some sleeping bags and a few quilts'. Once inside, they all very quietly settled down for the night, with almost everyone conking out within minutes.

Friday morning found a load of weary bodies wakening up with pounding headaches, dry throats, and emptier wallets. David Plain was first to be ready, and took great delight in jingling the car keys and constantly humming his favourite tune of the moment, '*Stranger On The Shore.*' 'Right, you lot!' he shouted. 'We'll be late if we don't all move out now'. Sluggishly, they all got in the car after thanking Tommy's wife for being their understanding host and set off quietly for work.

*   *   *

CHAPTER THIRTEEN

The Brothers

At the dinner table on Friday night, Mum said that she would give Allan a call to find out how he was, as he hadn't been home for a while. Ronald said, 'Tell him that we would come through to see him, but Alistair is scared', then laughed. 'Utter rubbish!' yelled Alistair. 'It was you that was scared, not me. I would go back anytime. No problem'. 'Alright then', said Ronald. 'Let's just see. It's a bank holiday here on Monday, so let's go through early in the morning. Just for the day'. 'Alright', said his brother, 'But we're not bringing Tilda '. 'Oh yes that's right, you're scared of her aren't you?' 'No I am not. It's you that's scared. I just tell her as it is'.

When the kitchen door opened and Tilda came in she asked 'Tell who what?' 'Oh nothing' said Ronald as he and Alistair quickly went through to the adjoining dining room to avoid further confrontation. She then put on the dining table, the cakes and other goodies she had bought for tea and told her silent brothers to leave them till after the meal. Putting a horror video on the table, she said, 'You might enjoy this boys, I saw this in a shop (display) window at a reduced rate'. 'It was still a bit pricey so I had to argue to get it reduced even further', then went to her room to get changed. Alistair muttered under his breath, that the shopkeeper had probably just reduced it to get rid of her. Ronald asked his Mum hopefully, 'Are those other cakes through there for tomorrow?' Mum shouted back 'No! she's taking these up to the old folks home on the way to visit that old lady that was a friend of your gran's'. 'Who is this old lady anyway?' asked Ronald. Mum came through and told them that, the old lady in question was only ever referred to as the 'old lady' because no matter how often Celia and Tilda asked her name they always forgot and were now too embarrassed to ask her again.

The girls love to visit her and listen to her tales of when she was younger. It seemed that she'd had a very full and active life when she was younger. Even now at ninety-eight she still has a twinkle in her eye, when Tilda told her she had lovely skin with very few wrinkles, she just laughed and said: 'Yes, just the one and am sitting on it'. she loves to hear of the younger ones antics, making sure they knew that she had acted the same way when she was much younger.

Alistair said 'Very nice but she's still not coming with us tomorrow anyway'. 'I heard that!' shouted Tilda from the hall. 'And keep your grubby mitts off those cakes'. Straight away the two pulled their hands back and waved them about in pretend obedience.

Their mum looked at them and pointed out 'Tilda wouldn't be able to come anyway because, as it happens, she is starting a new job tomorrow'. 'I wonder how long that one will last', 'now,now" now' said mum 'She's doing her best'.

When Alistair asked what had happened to her last job in the store of a Builder's-Yard, Ronald laughed and said 'She had to leave because of her bad language', 'I wouldn't have thought that would bother her' Alistair said while rummaging through the biscuit tin for any chocolate ones that Ronald and dad had missed. Wiping her hands on her apron, Mum said 'That's enough, you know pretty well that it was her language' 'Why don't you want to stay overnight, then?' Quick as a flash, Ronald said, 'I've a job to come home to. I can't just take time off willy-nilly'.

After tea, Mum made her quick call and told Allan his brothers would be through on Monday for the day. They would arrive at the back of eight, she said, as they knew he had to go to work, and Allan, who was still suffering from the previous night and was in no mood to disagree with anyone, told her that would be fine. 'Make sure they've got everything ready a night before they leave because I don't want to be late for my work, just because they are not prepared in time'.

Mum agreed to this. 'I'll make sure they make sandwiches for the journey for themselves'.

Next morning the two of them grabbed the sandwiches they had put in the freezer the night before, two bags of crisps, a box of twiglets snack, and half a dozen tins of beer to drink on the journey. They both said goodbye and ran along to catch the bus.

As soon as they got on the bus, Ronald took out a tin and offered his brother one. 'No', said Alistair, 'Wait until we get on the train'. Ignoring this, Ronald was about to open his tin when Alistair grabbed it from him, and said 'Not yet', while opening a bag of crisps.

When they arrived at the town centre they guzzled down a beer each, then went straight to the station where they finished their beers. The stationmaster, who had seen them drinking, rushed over, and told them they would not be allowed on the next train; they would have to wait for a later one so that any effects the beer may have had will have worn off, and that there would be no danger of them disrupting other passengers.

'Well, that's fine by me', said Alistair to his brother. 'I feel a bit queasy after drinking them so quickly, but if we get the next train we'll have to get a taxi from Stoopchurch to Strathmanor to be in time to meet him. I hope we'll have enough money'.

As they sat waiting, Alistair said, 'I'm hungry', and started opening sandwiches. Taking a bite from one and offering Ronald another, he said in a choking voice, 'These things are still frozen. Why did you put them in the freezer?'

'Well, I thought they might go off overnight. Besides, you never told me not to'.

When their train arrived, they left the sandwiches on the bench and sidled on quickly, hoping the stationmaster never saw them again, and settled down, praying they would be on time. Luckily enough, they arrived on time, having had to get a taxi from the station just to make sure.

The doorbell went at 8.05 A.M., just as Allan was finishing his breakfast. He picked up the newspaper from the floor and opened the door to let them in. 'Well, you're here nice and early. That's a relief', he said to them.

'Yes', said Ronald. 'That gives us more time before we go back home because he, "adding with a smile and nodding to Alistair", is too scared to stay overnight'.

Allan told them to put in the fridge; the steak pie that they had brought with them for lunch. 'Now, here's the spare key. Don't lose it, and don't make a mess. I'll come back at lunch'.

'No, it's okay', said Alistair. 'There's only enough for us anyway. You just go to your canteen, and we'll see you at tea-time. There are loads for us to do in that precinct'.

'I'm off to work, then', said Allan. 'Phone Mum to let her know you're okay, and I'll see you at tea-time'.

Straight away, the pair set about exploring the house. They looked over all the records that had been left in the house by the previous owner. Not being fans of classical music, they soon turned their attention to the many books on the bookshelves. Again, they found the choices available were not to their liking. 'Who reads Dosto-something-or-other-evsky, and a load of legal books just for fun in their spare time, anyway?'

'Look in here!' called Alistair. 'He's even got a piano. Why will he have that? He can't even play the piano'.

' Well, that must've been left in the house from the previous owner. Let's play chopsticks on it before we go out', said Ronald.

After a few feisty moments over who was hitting the wrong black notes, Alistair said, 'I am fed up with this now. Let's go over the road, and check out that precinct'.

'Yes, we will have a coffee first while we watch the end of the Flintstones, and there's a Tom and Jerry triple bill', said Ronald. They put their lunch in the oven on very low heat and put their cups in the basin for someone else to wash.

'Right, let's go. We'll just get some more milk and biscuits, come back, and watch more TV, then go to the precinct'.

The two of them grabbed their jackets, and on the way out, Ronald, pointing at the phone, said, 'Look – Mum is always moaning about us running up her phone bill... he'll never know'.

'Right!' said Alistair. I will phone my mate in Aberdeen'.

While he was talking for a good while, Ronald was looking in his wallet for the name and number of a French girl he had met at a disco a few weeks before. After wrestling the phone from his brother eventually, and saying, 'It's my go now,' he phoned Bridgette who he had met at the Squeezers, and had a good, long conversation with her.

Alistair pointed to his watch, and said, 'Right, two more – one each. We mustn't be greedy. Do you know Caroline in Canada's number? She is sweet'.

'No, but in my wallet, I have the number of Caroline's friend that I got when we were visiting over there. I will phone her. That's my choice'.

After letting the phone ring for a long time, a very groggy and annoyed voice answered, and said, 'Who is this? And what on earth are you doing phoning me at this time in the morning?'

'Ohh, what time is it there?' Ronald asked.

'It's three o'clock'.

'Ohh, really? What are you doing up at this time of the night?' And with that, he slammed the phone down.

Just as the phone went down, the postman posted a number of letters, then someone else posted a few fliers. Alistair picked up these, read them, and said, 'Let's phone all these numbers in this magazine over there for free catalogues and information about building products, insurance quotes, and everything else that will keep coming through the post, and confuse him'.

That took another good few minutes, by which time their attention span was exhausted, so they gave up on the phone.

'I can see from here that there is a sale on in some shops. Let's have a look round while we're here', suggested Alistair

'Yes' said Ronald. 'And that deodorant that he uses, they do a hair lacquer by the same company, and the container is almost identical. If we bought a can and switched it with his deodorant, he will never notice it until it was too late, so let's go and buy one of them'.

It appeared that almost all of the shops had a sale on, so the first shop they went to was a record shop. Apparently, it was a closing down sale, so they spent a long time there going through stacks and stacks of cut-price albums and singles, with Ronald, who worked as a part-time DJ, buying as many discs from new bands as he could afford.

Alistair looked at his watch and said that they should probably move on, as he wanted to look at the clothes shop across the way. Ronald, who was thoroughly enjoying himself looking through the records, but also flirting with the girl behind the counter, sighed, and raising his hands in submission, said, 'Right, let's go'.

As they walked over to the clothes shop, Alistair asked, 'Were you buying records or chatting up that girl?'

'Both, She was really nice'.

'True, but here's the Clothes Boutique now'.

The smell of rows and rows of brand new clothes always pleased Alistair. He was a bit of a fashion guru, well, both were really, and loved his clothes. He took a few pairs of trousers into a changing room to try them on, and after looking at himself in the mirror, decided they were not for him. He put them back on their hangers and took them over to the assistant. As he handed them back, he overheard another assistant chastising Ronald for trying on a number of t-shirts for size: 'You're not supposed to try on the t-shirts, Sir'.

'Who would want to buy a t-shirt someone has already worn? Well, certainly not me if it doesn't fit', said Ronald, thrusting them back indignantly into the hands of the girl.

They both then took two shirts each into cubicles, one large and one small, and switched the size labels when they both came out. They hung them up on the respective rails, then took two pairs of trousers each, again one large and one small and, after switching the labels, put them back on the rails. Frustrated, the shop assistant said, 'Couple of time-wasters'.

Alistair looked at his brother and said as he laughed, 'Maybe, but some anorexic person will be pleased to think they have suddenly put some weight on, and some fat bugger will think they have lost weight. That's our good deed for the day'.

Annoyed all the same by the shop assistant's leaving comment, Alistair said, 'They're not very friendly here, are they?'

'Oh look!' he said, pointing to an amusement arcade. 'Let's try that out'.

Once inside, Alistair went on the shooting range, while Ronald went on the space invaders. After that, they went over to the fruit machines after they exchanged some notes for change from the surly weather-beaten man behind the desk. Ronald put all of his change in the machine with no luck, borrowed a fiver from his grudging brother, then took it over to get more change. Alistair put his final coin in the fruit machine and was delighted when he hit the jackpot. Three gold bells! His brother came rushing over, and shouted vehemently, 'That's my money you just won! I only went to get change!'

'Well,though – it's mine now', he said with a smug look on his face, whilst patting his jingling pockets.

When they left the amusement arcade, still bickering jokingly, they noticed a pet shop. 'Look!' said Alistair. 'He is always wittering on about not knowing anyone, and he would like a dog. Let's go and see what they have'.

In the shop, which had the usual, obvious animal smells from rabbits, guinea pigs, and budgies, they had in the corner some cross-bred puppies. 'How much do these puppies cost?' asked Ronald. 'I never saw it in the window'.

'Well, they're designer dogs, so I'm asking a reasonable price. It's on the cage'.

'You mean a cross-breed! called out Alistair.

'Well, to the uninitiated, I suppose'.

'Well, I'm very initiated', retorted Ronald, 'And I know that it's just a bloody mongrel'.

'Look, if you two are not going to buy anything, but just muck around, get out of my shop, and let me serve proper customers'.

Ronald looked around the empty shop, and asked, 'Ohh, are these customers in the stockroom in the back, then?'

Getting exasperated by now, the shopkeeper called for his assistant to come and see if these jokers wanted to buy anything, as he was fed up with them.

Moving over to the aquarium section, Alistair said, 'You got gouramies, guppies, Siamese fighting fish, but do you have any Wandas?'

The assistant came over and looked in all the tanks, and looking perplexed, called back to his colleague Rob, 'Have you seen a fish called Wanda here?'

To which Rob replied, 'If that's Laurel and flipping Hardy laughing, just show them the door!'

'It's okay, we know where it is. We're not as daft as you look', and suppressing their laughs, they left the shop.

Wondering what to do next, they noticed a camping shop and ran over quickly to have a look inside.

Alistair explained to the cashier, 'We're only down for the day, and were looking around all the shops here. We've never been camping before, but might take it up sometime. What exactly should beginners buy?'

'Well', said the assistant pensively and scratching his head, 'Obviously you will need a tent. They are all over here in varying sizes'.

'You'll need a good sleeping bag '

'Nah, it's okay', interrupted Ronald. 'He will probably bring his girlfriend or pick up some floozy on the way'.

'A stove for cooking', continued the assistant.

Nah, our Gran will probably make sandwiches for us, and give us a flask', answered Ronald.

'And if it's hot you might need insect repellent?'

'Not with all the aftershave he douses himself in', Alistair said. 'That should see any beasties off!'

To which his brother immediately retorted, 'Yeah, and with his wind after all the curries he eats, that would see off even an elephant'.

'Yes, very funny lads, but are you serious buyers or just in for a laugh ?' the assistant asked, becoming impatient.

'Well, okay, but do you have any of those water pills I hear some old folk get? They would be good if we get thirsty. And do we need to add anything to them for them to work?' asked Ronald, defiantly.

'I don't think you're serious buyers, to be honest, and I don't have time to stand here all day being made a fool of. So, can you just leave my shop!'

The two brothers looked at each other in mock; acting surprise, and said in unison, 'Who, us?' and pointed to each other. As they turned to leave, one of the brothers looked at the large fire extinguisher on the wall behind the till, and said, 'Would we need one of them just in case?'

The shop assistant then ran out from behind the counter, shouting, 'Out, and don't come back!' Pointing to the door, he ushered them out.

As they sauntered nonchalantly back to the house, Ronald said, 'There's that pub he moaned about. Let's nip in for a pint, and you're paying out of your ill-gotten gains. You sneaky, money-grabbing git'.

"Well, if that's what it takes to put a smile back on your greeting' face – although you have cheered up a bit now. But, just the one beer mind'. Again, as with Allan before, the whole place went silent, with the few patrons in at that time turning to stare at the brothers.

'Shut that door, and keep the heat in!' rasped one of the regulars.

'And dinna you sit in that chair. That's auld Bert's. He's just gone out for his pension'.

As they sat down in a corner taking their jackets off, Ronald told Alistair to get the beers and picked up a newspaper from the seat. 'Oi! Put that paper back. Someone's reading that. He's just gone to the toilet', another regular shouted.

Ronald looked straight back, and quipped, 'Well, that's a novel trick, being able to read it from in there'.

After a while waiting to be served, Alistair shouted, 'Are we getting served or what!'

In a minute!' snapped the barman without lifting his head. 'Can you not see I'm doing my pools coupon!'

'Well, when you have finished it, could we get two steak pies for our lunch as well? And can we also get the darts? We'll have a game while we're waiting'.

Looking up fiercely, the barman said, 'No, they're only for regulars, and darts night is on a Thursday, anyway'..

One of the old men in the corner said, 'Aye, you're no' regulars here. Where are you from, anyway?'

'Oh, we're just down for the day visiting our brother who stays across the road'.

'Oh, I see!" the old man replied, as the barman said, 'Here's your beers', and slapped them on the counter.

As they went over to get their beers, their lukewarm steak pies were slapped on the counter as well. 'It smells as if it would be great if only it was hotter', said Ronald.

'It does', said Alistair, 'but I bet it'll never be as good as Gran's'.. With a startled look on his face, he said, 'Oh quick! We've left that pie in the oven!' And they both immediately ran out of the pub for home leaving their untouched beers and lunch on the counter, with the barman shouting, 'Oi, who's paying for these?'

When they got back to Allan's house, out of breath and panting, they argued over who had the key; each saying he thought the other had it. Agreeing eventually that neither had the key, they decided they had to call Mum for advice. Instinctively, they turned and ran over the road to a telephone box, where they reversed the charges to phone home.

Allan was sitting at his desk just after lunch when his phone rang from an outside line; it was his mother. She explained, 'I've just had a call from Strathmanor. Nothing to worry about, but those two have locked themselves out, and you can't just wait to tea-time because they told me that they put Gran's pie in the oven before they went out, so the oven is on. You'll need to go and sort it. And your Gran was saying last night –'

He interrupted his Mum by saying, 'Look, I need to go now. I have to hear this later'. He immediately jumped up, went through to the Boss to explain the situation and assured him that he would be back very quickly.

By the time Allan got back to the house, two worried-looking brothers were standing at the front door arguing. Ronald had just found the key under the doormat, and as they argued whose fault that was, Alistair put the key in the lock, but failed to get it to turn.

Allan jumped out of his car, and slamming the door closed, said, 'You pair of clowns. You can't even get the door open!' Saying hello to a passing neighbour, and explaining who the other two were and what they were doing, he turned the key himself, then looking menacingly at his brothers, he snarled, 'I don't know what you retards have done, but this doesn't work anymore.

He put the key back in his pocket, and running round to the back of the house, shouted for them to come quickly, as knowing them they could well have left a window open or even the back door unlocked.

They raced round to the back of the house and tried in vain to get in, until Alistair said that he could smell smoke from under the door. 'We'll have to go back and burst the front door in, and you two will need to stay in and get a joiner to fix the lock'.

The three raced back around to the front door and stopped dead in their tracks. Looking open-mouthed in astonishment at the now slightly opened door, Ronald said, 'What the heck is going on here?' Not waiting for any answer, they rushed into the house, and straight through to the kitchen. 'Well, I certainly didn't drop the key – I never took it!' Ronald said.

Alistair nodded in surprise agreement, and said, 'I don't know how it got there either. I definitely didn't take it with me'.

The smoke from the by now cremated pie had filled the whole house, the kitchen being the worst, and stank heavily of burnt lunch. 'Look at the mess you've made of my cooker and the kitchen. Get all the windows and doors open, and make sure that by the time I get back, you have this cooker as clean as it was when you got here'. In disgust, Allan gave Ronald back the key and stormed out of the house, and went back to work. 'They'll have some explaining to do when I get back tonight'.

Ronald turned to Alistair, handed him a cloth, and said, 'I will use this air freshener spray'. After depleting the contents of the can, and seeing his brother being less than enthusiastic, he said, 'That's good enough for me. If we are here when he comes back, he'll only moan again, so we got to get out of this place'. Grabbing their coats, and still laughing and joking, they headed for the bus station to go home.

Allan stayed slightly later at work that night to make up the time he took, and was disgusted to find the house still stank, and the cooker looked like it had only been rubbed over with a damp dishcloth. As he went to put the kettle on, he noticed a note.

It said, 'Sorry'. That was all.

Allan immediately phoned home. 'Hi Mum, it's me. Are those two in? I want a word with them'.

'No', she said, 'they've gone out. They came home early telling me they couldn't get any peace to watch TV because of a big dog barking all afternoon'.

'Oh, that's what they told you, is it? Well, here's what really happened'. He went on to tell his mother what had really happened, and trying to calm down, he asked, 'How was Tilda's first day' Mum took a big sigh and said ' Oh, not too well' she walked out, she said she didn't do all that studying just to sweep up hair' 'If I were a swearing man you'd hear me swear. I'd best go now, Mum. I need to clean a bit more, and eat something before I lose my mind. Then, saying goodbye, he had an extra-large scotch, and ran across for a fish supper, as he didn't want to cook anything before he cleanse the cooker.

The road was very busy, and as he waited for a gap in the traffic to run across, his mood got darker and darker the more he dwelled upon the mess. As soon as there was a gap, he belted across, and straight to the chip shop which was just about to close. Six o'clock on Mondays, 'I'm glad I just got you', he said.

She replied, 'Yes, but hurry up, as I'm just about to close'.

'I'd fancy a chicken supper. Do you have chicken breast?'

'Yes, but hurry up. Is that what you want?'

Looking at her sour face, he said, 'Ohh, no, don't bother. Just give me a bag of chips then fluffy tits'. She served him without another word. Allan paid her, and grabbing the chips, started to run for home.

Allan sat in front of his TV, and as soon as his chips were finished, phoned home to check-in. As much as he tried to keep the conversation about the other two, his mother always seemed to just agree with Allan, and then cleverly steer the conversation around to events back home. 'Well, Mum', said Allan, 'Sorry to interrupt you again, but that's Panorama just coming up now', and saying goodbye to his Mum, he settled down with a drink to watch Benny Hill.

The combination of watching Benny Hill and more whiskey raised his mood greatly, so Allan started to watch a new program called, 'Choose A Mate' because it sounded like it had prospects. After which he just decided to call it a day, and trudged wearily upstairs to put the day to rest.

At his room, Allan stopped in his tracks and looked down at his bed, puzzled. The bed he always made up meticulously before leaving in the morning had no bedclothes on it at all; instead, they were in a heap at the bottom. Sensing there was something strange here, he checked that all windows and doors were closed. Then, went back to his room, made up his bed again, took another large swig, and got into the bed, wondering what had happened there. Eventually, he just drifted off to sleep.

*   *   *

CHAPTER FOURTEEN

The Nanny

At 6.05 A.M., Allan was wakened by the milkman, so he sighed, jumped out of bed, and said: 'Right, today is the start of my new regime'. He put on an old tracksuit that his brother didn't yet know he had borrowed, picked up the sports bag that his other brother didn't know about either and made his way downstairs with his work clothes in a supermarket carrier bag, put the bag in the car and drove off to the swimming pool.

'You are a new face here' , said the attendant. 'Yes, I'm new to Strathmanor, I'm a fitness freak, so you will see a lot of me'. The attendant nodded and looked at Allan's beer belly and said 'The gent's pool is straight ahead, the mixed one to the right'.

As Allan left him and walked through to the right, he heard the attendant shout: 'Since it's quite early, it will be very quiet in there, so you will probably be allowed to stay in the pool much longer'.

There were no other bathers in the pool yet, only a lifeguard sitting in the high chair at the side, reading a book. For a few seconds, the water seemed cold, bracing himself, a quick length with breast stroke soon warmed him up. As he turned to swim back down, an oversized elderly lady climbed down the ladder into the pool, so Allan diverted slightly to allow her more room.

As he swam in the other direction, another, heftier lady waddled out of the changing room, and without any trepidation, jumped straight in the water. 'That was some dive bomb! I'm surprised, that there's any water left' thought Allan as he reached the far end. As she sidled along the edge of the pool to join the other lady, Allan swam further into the centre to allow her some room. By the time he had completed his next length, two other rolly-pollies had joined in.

Allan was being pushed further and further over to the same side the lifeguard was at, who called down to him: 'There is not much room for you, mate, you must've picked a day when there is a special offer on at the Bingo, where they're off to after this swim' . 'Yes', laughed Allan, 'But after all, they are entitled to be here as much as me and I hope I'm still getting out and about; when I'm at their age'. As Allan swam down once more, two more ladies wedged themselves in amongst their friends and since they were all just standing and chatting, none of them were actually swimming, not even the one with the water wings or the one next to her with her own built-in rubber tyre and bathing cap that resembled a bowl of fruit, Allan decided, maybe I need to just to give in for the day and come back another time.

When Allan was coming out of the water to go back to the changing room, a beautiful blonde, in a bikini, passed him on her way to the edge of the pool, where she dived in and took off like an Olympic swimmer. When she reached the end, she quickly climbed out and nodding to the guard climbed up to the high diving board. Allan stood mesmerized by her beauty while she poised herself on tiptoes at the end of the springboard, then suddenly dived backwards. When she swam down to the end of the pool and climbed out, Allan went over to speak to her but she just shouted over to the guard: 'That will do for me diving today, I will just swim now to keep my body trim'.

'What kind of a brother are you anyway, that doesn't get me fixed up with a decent boyfriend?' she said jokingly to the guard as he started to climb down the ladder. He replied: 'One that is glad his shift is finished and his wee sister is taking over, so get yourself up here. You better hope, the manager doesn't come in and see you in that bikini when you are on duty. You're meant to wear a uniform'. He picked up a towel from the stack at the door to the showers, and went in, followed by Allan. In the shower, Allan began a conversation with the guard. 'I think, I will try to come in here every morning before work. I found it a bit more tiring than I expected'. When he turned to face the guard, he noticed his midriff had a six-pack to rival Arnie's. 'That's impressive', said Allan and pointed to it. 'Far more impressive than mine' as he looked down on himself.

'What are you talking about?' growled the guard who was somewhat taken aback.

'Ohh, just your abs, very impressive' . Realising that he might have been misunderstood a bit, Allan tried to recover the situation by saying: 'I hope you didn't think I meant anything else by it'

'Like what?' He was asked. 'Well, you know, I'm not that way inclined, hop3

e you are okay with me. So maybe you can put a word in for me with your sister' . The swimming guard thinks to himself 'Okay, I will fix you up with my sister, alright' . Allan never heard any reply, as another guy came in to get changed and pecked the brother on the cheek, and said 'Sorry, I'm late, darling, I had a meltdown earlier in the kitchen and my mum was consoling me. So I'll just do a quick ten length and meet you at the canteen'. 'Sure, sweetheart, will see you there'.

Feeling quite uncomfortable, Allan thought it would be best just to get dried, dressed and out as soon as possible. In silence, he opened his bag and was shocked to find there was no towel. There certainly had been when he packed his bag but now there was only a face cloth. The cloth was still damp from when he washed his face this morning. Wondering how the two could've switched, he bit the bullet and asked the attendant if he could get a towel. 'Of course, there are loads out there, just help yourself'', said the Attendant, and left the changing room.

With no one in the changing room now and Allan needing to get to work soon, he poked his head out the door and told the bikini-clad girl his predicament. 'Oh it's okay'she called down. 'I've seen it all before and I am sure these ladies have as well. And if they haven't, then at their age it's time they had' . The older ladies heard this and immediately, one called back 'No we've not. We are not prudes though. Come out' and continued the catcalling.

'Right' said Allan. 'You asked for it. Here I come'. Allan came out for a towel with his face cloth in front and his bag at his rear. He picked up a towel and went back into the changing room. The Boos and hisses and calls of coward from the older ladies were still ringing in his ears when the young girl shouted down from her high chair. 'What a spoilsport. And with us having nothing to look forward to now'.

Allan smiled back to her and rushed into the changing room to get dried off, dressed up, then left immediately for his work. 'See you soon Adonis hopefully' as she waved to a red-faced Allan. Glad to be out of there but wondering what kind of an impression he had made on the girl. Allan vowed to himself to try to make it a more regular occurrence because he would have to do all the chasing as her brother would probably be of no help.

Allan, feeling that he may have now blown his chances of a message being passed on to the bikini-clad beauty headed straight to work, where Ivan commented on the cheap aftershave he was using. 'Eau De Chlorine' he called it.

'Oh Allan!', called the Boss. 'Could you pop in here for a minute?' It was first thing in the morning, and he hadn't yet planned his work for the day, so Allan went through to the Bosses office as requested to see if there was anything, in particular, he wanted him to do that day.

'If you haven't planned today as yet, maybe you could do me a favour?' Pleased to hear Allan had nothing planned, he continued, 'When I was in France setting up an office for our foreign branch we had a nanny for the children, called Irene. She's coming over today to stay with us for a fortnight. I'm too busy to collect her at lunchtime, so will you go and collect her and her friend from the train station in Edinburgh?'

Agreeing, Allan went into his own office to tell his office mates where he was going. Geophrey said that would be a nice skive for him, but since he didn't know the girls in question personally, and so wouldn't recognise them, it would be best to make an Idiot Board with their names on it. This took up a good half-hour, with the two of them doing so, and with it in hand, Allan set off for the station.

The traffic was heavy, with a few minor hold-ups, which bordered Allan, but he was relieved when he looked at his watch to see that the train was not yet due. He found a place to park his car, bought a sausage roll and a tin of coke for his lunch in the station, and sat on a bench to consume it while waiting in the sunshine, which wasn't expected to last according to the weather report. At the other end of the bench, someone had left empty coke cans, crisp packets and old newspapers. He thought this wouldn't give a good impression to tourists, and after putting them all in the bin, except The Sun, he sat back down to await the girls.

After a few minutes waiting and chatting to a girl who was waiting for a train to Glasgow, he began to wonder if perhaps he had missed the train after all, as there didn't seem to be any sign of a train arriving. Allan looked down at his watch checking the time after the girl left to get on her train, and by now was convinced he had missed the train after all. 'So, what will I do now? With me standing here looking like a fool with an Idiot Board on an empty platform'.

Phoning back to the office for further instructions, he was told by the Boss, 'Well, just wait ten more minutes and head back'. Allan sat down on the bench to read the newspaper that was there, and after a good fifteen minutes, decided it was probably time to call it quits and go back to the office.

Just as he walked past the ticket office, a couple of girls were coming out of the snack bar in the station. Allan said 'Hi' to the girls, and caught the name Irene on one of the girls' suitcases. 'Irene!' said Allan to them, and one of the girls looked up, surprised to see her name on the card they had made back at the office. 'My name is Allan, and I was sent by my Boss to collect you'. Taking both suitcases from the girls, he said, 'Your carriage awaits. The car is just over there. I thought I'd missed you when I didn't see you for a while'.

Irene said, 'Well, I'm glad we found you because we wouldn't have known what to do. It was a long journey, and we took the opportunity for a snack'.

'Well, all's well that ends well. I'm all yours now', and after putting the suitcases in the boot of the car, Allan opened the door to let them in, and started off to Strathmanor.

184

The girls in the back were chatting and laughing to themselves, and every time Allan looked in the mirror to make eye contact and be friendly, they smiled and fixed their hair, or so he thought. Seeing this as a golden opportunity to ingratiate himself, he asked them if they fancied stopping off for something to eat, to which they politely said no, as they had just eaten at the station.

Chatting away to his passengers, Allan remarked, 'Phh, there's a hitch-hiker. A dodgy character if there ever was one'. The long-haired youth standing at the side of the road with his thumb out looked hopeful when he saw the girls pointing at him and talking.

'Let's stop for him', said a voice from the back. 'It looks like he has many bags with him'.

'Well, okay then', said Allan reluctantly, as he pulled into the side of the road. It turned out that he was going much further than Strathmanor, but Allan agreed to take him as far as he could, where he could probably pick up another lift. The hitch-hiker agreed happily, got in the front of the car, and they set off again.

After a few miles of chat, mainly between his passengers, the hitch-hiker said he was hungry and asked to stop near a motorway station. Allan said to him gruffly, 'Well, we don't actually have time. I'm supposed to be at work'.

Immediately, one of the girls from the back interrupted, and said, 'Yes, that sounds a good idea! We probably didn't eat enough back at the station. Let's stop at that one over there'. Cheesed off at this reply, as they had already said no to

Allan's offer, he relented and pulled in to the approaching service station.

'We'll need to be quick', said Allan, as he marched briskly into the diner. Here, he only allowed them enough time for a burger and a coffee, while all the time his conversation was paid little attention to, and the hitch-hiker was listened to attentively by the girls.

Allan went over to pay the bill and was more annoyed to discover that he had been given the bill for all four of them. Hustling everyone into the car, one of the girls said, 'You sit in the back with us, as Allan will probably need to concentrate on the road'. The two girls got in the back, with the hitch-hiker happily seated between them.

Two or three miles down the road, the hitchhiker said, 'Do you mind if I smoke?' To which Allan of course replied, 'I'd rather you didn't smoke in the car. I've just given up, so if it's all the same to you...'

'Oh, let him,' said Irene's friend. 'We're just about to light up, anyway'.

'Well, I suppose so', grumbled Allan as he wound down his window, 'but no fag ash on my carpet!' he said as he settled down in a huffed silence. They continued along the motorway with Allan struggling to get a word in edgeways, until it was time to turn off, where they left the hitch-hiker along with his bags, and his thumb.

Allan said to Irene's friend, Freida, 'How do you two fancy coming out for a drink with me one of these night? There's a nice Inn up at the village you'll be staying in. I could meet you there, or, we could do something else?'

'Yeah, that sounds a good idea. We'll organise something, soon'.

Just then, they rounded a corner, and Allan said, 'This is where you're staying girls. I'll take your suitcases in'.

Irene gasped as she looked up at the big house, and said to Freida, 'Look at that house. Like a mansion, really! It's very impressive! I must have a picture taken outside to take home.' Thinking that he would be also part of the picture, Allan started to fix his hair, only to be handed the camera to take the picture with. He took three or four snaps from different angles, then just said 'cheerio to the girls', and headed back to work.

Back in the office, Allan went straight to the Boss and told him, 'That his guests arrived safely at the house'.

'Yes, I know; they have just called me. Thanks, Allan. I was worried they had missed the train'.

'No, everything is okay. I will go and see what's been happening here'. As he turned to leave the room, he was called back again.

'Oh, Allan, you seem to have struck a chord with Irene's friend Freida. She said that you were going to take her up to the pub'. He went on to say, 'She will be leaving us to go to Edinburgh for a few days, so you best do it tomorrow night'.

Later that afternoon, when he was sure there were no eavesdroppers around, Allan telephoned Freida. 'Hi, Freida, it's Allan. I know you're going away soon, but I have to stay in tomorrow night to wait for a heating engineer'. After hearing Freida sighing which made him think she was still quite keen, he asked her if she would come around to his house for a drink.

'That would be fine', she said.

Allan, pleased with himself, explained the slight change of plan to the Boss: 'This is the third or fourth heating engineer I've asked; the other ones just didn't turn up. So, hopefully, this time I will be lucky'.

The next day, the aroma of expensive aftershave was wafting around the office, and was commented on by the others. It was obvious Allan was planning a special night.

As soon as five o'clock came, he was out of the office and over to the canteen, like the proverbial bat out of hell. Eating as quickly as he could, ignoring the jibes from the others, and not lingering to chat anyone up, Allan went to collect Freida and brought her back to his house.

'I see there's a pub across the road there', said Freida. 'Let's pop over for a quickie'. Reluctantly, Allan crossed the road with Freida. When they entered the pub, yet again the place went silent as everyone turned and stared at the pair.

'It's not very welcoming in here. Let's just go', said Allan.

'No, no', replied Freida. 'I told you, I really fancied a quickie'.

'Well, so do I, but let's just have one drink here and then go home'. Sure enough, they had just one drink, then left the hostile environment and went back across the road.

Allan opened the door to a very cold hall. He explained to Freida, 'You see, this is why I have to get the heating engineer; it's always cold here. I'm only warm in bed under the quilt. Let's get the kettle on for something warm'. Allan put the kettle on, and they both went through to the living room to sample Allan's home-brew. This was the home-brew he had made with Alice, some weeks ago, hence, it should now be ready for consumption.

In the living room, they sat together on the sofa with the radio on in the background. 'Give me your honest opinion of this beer. It's one I made from the Bosses new recipe. I've never tried it before', Allan said. 'There's the kettle boiling now. You open a couple of bottles, and I'll come through with some tea. That should get some warmth into you'.

Two minutes later, Allan returned from the kitchen, saying, 'I definitely heard the kettle whistling, but the water's stone cold'. Shrugging his shoulders, he sat down next to Freida on the settee and drank his beer.

After finishing a bottle each, Allan said, 'Well, I'm fairly impressed with that, but I do think it could have stayed fermenting in the bottle a tad longer. I have some wine here. Let's have some of that instead'. Freida chose a bottle from the wine rack, and once back in the living room, the two of them spent the rest of the evening chatting, flirting, and finishing three bottles of wine.

'I feel quite tipsy now', slurred Freida.

'Same here', said Allan, as she rested her head on him. Putting her hand right around his shoulder and pulling his body closer, they started to kiss.

Freida pulled back abruptly, and said, 'Oh wait! It's late. How will I get back home? You can't drive in your state'.

'True, said Allan. 'You'll need to phone the Boss to come and collect you'.

'Oh, no. He'll go mad if he sees me in this state, and he won't be very pleased with you, either'.

'Well, the only alternative is that you stay here for the night'.

With that suggestion being planted in her mind, her face brightened up, and she said, 'Well, it's quite late. Let's just finish this bottle and then go to bed, and would you phone to let him know'.

Allan's face beamed as he told her where the bedroom was. 'Yes', he thought! 'This is my dream come true'. As Freida went up to the bedroom, Allan phoned the Boss to say she was staying overnight. There was no answer so he had to leave a message on the machine. He put the phone down and ran expectantly upstairs.

'Here I am!' he called as he opened the bedroom door. When he looked in the bedroom he was dismayed to discover that the many glasses of alcohol had taken their toll on Freida and she was out for the count. No amount of coaxing and prodding could stir her, so Allan gave up and went through to sleep in the spare room, wondering what might have been, andwhat he would say to the Boss the next day.

, Allan opened his eyes in the morning to see Freida standing in the room with a cup of coffee. With an apologetic look on her face, she mumbled the that kettle seems to be working okay now, and how sorry she was about the previous night.

'Don't worry', said Allan. 'I'll take you back home before I go to work'.

Looking down at her feet, Freida asked, 'What will he be more annoyed at; you being late for work or me staying the night here? '

'Neither', said Allan. 'He's very understanding as long as I make up the time, and he'll just be glad you're safe'. Leaving it at that, Allan phoned the office to tell them where he was going, then took his charge back.

After dropping Freida off, while driving, Allan wondered all the way back to the office what kind of a reception would be waiting for him. He had brought with him two bottles of his home-brew ale, and went straight to his Bosses office to explain things. He knocked once on the open door and went in. 'That's Freida back at yours, safely. I'm really sorry about last night, but we got carried away with your home-brew'. Seeing the Bosses eyes light up with this back-handed compliment, Allan handed his home-brew ale over. 'We were enjoying it so much we finished all of yours, and then started on mine. We didn't think it was quite ready yet, so here's two bottles for your opinion'.

'Just put them under that shelf, and I'll keep an eye on them and tell you when they're ready'.

After a long and tiring day at work with a hangover, and back in his house for the evening, Allan tried out the new kettle he had bought in the precinct to replace the one from yesterday, and for some strange, reason he was relieved to hear this kettle, a brand new kettle, starting to boil. He had eaten his tea in the canteen, so all he wanted to do now was relax in front of the TV with a drink, but first, he telephoned home.

There was nothing new happening at home; everyone was well, but his brother Ronald who had just bought a flat (an apartment), had some reflection, decided to stay at his Mum's, and rent the flat out instead. This seemed a good idea to Allan; he would look into this himself and possibly do the same, after all, it would be an interest as well as an added income.

Still trying to make amends to the Boss for the Freida scenario, Allan told him of his flat plans, and the rest of the week was spent checking out as many possible flats as he could.

Allan had given his flat-looking parameters to his workmates who wanted to help in his search and an off-the-cuff remark from an engineer resulted in a glimmer of hope; the engineer's sister, who was now working abroad, had been trying to sell her flat for some time, and now fed up with her estate agent, had decided to sell quickly, and her brother was dealing with it himself. 'It could well be what you are looking for, Allan, as I don't have the time to deal with it especially when she is off gallivanting abroad. I'll throw in all the furniture and fittings as well because I can't be bothered waiting for a buyer anymore'. Allan's face brightened up and he jumped at this opportunity, and the two arranged a viewing that evening.

After viewing the flat, Allan said he was very interested, even more so, if all the extras mentioned were thrown in. 'First thing tomorrow morning I will sort things out with my solicitor and will get the ball rolling as soon as possible'.

At last, he had found one that seemed to have rentable possibilities; it was fully furnished and ready for someone to move in. He bought the flat as quickly as the paperwork could be done.

To celebrate the completion of the transaction, and to thank his workmates for helping him to find the flat, Allan treated some of them to a beer in the 'The Drovers.' They all sat in the corner, passing funny comments on everyone who went by. 'Look at the size of that thing', said Gregor McAndrew, pointing to a very portly lady. 'She'd need to fart to give you a clue'.

Just as they were finishing their last beer and were about to go back, the barmaid Morag who was collecting their tumblers asked for a quiet word. 'I couldn't help overhearing you, but I heard you talk about a flat you just bought up the road. Could I come and have a look? I've just split up from my husband and want to move out'. This seemed to be an ideal proposition, and Allan agreed to take her there that night before she started work.

When he arrived at the pub to see his possible new tenant, she told him, 'I'm sorry, but I don't think it will be suitable after all'.

Slightly disheartened by this, but trying not to show it, he just said, 'Well, never mind, there's bound to be someone else out there who will want it'.

'Well, on that note, we have a tenant staying in the hotel, but she has to go back down south tomorrow, and will need permanent accommodation when she comes back. She's just left to go to the train station to find out the times for tomorrow. If we run we can catch her'. She called over to her colleague at the bar, 'Can you cover for me?! I'll be back very soon!' The pair of them grabbed their coats and ran as fast as they could to the station.

Breathlessly, they asked the old, grey-haired stationmaster of her whereabouts. 'Oh yes, she's just been here, bought some tickets to go down south, and has now gone back to get her suitcase, as she wants to leave tonight', he said. 'Her ticket's valid for any time this month, though', he added, running his finger along with his notes.

'Great! Thanks', they said and rushed over to the phone to call the pub to tell her to wait there for their return or come to the flat. They were told she had just come in with her tickets, and had overheard the conversation, and would just get a taxi straight away to meet them at the flat. Deciding his dream job was getting better and better, they walked off to meet her at the flat.

On the way, Allan asked many questions about the possible new tenant, and was slightly intrigued when he was told she was at college studying, 'Paranormal Occurrences and all that entails'. "What kind of a person is she?' asked Allan.

'Well, she's quite loud and a bit of an extrovert. I didn't have much to do with her because I'm quieter'.

'Well, as a thank you for getting me a tenant, and because I'm new to the area and know nobody here, would you come out with me some time for a drink?'

'Yes, I'd love that. We'll sort something out next time you're in'.

'Yes, it definitely was getting better and better', he thought inwardly as he opened the door for her.

By the time they got to the flat, someone was waiting outside with her luggage. 'Hi, I'm Allan. Let's just go in and discuss things. What's your name by the way?'

'Carrie', she said.

Allan eyed Carrie up and down. She was an unusual-looking girl, with thigh-length black leather boots, long black elbow-length leather gloves, a bright red jacket, a bright purple head scarf, and big, long earrings which matched the many bangles on her wrists over the gloves. She had no handbag; just a carrier bag, with her purse and makeup. Her face was heavily made up with black, red, and purple makeup, and as Allan picked up her suitcases, he noticed she was studying him intently.

Inside the house, he put the suitcases in the hall, and said, 'If someone puts the kettle on I've left some milk, coffee, and the like in the kitchen. As you can see, the house is fully furnished, but it was the lads in the office and myself that bought it; there was no female involvement, so it might need a few more homely touches. If you need anything or any help just phone this number'.

The barmaid was about to leave to go back to work, but Allan asked her to stay for a coffee to keep Carrie company. 'Sure', said Morag, 'I'll act as a chaperone', she laughed, 'Because we don't know what will happen if you're left alone with her'.

'Well, yes! Stay with us for a while'. Carrie replied. 'But I'll be perfectly safe with him. I can tell'. The three of them sat for a while drinking coffee and discussing Carrie's peculiar studies.

'I've always been sceptical of these things', said Allan.

'Yes' said Carrie. 'I knew you were going to say that'.

'Although I do have an open mind, and I am willing to learn more', said Allan. 'Would you do a séance or a talk at my house if I get a decent crowd from my work? They are great guys, and I'm sure that they would be up for that'.

'Well, sure, as long as it's not just men. Sometimes when men have a drink they can be quite boorish and rowdy'.

Amidst the polite laughter, Morag said that Allan had just moved into a new house. 'Yes, he got a really good deal. I bet you didn't know that?' 'Well, I get that feeling...'

A dark look came across Carrie's face, and she glowered at Morag. Then, looking down at the table, said, 'You better get out!'

'Oh, right', said Morag, who stood up to leave.

Carrie looked at Allan with a more serious face, 'I meant you – out of the house as soon as possible'.

Allan said, 'Okay. I'll leave you to sort your stuff out'.

Morag nodded, and said, 'I best get back to the pub. I'm meant to be working'.

At that, they both said they would see Carrie soon, and hurried   off   back   to   The   Drovers.

CHAPTER FIFTEEN

The Piano Lesson

It was a nice warm Monday morning as Allan drove to the refinery, quite looking forward to telling his workmates about his tenant. He was the first to arrive so left his car at the front of the offices to leave room for everyone else, as he was usually in and out of the office all day. One after another they appeared almost at the same time, as though they were all using synchronised watches. He was eager to tell as many people as he could about Carrie.

Full of enthusiasm and excitement, he told them more about his tenant, and when he said she was a clairvoyant and had agreed to do a séance at his house shortly, the bewildered looks of trepidation and horror on everyone's face indicated there would not be very many willing participants from here, and that not everyone would be keen to attend. The last one he told was the Boss, as he was unusually a few minutes later than the rest today. 'I'm really pleased for you, Allan. I'm glad we could all help'.

'Yes, but I'm trying to convince these guys to come to a séance at my house, with the tenant'.

'Oh, come on lads, let's all go', said the Boss. 'It will be a laugh. It's a lot of rubbish, anyway – reading tea leaves is more dangerous'.

'Alright, then. I'll come', said Curtis. Then, everyone else decided to go when Allan said he was inviting some girls.

'Oh, Allan!' shouted Gemma. 'I've left a phone number on your desk of the piano teacher. Will you phone her this morning?'

'Sure, I'll do that straight away'. Sitting down at his desk with a coffee, Allan picked up the telephone and dialled the number. Telling the teacher he had been given her number on a recommendation, he made arrangements to come to her house that evening. Eager to start his new lessons, he just grabbed a few rolls after lunch from the machines so he could go straight there.

Allan hadn't really got many girls to come to the séance; he had just said that so it would possibly attract some of his younger colleagues. This he felt he would have to rectify immediately so that he wouldn't look stupid. As he sat at his desk, he wrote down a list of girls in the refinery that he could possibly ask. The first one he wrote down was Linda, the girl from the typing pool in the main building. This was the girl who had mentioned a wedding she was going to.

There was a call from one of the adjoining offices: 'If you're going over to the main office anytime today, Allan, would you deliver this to one of the engineers for me, please?'

Seeing this as the opportunity he was looking for, he seized it, and replied, 'Well, I'm a bit busy actually, but I'll go over right now to get that out of the way'. Putting his jacket on, he went around the office collecting anything that anyone else needed to be delivered. As there were a couple of girls in the nearby office, he nipped in there to say hello, and tell them about his séance. They all looked horrified and said 'No thank you', and even with Allan explaining most of his office were going, they declined strongly. He felt he hadn't done his cause any good here, as the girls viewed him with mild suspicion now as he said goodbye. Turning back, he looked at one of the girls, and said, 'What's that perfume you're wearing? It's really nice'.

She looked embarrassed, so he turned to the other one, and said, 'And what's the one you are wearing?'

'That's lovely as well', he said to the other one. 'Well, if you change your mind let me know, girls. There's some coming from the typing pool as well'.

'What's this, then?' said a deep voice just coming into the office. Allan turned around to see big Chic, an engineer, collecting some documents from the girls.

'Allan was just telling us about a séance he's organising at his house. He's invited us, but we're not too keen yet. Why don't you come along, Chic?'

Chic took the last of the documents off the desk, and taking a deep breath, told them that he would most certainly not be going to anything like that. 'You shouldn't go either. Nothing good can come of it. It's not a thing to be taken lightly!' Lifting some mail that was for him, he looked at Allan, and said, 'You should be ashamed of yourself, trying everything to get girls to come back to your house'.

'But there are lots of people coming, Chic. It will be okay'.

'Well, it won't be. You're heading for a fall, young lad. Mark my words'. Allan was taken aback by this unexpected tirade, and as he opened his mouth to reply, Chic put the large envelopes under his arm, pushed him aside, and said, 'Get out of my road!'

A stunned Allan turned to face the girls who had burst into uncontrollable giggles. 'Well, take that!' one of them laughed.

'You can safely count me in now', said one.

'Make that two,' said the other.

'Great, I'll come back over when the details are all sorted'.

'Well, that turned out okay, eventually. I was a bit worried until big Chic came in', thought Allan, as he drove straight across to the main refinery building to seek out Linda, all on the pretext, of course, of delivering some work to the engineers.

A horn sounded from a car going in the opposite direction. This was full of some of the refinery workers he knew vaguely and had met in pubs occasionally. Outside the main office car park, one of the younger engineers called out, 'Hi Allan, come and have a look at this car'. There was half a dozen or so gathered around an old veteran car that was in pristine condition. They all studied the car with envy, with no one really knowing what kind of car it was, or who owned it. Each ran their hand along the highly buffed gleaming bodywork and admired the walnut dashboard, burgundy leather seats and chrome wheels and additional frog-eye spotlights. 'Hope it doesn't rain or he will get a soggy bum', said someone. It turned out it was just a visitor's car, and no one ever saw that car again.

'Well, that's our fun for the day', said one of them, as Allan waved goodbye, and jogged off to the typing pool. Thinking it didn't look very cool jogging, he straightened up to a smart walk and went straight to the typing pool floor.

On the entrance door of the typists' office, there were highly polished brass plates. These made excellent make-shift mirrors for him to make sure his hair was alright, his tie was smart, and he was looking as presentable as he could. The door opened, and as someone came out, Allan said, 'Oh, I'm glad I've caught you there. Here's a report I've got to deliver to you'.

'That's great. Just leave it on my desk for me, and I'll get it when I'm back, thanks'. Allan and the engineer talked for a few minutes and discussed what they had done over the weekend. Allan was pleased that the door was open and that the girls could see him making general chit-chat with this senior engineer. Straightening his tie and smoothing his hair, he listened at the opened door to the clickety-click of the many typewriters and the hubble-bub of everyone inside chattering about their weekends; who they had seen and what they had done, while pretending to be interested in everyone else. When one of the girls looked up and saw him, her smile was his cue to enter the room.

He loved the smell in that room: that of a dozen different perfumes and hard work. He marched straight over to the senior Italian lady in charge; the Strega the girls had dubbed her, and was pleased to hear her shout, 'Will someone get the laddie a coffee! He's probably made up this visit just to see you all anyway'.

'Hi, girls', said a slightly red face Allan. I'm just delivering some reports, and thought I'd pop in to say hello'. The girls were all pleased to see him, as this was a little unexpected break they could have. He was especially pleased that the senior typists had instructed them to get him a coffee.

'Did I hear you say the last time I was over here, that you had to go to a wedding, but didn't have anyone to go with yet?' he asked one of the girls.

'Yes, that's right. It's my cousin's, and I've split up with my boyfriend, so I can't go'.

Allan took the coffee, and sipping it slowly, said to the girl, 'Oh Linda... Well, like I said before: I'm new here. I don't know many people yet, so I would love to go with you, if that would help you. I hope that's not too presumptuous. If it is, I'm sorry'.

Linda's face lit up immediately, and she said, 'I'd like that, thanks', and she wrote down the date, the venue, and her telephone number.

Allan, pleased with this turn of events, explained to her and all the rest about the flat he had bought, and that his tenant was a spiritualist. 'She's going to hold a séance, and some of my colleagues are going. Would any of you girls like to come as well? A glass of wine, a few nibbles. It should be a laugh'. Most of the girls agreed to come along, and Allan left them saying he would come back with the date and the address.

He quickly went back to his own office and told everyone he had got more girls, and that as it was nearly time to go home, he would just eat his rolls here, and then go to his music lesson.

Just as he opened the door to leave, there was a shout from one of his colleagues: 'Allan, before you go! There was a phone call from one of your old college mates. He said that you'd promise to have a class reunion down here. He said to give him a call to make arrangements'.

'Right, okay. Thanks! I might do that tonight after I come home from my lesson. That's me off now'.

As he walked up the pathway, the door opened and Allan was met by a young blonde girl at the door. 'You must be Allan', she said. 'We'll soon turn you into Liberace or Barry Manilow. Smiling, but not too pleased at the likeness to the piano players mentioned, he followed her through to the room where the piano was.

Looking around the immaculately tidy living room, he commented out loud when he saw a toy box in the corner, 'Well, this room is amazingly tidy for someone with children', and pointed to the toy box.

'No', she said, shaking her head. "That's my nieces" when they come to visit', and pointed to a photograph of herself with two young children. 'My husband and I aren't that close anymore. I don't have children, and never wanted any'.

Allan agreed with her, and said, 'I've never wanted any either. That is another thing that we have in common'.

Looking at the piano, she said that although he was a novice she was sure he was quite smart and would pick it up quickly. As she sat down at the piano, she told him her name was Mandy. 'Okay, back to Barry Manilo again', said Allan.

Taking his hand in hers, she said, 'Now, let's get in the right position', and placed his hands on the keyboard. She looked deep into Allan's eyes, and he wondered what she was thinking.

'Well, she showed him the basic rudiments, she asked him, 'How far do you want to go?'

Allan replied, 'I want to go all the way, but as you can see I do not have any clue about this. But I would eventually like to be able to play some Beethoven eventually'.

Mandy nodded, and said, 'I like a man with ambition, but that will be quite some time off, so we best crack on'.

Allan looked around the room and said it was a very nice house, and asked who all lived here. 'Just myself and my husband', she said, pulling a face.

'Have you been married long?'

'Yes, too long. Eight months now. The biggest mistake of my life so far'

Allan tapped Mandy's elbow, and said, 'Well, what's next then?'

'Well, since it's your first lesson, I won't charge you. I'll just play some Beethoven for you to remind you of your goal. You can pour a couple of drinks for us, and just listen to me'.

After a few drinks and much laughter, they had edged much closer together, and as Allan leaned over to the piano, she stole a quick kiss. 'Oh, sorry, I shouldn't have done that'.

'No, probably not', said Allan, 'But I will even it up'. With no hesitation only impulse, he drew her towards him, and with his arm right around her, gave the unexpecting Mandy a long lingering kiss. Allan had certainly not been expecting this when he left his house but welcomed it eagerly. When she pulled back to look at him for a reaction, she smiled, and slowly began to unbutton her blouse. Allan could tell by now that she wasn't wearing a bra, so slid his hand deftly up the back of the scant shirt. They got more and more oblivious as to why they were there and worked themselves into a wild frenzy. Just as he slid his hand slowly nearer the front, the passion was suddenly interrupted by the sound of a car coming up the driveway. 'Oh quick!' said Mandy. 'That's my husband! I didn't realise the time'.

'Well',said Allan, as they both hurriedly made themselves presentable, 'neither did I. If you like you can come to my house and do the lessons there some time, and we won't be disturbed'.

'Yes', she said, with a gleaming, white smile.

As he stood up to leave, he quickly wrote down his address, and asked her if she could make it the same time next week. Gazing into each other's eyes for the last moment, their lips touched briefly just as the door opened. Allan grabbed his coat, said goodbye, then nodded to the husband who viewed them both with deep suspicion, before anyone broke the uneasy silence.

Her husband said to her curtly, 'I'm off upstairs to get changed. You see him out'.

Once inside his house, just as Allan was about to go through to the kitchen, his telephone rang. Grabbing the receiver, and saying hello in his best telephone voice, he smiled as he recognised Mandy's hush voice. 'Hi', it's me, she said. 'I'll be quiet. He's gone upstairs for a shower. I thought we got on very well tonight, and I was just thinking, I have tomorrow night free. If you want me to continue, I can come round tomorrow'.

'Yes, that would be great', said Allan, quite cockily. 'I don't think I have anything else on tomorrow, so I'll see you here at the same time'. Explaining to her that he knew that she still had to teach him a lot more on the piano before he could play anything seriously, he asked if she could bring some sheet music to leave here as a reminder of what he was aspiring to. 'Will do that' said Mandy. Just then a dog howling in the distance made his eyes cloud over, as he was reminded of his lost friend, and so decided to go for a quick jog to clear his mind. 'Not too far this time', he thought.

Seeing that some shops were still open in the precinct, he made a quick detour to the music shop. He browsed through many catalogues, and told the assistant who had offered to help that he was a piano player, and was just looking. When she said that she also was a piano player, Allan asked her if she would like to meet for a drink some night, on condition they don't talk shop.

'Yes, we can do that sometime soon, and I promise I won't ask about how good you are'.

Sighing with relief at this get-out clause, he said, 'I don't think I'll be as good at it as you are'.

'Maybe not' she said, 'But practice makes perfect, and I might be able to help sometime', Allan said thank you, left the shop, and thrust the music through his own letterbox.

As a bus was approaching, he lingered for a minute or two, and when no unsavoury characters came off the bus, he started jogging. Twenty minutes out and twenty minutes in, was his plan until the end of the month, after which he intended to increase the duration.

As Allan reached the 'The Drovers' pub, he checked the time. That was the twenty minutes up, so he toyed with the idea of nipping in for one or just to go home. 'No', he thought. 'I'm going straight home. The Incredible Hulk's on tonight. I'll just watch that, and read something'.

Panting at the front door, Allan looked behind and nodded to three other joggers who waved back whilst running in the opposite direction. When Allan opened the front door to a still-chilly hallway, he forgot the sheet music he had put through earlier, and ran upstairs for his usual shower, then straight back downstairs to sit in front of the TV with his trusty bottle and glass next to it.

During the adverts, he picked up his professional magazine, looked at the models modelling fast cars, then put it back down. 'Nothing much of any interest in there', he thought, as he poured himself another drink.

When his programme finished, he made a quick phone call home to see if anything exciting had happened. Apparently, nothing had, and none of the boys wanted to come to the phone, as Star Trek was coming on. 'Okay then, Mum. I won't hold you up. I'll leave you all to it. Speak soon'.

'Star Trek, eh?'

'I'll have time for another quick scotch, and I'll just switch channel as soon as The Incredible Hulk finishes. Ah, this is the life right enough', Allan said to himself, as he watched TV.

In the mood for a drink tonight, and having finished the last of his scotch, he decided that since the weather was fair he would nip across to The Drovers, after all, to see what was happening. Allan was looking at the newspaper on the settee wondering how it had got there as he knew he hadn't bought it. Confused, he stood up to put on his jacket, and when he heard the front door unlocking, he stood motionless and silently in the hallway, with bated breath.

As the door started opening he took a backwards step, retreating towards the living room. Not quite knowing what to do now, he reached for the telephone and was hugely relieved as Evelyn the cleaner came in.

'Hi Allan', said her familiar voice. 'I'm just here to collect my money that I forgot this morning. I was a bit pushed for time. I wondered what that awful-like smell was when I came in earlier, then I saw that the oven was quite bad. It looked like it had been in the wars. It looks like steak pie or something ingrained in it. I didn't think you used the cooker that much'.

'Ohh, that would have probably been my younger brothers when they were through'.

As they walked through to the living room, Allan teasingly said, 'Your mind was probably taken up reading the newspaper. I must reduce your time if you have so much spare time on your hands'.

'No, no!'she said, with a worried look on her face. 'I read that on my tea break. You said to help myself to tea and biscuits, anyway'.

'It's okay', said Allan, patting her shoulder. 'Don't look so worried. I was only joking, my dear'.

'Ohh, that's good', said Evelyn, as she bent down to take the paper away.

'Auch!'' screamed Evelyn, as she stood up clutching her rib cage.

'What's wrong? Is it your heart?'

'No, nothing like that. The underwire of this stupid bra has snapped, and it's digging into me. Ohh, it's really sore. I'm sorry, Allan, I need to take it off in the bathroom. I'll be okay with just my blouse and jersey until I get home'.

'Ohh, that's much better', she said when she came back, clutching an enormous black, lacy bra.

Evelyn was a heavily built, older lady, and when Allan saw her clutching that enormous bra, he laughed, and said, 'What the heck are you doing with a bra like that at your age?' Then hesitated, and said, 'No offence'.

Evelyn said, 'My son-in-law gave it to me for Christmas as a joke'.

'Can you leave it here? I could have a laugh with that', said Allan. He handed over her bevvy money as she used to call it, and said, 'Now, don't spend it all at once!'

'No, I'll try, but I'm going to The Drovers this weekend with young Evelyn and my son-in-law, so I might. Thanks, anyway. I will see myself out'.

Allan rushed upstairs to hide the bra in a safe place, then came back down. He went through to the living room and saw a newspaper on the settee. 'That's funny, I was sure Evelyn just took that newspaper with her', but picked it up anyway to take a glance when the TV show's Question Time was on, as he thought it would be good to at least know who was on it tonight. 'Boring muck. I hear the pub calling'.

Inside the pub, he was pleased to see some faces he had spoken to before, so went over to join some girls, and sat down at their table.

As the evening wore on, the spirits got higher and higher, and everyone was in a really happy mood. Someone shouted out, 'Hi! Come over here, lads'. Allan looked up to see who had come in but was disappointed to see the two lads who he had met before. Trying to disassociate himself with them and not let anyone know he knew them, he focused his eyes on anything within eyeshot, trying to appear very interested in the surroundings.

'Oh, hello there. We meet again, old friend', said one of the two, putting his arm around Allan and hugging him.

'Oh, if you're well-acquainted with these two, I won't introduce you, Allan', said one of the girls. With a cheesy, embarrassed grin on his face, he wondered how he could ignore these popular guys, and concentrate more on the girls. This would really cramp his style.

'How well do you know these two?' asked the blonde. 'I believe you were over at their house one night?'

'They really are very adventurous guys', said another. 'They're very open-minded, and will try anything. Are you the same, Allan?'

'No, not really. I'm a bit quieter...' he answered, not liking the way this conversation was going.

'Oh, that's a shame'.

Allan was released from the embarrassing hug, when the door opened and a beautiful girl came in, wide-eyed. She smiled, and looking in Allan's direction, shouted, 'Hi, darling, have you missed me?' Then, rushed over towards him, arms out wide. Thinking his luck had changed for the better, Allan stood up expecting a big hug and a kiss, when the girl bypassed him and threw her arms around one of the other guys. 'Hi, I've really missed you, and I'm glad to be back. Did you manage fine with my brother sharing for the fortnight?' Allan sighed both with relief at this revelation and with disappointment that the beauty was with one of the blokes. The double bed was not for the two guys, and as for a threesome, well, he had got that wrong.

Allan bought drinks for the four of them, stayed to get his drinks back from the guys, then said goodnight to all, even getting a peck on the cheek from a couple of the girls. Just as he was going out the door, he shouted over goodnight to the barmaid, who called back, 'Don't forget the séance you mentioned! I'm definitely up for it, and I'll ask a few friends as well'.

'Great!' said Allan, and opened the door to go outside. As the door closed behind him, over the cacophony and laughter within, he was convinced that he heard his dog. Going a few hundred yards in the opposite direction to look for it, Allan stopped dead in his tracks, and thought to himself, 'Don't be such a fool; the dog's dead and every other dog of that size sounds the same'.

Turning back to his house, he made a quick detour to the off-license for more bedtime company. The assistant smiled, and said half-sarcastically, 'Not seen you in here for a wee while'.

'No, I've just been doing some reading'.

Pleased that she hadn't asked what he was reading, he nodded as she said, 'Would you like to try this special offer of Laphroaig?' "It's a bit too peaty for my liking, as well as a few of them'. He agreed to buy a bottle of the Laphroaig, and a milder one as well, but only if she would come over one night to help him drink it. Her face lit up at this, and they swapped phone numbers.

On the way back home, the girl from the music shop was just locking up, and Allan shouted over to her, 'Hello, we must get together for a drink sometime!' Receiving a thumbs up from her, he ran the last few hundred yards, went inside, poured himself a drink, and went to the hall to phone his classmate Craig Andrews. 'Hi there, it's me, Allan. You have everybody's addresses! So, can you get everyone organised to come to me in a fortnight? We'll make it one heck of a fun boozy weekend'.

Craig agreed, and said he would call back just to confirm it in a few days but, 'It was pencilled in now'.

Switching off everything in the living room, Allan saw his new bottle. He thought this has been a great day, so took it, and went upstairs for an early night to listen to the radio.

Halfway through the news the radio went silent and Allan just lay in bed thinking about the day that had just been, the hair on the back of his head stood up as he heard whispering from downstairs. More curious than worried he ran downstairs to see..... no one!! inwardly cursing he went back upstairs to bed.

The faint sound of sobbing from downstairs only encouraged Allan, who by now couldn't care, to try to get the radio back on and then tuck himself back into bed.

* * *

CHAPTER SIXTEEN

Snood's

Friday morning came, and when Allan jumped out of bed quickly for his shower, his thumping headache which wasn't usual, made him think that maybe this whiskey wasn't ideal for him. Perhaps that old wives' tale he had heard about drinking lots of water before bed had a bit more truth in it than most folk believed. 'That's a great excuse for getting drunk tonight, and trying that theory out', he thought. He also remembered the phone call he had received about a college mates' reunion: 'It's pencilled in for a fortnight today'.

He was looking forward to a great weekend as he made his way to the office. Holding back to open the door for Gemma, he waved to some of his colleagues as they filed in. When he saw Gemma pull up next to him, he checked his hair and tie as usual, and followed her in.

The lovely aroma of hot coffee filled the offices. He poured himself a cup, and sat down at his desk to call some of his mates about the reunion. Just as he was about to pick up the phone, he was asked to pop up to Snood's stationer, and at the same time pick up more of the special coffee they all enjoyed.

He asked every one of his colleagues as he went past them if they required anything in particular from the stationers. The longer the list of things to be bought, the longer he could spend chatting up the assistant, while she gathered the things together.

The last office on the way out belonged to Gemma, and he popped in just to say her perfume smelled lovely. Just a cheesy practice run. Gemma thanked him with her usual coy smile, and said, 'It's nice to see the sun out again. It makes everyone cheery and happy. I love the sunshine, don't you?'

Allan said, 'Oh, yes, but you are my sunshine'.

She smiled briefly, then said, 'Not to bring up a touchy subject, but is there still no sign of that dog?'

'No, I try not to think about it now'.

'How's your friend at the pound? I may pop back up and see if she has any more news for me at all while I'm out. I'll see you when I come back', and with a wink, Allan casually sauntered off with his shopping list.

Snood's was a family-run stationer, and as Allan approached the door, he noticed through the window that the crotchety old owner was behind the counter today, but his daughter was there as well, filling some shelves. The shop next door to Snood's was the one where the office got their special coffee from. 'I'll just go in here and get some more coffee for the office', hoping that would waste some time, after which Mr Snood would have left the shop leaving his daughter in charge.

The coffee shop attendant, a very pleasant girl in her early thirties, although somewhat obese in Allan's eyes, presented him with a cardboard box full of the freshly ground coffee. Taking the box from her, he settled upon the account, and agreed with her when she said that he should really buy it at the start of the week and not at the weekend. Allan agreed completely and said ' Yes, but I'm up here to get some stationary anyway so It saves me coming back on Monday' .

'Oh well, you best hurry. There's Mr. Snood leaving now', she said, looking over her shoulder and out the window.

'Great', thought Allan, and as he went to put the coffee in the car, he checked in the mirror that he was presentable, and went back over the road.

Mr Snood's daughter looked up when she heard the doorbell. Allan walked in and told her he had a fairly long list of things to get which she immediately set about collecting. He watched her every move as she stretched her slim lithe body while on the step ladder, and asked if she required him to hold her steady.

'To hold my steady what?' she laughed.

'Oh, if only', smiled Allan.

'Oh, by the way', he said, 'I have a few old college friends coming through to stay with me in a fortnight for the weekend. Where's the best place to go with them? We usually go nuts for the weekend when we get together. So, where should we go?'

She turned around to Allan, and said, 'There's a nightclub here in Stoopchurch that I always go to with my friends. We always have a good time, but you have to go early if you want to get in'. He wrote down the name of the club, and a few pubs that she said were quite trendy and offered good fun at the weekends.

The sound of the door chime caused Allan to turn around to see who was coming in. It was an older lady, who smiled at Allan, and said, 'Don't you just love the smell of a stationers shop'.

'Yes, but there are other attractions to this place as well as the merchandise'.

The older lady smiled, and looking at Mr Snood's daughter, said, 'Yes, there certainly is'.

When Allan picked up the stationery to leave, he gave the small parcel a satisfying sniff. 'Yes, it's lovely isn't it?' said the old lady. 'Just like the coffee shop next door'.

Mr Snood's daughter said, 'I love the smell in bakers as well'.

The other lady, while looking at some shelves joined in with, 'Yes, but my favourite is a chemist. Oh, and I really hate the butchers'.

Allan nodded to them both, and said, 'I can't stand the smell of oranges myself, well, I'd love to stay and have a long discussion about shop smells, but I'd better get back to work'.

As he opened the door to leave, he overheard one of them say, 'Oh, I love the smell of freshly ironed laundry'.

'Oh yes, I love going to bed on newly ironed bedsheets, especially cotton ones', said the other. Ignoring the impulse to make another comment, Allan just went back to his car carrying the parcel of stationary. When he bent over to put his purchases in the back of the car he saw a second-hand junk shop over the road. He had made good time so far, and checking his watch, decided to nip in and have a quick look around.

There were lots of very interesting items on show, all of which someone had no further use for, or decided they could get some quick cash for. Everything Allan looked at because it was second-hand, obviously had some tale to tell, but couldn't. Out of all the interesting items on display, Allan bought a second-hand electric fan, as his office got very warm in the afternoons; an old Charles and Diana wedding mug; and he asked if he could come back for the portable TV which he could watch in the kitchen while doing some ironing. These, he bought for £5, and tempted as he was to haggle over the price just for the fun of it, he paid; and his attention was caught by an attractive lady with a baby in a pram, who was talking to the other assistant.

'Yes', she said, 'When my husband walked out I was really lost. Well, it's a bit worse for me because of my working arrangements; he gets custody, and I only see the wee once at the weekend, but that will change at the court meeting next week'.

As the two ladies cooed and billed over the baby in the pram, Allan peered in to have a look. His face turned ashen white with shock when he saw the baby was not quite as lovely as the other two had made out. They continued their chat, saying that the best thing to do would beto get right back into the fray and start dating and forgetting their troubles. 'Bye now, see you soon', called the assistant to the lady with the pram as she left the shop.

Allan went back to the counter, and lied, 'What a cute baby. Do you know them?'

'Yes, she is a neighbour, and her husband is a rat and didn't deserve her'.

He had taken with him to the counter a very large teddy, a smaller one, a *plaything* that Allan could not understand, and a few other things he had seen on the shelf he thought a young mother may find useful. After paying for his goods, he said a quick goodbye and thank you, then left the shop, quickly.

'Excuse me!' he shouted after the mother. 'I overheard you speaking in there, and I think your man has been really nasty to you. I cannot understand how men can be like that to women. How can he leave such a beautiful wife and child? I believe the children are our future, cherish them. Take these gifts I bought in the shop for your beautiful baby. Please, I'm sure you can make good use of them'.

'Oh, thanks very much', she said with a smile, as she preened herself a little. 'The world could do with more men as courteous and considerate as you'. Allan swelled with pride, as he thought he had made a very good impression. She then went on to say, 'This teddy will make up for the one my new boyfriend gave me which the dog, unfortunately, chewed up. His was bigger than yours, so maybe this one won't intimidate the dog so much, and hopefully, my boyfriend may never know the difference. I don't know how to thank you'. Deflated on hearing this final comment, Allan just said goodbye and set off back to the car with his purchases.

He drove back to the office pleased with the information he had gleaned from Mr Snood's daughter about the local nightclubs. 'Should make for a good night out', he thought to himself.

When Allan got back to his desk he started calling around some friends to remind them of the reunion. Picking up the telephone, Allan called Craig Andrew and asked how many people he had rounded up so far for the reunion at his place. 'Well, so far', said Craig, 'I have Grant Michael, Andrew Richardson, Basil Reed, and a few others. Can you think of anyone else in particular?'

'No, not really. I don't know where anyone else is-- at the moment, that will probably have to do for now I'm bringing my friend Ewan Stevens. That's all the room I'll have. If you round everyone up, we can all meet at 7.30 P.M. at mine, then move on to my local, The Drovers. We'll have a couple there, then move on to the nightclub. So, if I don't hear from you, I'll just see everyone on the day. Cheers, now. See you'.

Quite satisfied with developments and the progress he had made, he spent some time reading over some contracts, then hearing everyone beginning to leave, gathered his things together, and started to leave as well.

As he passed by Gemma's office and was about to say something nice and cheesy as usual, she said, 'I'm glad I've caught you. My friend from the pound phoned to say there's a dog been handed in that seems very similar to yours; so similar she thinks it might be from the same litter. It's late-night opening tonight, and she'll be on duty.It's probably best to go up after your tea, however, am staying here for a short while and I will just eat this orange in place of tea to keep my figure in trim'. Allan looked at the orange and her and said 'I would stay with you for a while because I love oranges as well, but I better be off to the pound'.

All excited with hopeful anticipation, he went straight home, and decided a few rolls would do for tea, since he was dying to go for the dog.

As he went for his car in the car park of the offices beside his house, he noticed the lights were on. So, he thought he would take this opportunity to speak to the Manager. Allan popped into the office to remind the Manager his friends would be using his car park. 'Oh yes, that's no problem. You use it yourself anyway; some more cars won't matter, Allan'. '

'Great, thanks very much. Here's a bottle of malt, by way of appreciation. The Manager took the bottle, and gave it to his secretary.

'That will do me nicely for the new year'.

Allan noticed out the corner of his eye the secretary straightening her skirt and teasing her hair as she was putting the bottle in the cupboard next to a couple of other malts, presumably gifts. Looking at Allan, she asked, 'What does this Laphroaig taste like?'

'Well, to me it's like drinking whiskey with a lump of coal in it – very peaty. I don't like it. You probably wouldn't either'.

'No, I don't drink very much. I prefer a cup of tea'.

'Same here. Why don't you pop in some night after work for a cup of tea and a chat?' Allan asked.

'You're on', she said. 'I'd like that. Which house is yours?'

'I'm next to the doctor's… Just pop in anytime. Here's my phone number, if you like'. She looked at her boss while putting the telephone number in her top pocket.

The Manager looked up, and asked, 'Did you say… next door to the doctor's house?'

'Yes, that's right. Well, enjoy the whiskey', and tapping the secretary on the elbow, said, 'I'll hear from you soon'. Smiling inwardly, he set off home with a spring in his step.

Once in his house, Allan saw his, as yet unused, bicycle in the hall, and decided to wolf down the rolls he had brought home, get changed, then cycle to the pound to see if this was a suitable replacement. If it was, he would just collect it the next day. 'I look a proper Charlie', he said to himself. 'The bicycle clips don't give off the sexiest look.' As he wheeled the bicycle down the path, he took a long hard look both ways up and down the street, hoping he would not be seen in his less-than-elegant attire. 'Mind you, anyone I see will think I'm a proper keep-fit fanatic'.

The street was still quite busy with people coming home after work. As he smelled the air which was full of lovely cooking aromas of many different teas, all being prepared for families returning home, he pushed the bike forward and sat astride the saddle. It took a while for him to get his feet into the racing bike's pedal housing, and after a wobbly start, just as he thought he had got into the groove, the chain came off. Quickly, he carried the bike back to the house and put the chain back on. With the chain in place, he ran back upstairs to scrub as much oil off his hands as possible. 'Good stuff, this Swarf'.

Back downstairs, he looked in astonishment at the bike. Both tyres were flat, and they weren't when he had brought the bike in. It was a long time since he had mended a puncture, but it needed to be done.

By now, it was later than he had hoped for him to be setting off for the pound, so he telephoned to let them know he had been delayed, but was on his way now. 'Not to worry', said the receptionist. 'We're open late as you know. See you soon'. Relieved at this, he decided to have a quick coffee, then set off once more.

He pushed off, and after pedalling two or three times, the central locking nut on the handlebars loosened, rendering the handlebars useless, and the bike uncontrollable. 'Damn', cursed Allan, as he picked up the bike, and threw it in disgust into the garden.

'You're not having much luck with that', said two of his young neighbours who had been watching the proceedings from their garden.

'I know', said a very disgruntled Allan, ' Andjust when I'm in a hurry. I'll need to run if I'm to be in time'. When the older of the two lads volunteered to fix the bike, a delighted Allan jumped at this offer, saying he would be back in about an hour,then set off on his errand.

He never stopped to chat to the many neighbours he met along the way; instead, just gave a smile, a nod, or a wave. The rolls Allan had wolfed down quickly were giving him a touch of heartburn, but he was more concerned with getting to the pound and ignored the thought of going back for something to ease it.

At last, he could hear the yelping of many dogs and hounds in the kennels. As he opened the door to go inside, he was met again with the mixed smells of disinfectant and damp dogs. There was no one at the desk, so Allan rang the bell on the counter a few times, quite impatiently.

Eventually, a receptionist came in and said to Allan, 'Oh, I've been waiting for you. Come and have a look at this dog'. Allan eagerly jumped to his feet and followed her through to the back. The yapping and barking increased, and all the dogs were jumping in a frenzy, but were restricted to their respective pounds. All except one dog that seems replica of Allan's original dog that he had lost, and was still pining for. He was almost driven to tears when it came over to him, tail wagging frantically. Trying to jump up to get to Allan gleefully at this point, Allan could contain himself no more and could hardly speak, when he tried to say, 'That's it! That's my dog. Can we go home now?'

The attendant looked down, shook her head slowly, and said, 'No, I'm really sorry, but that is not your dog; the microchips do not match, so unfortunately it clearly is not your dog. We can't let you have it'. As much as Allan protested that it was his the girl would not relent, so she didn't let Allan have the dog.

After a fairly heated conversation, they brought over the supervisor to calm things down. She explained to Allan that she had been the one who had to incinerate Allan's original dog, and reiterated the fact that the chips were not the same. Besides, this dog has a floppy left ear; his dog didn't.

Still protesting, Allan resigned himself to the fact that they would never agree to let him take the dog, especially when he was told he was probably too attached to the first one anyway to give it the attention it needed. With one last look back at the dogs, he bowed his head and set off slowly for the homeward journey.

At every house he passed, his thoughts alternated between realising that someone out there was looking for the dog that was in the pound, so he couldn't have it anyway, and with thoughts of how convinced he had been that it was his dog.

'Heaven knows I am miserable now' . As he toyed with the idea of going to the pub to cheer himself up, he remembered the girl from the swimming pool and as he had her number etched into his memory, in case her brother never gave it to him again, he called her up. The phone was answered by the swimming pool guard who said he was just off to work, however, he had intimated hissister about it days ago, therefore he could just come around. When Allan arrived at the address he had been given, and rang the doorbell, a mature lady answered the door, he was slightly taken aback when she said 'Hi Allan, I was waiting for you'. They went in and sat down together on the sofa in the living room. Allan, holding onto the flowers he had brought with him, as she made herself comfortable, said 'You have no idea, how lovely this is, it's been so long since my last date. My brother always promises to fix me and my wee sister up but never does. Do you go swimming often? I might take it up again now. My life at the moment is just cooking, cleaning and work. But now that I've met you that might change. I've been looking forward to this especially since the children won't be back tonight, they are at their father's. I will make sure that you will have a good time tonight" as she glanced upstairs.

Allan, thinking how he could get out of this situation, said to the lady, 'Am sorry but I can't stay, I just popped in to say that I will be taking my friend up to the hospital to see his sick mother' . 'Oh that's okay, So that's what the flowers are for?' Quick as a flash he said 'Oh no, these were for you' as he handed them to her. 'Well thanks very much', she said. 'You're a very sweet person but I think she would really appreciate them' and offered them back.

Taking the flowers back, he thanked her and said 'I am sorry I can't stay' . As he got back into his car, he nodded and waved her goodbye, breathing a heavy sigh of relief. 'That was close' he thought. And set off home to watch Bay-watch instead.

As he turned into his street, he could see that his bike was still in bits in his garden, with the younger of the two neighbours in the street saying we've not fixed your bike because my brother wouldn't go in your garden. Allan shrugged his shoulders, picked up the bicycle parts, and went inside, intending to put it back together himself. Allan closed the door ,left the bike in the hall, and picked up the phone that had started ringing as he moved up the path. It was one of his classmates confirming that he would make it.

As Allan was watching the news, and getting more and more annoyed without his dog, he decided, 'I'm off to bed to read and listen to the radio, and I'll go home this weekend', As he passed the telephone on the way, picked it up and phoned home to say that he would be back this weekend to see everyone, 'And to get your washing done', added his mother. After saying, 'Oh well, if you insist, Mum. I'll bring it home, thanks', he put the phone down and ran upstairs. In bed, he was glad to get all tucked up and cosy. 'I'm glad I am in here now, as the wind is picking up out there'. He lay there listening to the sounds of the elements outside, and strained to hear not for the first time the sound of a faint voice being carried on top of the wind, whispering very slowly, 'Leave, leeeeeeeaaaaavvvvveeee... Gooooo hoooommmeeee, goooo hooommeeeee'.

CHAPTER SEVENTEEN

College Mates

Allan woke up before his alarm clock rang. Eager to get the day underway, he jumped out of bed and ran downstairs, as usual, to see what mail had arrived.

'None yet'.

This was the day he had arranged for all his college mates to come through to spend some time with him, and go to the nightclub he had heard of. His friend from back home, Ewan Stevens, was coming down that evening as well, and he would probably arrive first and need to be collected from the station.

The weather was quite sunny and still quite cool, as it was early in the morning, but the weather didn't really play very much on his mind; his thoughts were firmly fixed on what a good time he would have with all his friends.

Just as he left the house the mail arrived. 'The postman must've forgotten some of the houses', he thought. 'Serves him right, having to come back. He probably won't do that again'.

The cool air hit him as soon as he opened the front door, and he saw that one of his neighbours was having difficulty starting her car, so, ever eager to help and impress a lady, he volunteered to give her a jump start.

Once the car was revved up and ready to go, Allan wiped his hands on the cloth he kept on the windscreen for condensation and headed off to the newsagents to collect his morning paper, buy the milk for the office coffees, and see who was out and about that he could chat to on the way.

He took the long way so he could pass by the dog pound, just for nostalgic reasons, as he knew the dog scenario was to be left in the past. Still, he might get a wave from the girl if she sees him.

Pleased with the thought of the newsagent girl maybe being there, he nipped into the adjoining shop to buy some rolls, some eggs and two more pints of milk, just in case everyone was thirsty in the morning.

The girl behind the counterreminded Allan that as there was only one nightclub in Stoopchurch now, and it filled up quickly, he would have to be in early. 'You told me a few days ago that you were going tonight, but unfortunately I can't make it until later. But as I know the doorman I will still get in, so I will expect a dance', she added.

As Allan headed for home, he saw his neighbour returning too. Waving to her as she came out of her car, Allan ran inside with his groceries. Leaving everything on the counter in the kitchen, he looked at his watch, and decided to get to work early so he could ask the Boss if he could leave sharpish, to pick up Ewan.

When Allan arrived outside his office, he was not surprised to see the Bosses car already there; he was almost always the first to arrive in the morning. 'That's good; means I can ask to get away early without anyone else knowing'.

'Morning!' he shouted, as he went into the Bosses office after knocking once. 'I was wondering if I could push off early today, as I would like to collect an old friend from the station for a college reunion we are having in Stoopchurch tonight?'

'Yes, that's no problem, but I would like you to do me a favour in a few weeks. I would like you to work at the weekend to deliver a load of last-minute reports to the engineers' pigeon holes. You should enjoy that; there will be no distractions, and you will be able to stock up on the freerolls with nobody noticing', he smiled.

'It's a deal', said Allan. 'Just let me know which weekend you want me to work. I'll just see if there is anything to be taken over to the main building'. Allan went around all the offices of his colleagues to collect some reports and then left immediately.

He made a point of going to the typing pool to ask Linda, who had said she would take him to the wedding, for the details. She told him that the wedding was in four weeks, and gave him the address where he could pick her up from.

'Okay, well I will see you on Monday. I'm off early to pick up some mates from the station, as we have a night out tonight'. He was just about to tell her where they were going when he changed his mind; he didn't want her turning up and cramping his style, instead, he went straight back to the office to tell everyone the reports had been delivered and told the boss that he was off to the station.

By the time Allan got to the station, Ewan was already outside and waiting. Looking at his watch, he said, 'You're a wee bit late."

'I know. Sorry, I had a few things to do. Let's get back straight away. The others won't be too long'.

Just as they turned to go back to the car, someone called, 'Allan!' They looked at each other, and Ewan pointed to someone running over with a suitcase. It was John Ambrose, another classmate.

'Hi John '

John interrupted Allan by saying, 'I got a phone call last night from one of the lads. He said that you were organising a reunion in Strathmanor where you're working, so I thought I would pack a case, and come and join you. Lucky I saw you there, as I was just about to hop in a taxi, so that will save me a few bucks. Hope there's room'. They all shook hands with a laugh, loaded two suitcases in the back of the car, and headed for home.

On the way, John added that he had been speaking to the Sunderland twins, Callum and Graham, and they had said they would probably make it too.

When they got back to Allan's, two cars pulled up, and out of them came Andrew Richardson, Basil Reed, Craig Andrew and Grant Michael. As everyone filed into the house, a high pitched ringing was heard from Andrew Richardson's pocket, 'What's that noise?' asked a very surprised Michael Grant,

'That's just my mobile phone, remember that young lecturer we had, that told us these things where in the pipeline, and none of us believed him, well, this is one of them, I use it at work. It's Blair Frazer, he's come with Duncan Williams on his motorbike, he's on this street and wants to know the number' Allan took the phone and gave the number. The house was the fourth house into Strathmanor and Blair and Duncan were at the call box across the road.

'Tell them just to come over and leave their stuff'. After a few minutes, Blair and Duncan rang the bell and came in. They all took a few minutes to re-acquaint. Duncan told them that he was employing a student to do his Industrial Training and when Munro Neal came out from the College to visit, he had told him about the reunion.

'What about you Blair?' Frazer put down his crash helmet and said Am now a school teacher and guess whose children am teaching' and pointing to Duncan, added 'And for heaven's sake don't tell your kids you all call me Fuzz' Ewan laughed and said, 'Why do they call you Fuzz?' 'Oh, right enough look at that huge mop of curly hair'. Ewan offered Allan a cigarette.

Shaking his head and refusing, he said, 'I've stopped smoking now, so there's no smoking in the house'. Everyone brought their overnight gear into the house, and they discussed old times and caught up with what each other had been doing over the years. Just then, the doorbell rang. It was the Sunderland twins who had made it after all, and Jerry

Paul from Arbroath, who had also heard of it through the grapevine.

After overhearing one or two of them admiring the house, but also saying it was creepy and had a somewhat eerie atmosphere, Allan telephoned for some taxis. 'Well, that's a real nuisance', he said to the rest. 'All of those taxi firms say that they cannot take us to Stoopchurch, as it's outwith their licensed area'.

'That can't be true. Have you annoyed them before or do they just not like coming to this house?' laughed Grant Michael.

'I've always had problems getting taxis to come here, so we will go over the road to the pub, and phone from there. I call it, 'The Hostility Inn' because they're not very friendly, but we'll soon liven it up. The last one in pays for the first round!' shouted Allan, as he laughed, and made a bolt for the pub.

Unfortunately, he was overtaken by everyone and was the last in, so headed to the bar to order the beers up. Although it was not busy, the barman just continued speaking to a friend at the other end of the bar. When he was asked, 'Could we get some service here, please?' he just looked up, and said, 'I'm busy speaking. Just wait your turn'.

A number of other people came in and were served, but still, none of Allan's friends could get served. Coupled with the fact that they had still no luck getting taxis, they decided to just walk, and have a pub crawl on the way.

The first pub they came to was The Drovers, where they were served quite happily by the barmaid. 'If you are all going to

Stoopchurch there is a bus leaving from outside in about five minutes', she informed them. That was their problem solved, and they all went outside to board the bus that just pulled up.

Everyone got off the bus and filed into the pub next door to the club. This pub had a large stuffed gorilla at the door, taking the place of any doorman. 'I wonder if this gorilla could take the bear in Churchill's in Dundee?' thought Allan. One of his friends, Ewan, after a few drinks, decided to do a slow dance with the gorilla. This did not meet with the barman's approval, and he asked them to leave. They were all in high spirits by now, and so just laughed and said sure, and went across the road to another pub.

Craig, ignoring the rest of the gang who were mixing and socialising with the girls, spent some time on the puggy machine. He was not having much luck, and he just kept putting money in until, in a desperate act of frustration, he punched and kicked the machine. This immediately caught the attention of the head barman, who rushed out from behind the bar, and said, 'Right, out! The lot of you. Now!' Laughing hysterically, they left and decided that since the nightclub got filled up early, they had probably best just go there now. With the barman still hurling abuse at them, they headed off towards the club.

The doorman at the entrance blocked their passage, and said, 'There's too many of you. We don't accept large groups of males'. Wondering what to do, they decided to split up, walk around the block a bit, and come back in smaller groups and from different directions.

Looking over their shoulder to make sure the doorman had not heard them, they walked around the corner and came back later in much smaller groups. This time they had more success, and as the last three went in, the doorman said, "In you go, lads, but do have you any idea how many folks have tried that trick before? Be careful. I've got my eye on you!'

The nightclub which was called 'Flicks' was a converted cinema. It had been a cinema initially for a long time but had since then been converted into a bingo hall, used as a gym, and was now the main nightclub in the area. The strobe lights from the disco shone everywhere after reflecting from the glitter ball in the centre.

The lads got themselves a table next to the bar. This meant they could see all the girls as they came up for a drink. 'Come on lads, there are lots of girls here, let's get moving'.

Two blond girls came up to the bar and sat next to Fuzz. The taller one asked him if he was here on his own or if he was looking for some company. He told her he was in with some friends and that he was called Fuzz by friends because of his hair. Running her fingers through his hair, she said, 'am on my own tonight, I could be your friend and keep you company', 'No, it's all right, thanks' said Fuzz, 'I already have a girlfriend back home so pay no attention to that lot' .

Taking a sip from his glass, Allan commented on the fact that the girls were dancing around handbags, just like they did back in Dundee. Grant and Basil, never being slow on the uptake when it came to women, saw the surplus of girls dancing on their own, and rushed up to join them.

236

Allan, as usual, sat quietly on his own in the corner to start with, just eyeing up all that he called, 'The local totty'. As he looked around, his eye was caught by one smartly dressed slim girl, clutching her drink, walking towards the mirrored wall. Drunk and confused, she went from side to side to avoid her reflection.

The twins, who were just coming off the dance floor, saw her and saw this as an opportunity to chat up what they hoped could be an amiable, albeit vulnerable, conquest. They hurried towards her, each trying to look cool, but wanting to get there first. When the girl, who was very confused at seeing her reflection in the mirror, saw the twins in duplicate descending upon her, she found this too much to comprehend, and in trying to avoid all the reflections, smacked right into the mirror.

Back at the table, everyone laughed out loud at this, except Allan. 'Oh! That's the funniest thing I've seen in ages', said Jerry Paul. 'Don't you find that funny, Allan?'

'Yes' he said and shaking his head smiled in his best Charlie Watts impersonation, sighed and said, 'But I've seen it all before'.

The DJ, Randy Andy, as he was known by the locals, then played a sequence of punk songs, and most of the lads laughed at the locals' pogoing. Even though it was very popular at the time and many girls joined in, the lads still tended to look down their noses slightly, and just enjoyed watching.

Andrew Richardson brought out of his pocket a large thick cigar which was frowned upon by the rest, as the smell tended to keep the girls away. 'That's just like mosquito repellent', said Basil, when he came back for a seat and a drink.

Realising the disapproval that was being shown amongst his friends, Andrew stubbed out the cigar and immediately tried to turn the attention over to someone else. 'Grant', he said, 'I think it's about time you bought a round of whiskey. I'll just have a large whiskey'. Everyone else gave Grant their order, and he went up to the bar, accompanied by Craig.

By the time they came back with a tray full of drinks, the club, as they had been warned, was really full. It seemed most of the girls were pairing off with the locals quite early, so they thought they had best move a bit quicker.

When some slow dances came on, Allan looked around frantically to see if the girl from the newsagent's had made it. When he saw her amongst a group of her friends but surrounded by blokes, he was a bit disappointed. Nevertheless, he decided to try and catch her on her own for a dance. Soon, she went to the ladies' room, and Allan seized this opportunity when she was on her way back to make his move. 'Hi there', he said. 'You said you wanted a dance. Well, I'm here now, so let's have that dance.

Smiling and blushing slightly, she agreed, but said, 'I only dance with boys to Leo Sayer's, "*When I Need You.*"'

'I know this song. So, honey, your wish is my command. I will go up, and request that, especially for you.' Allan immediately went up to ask the DJ for the request. On the way, of course, he said hello to a few girls, and one grabbed hold of him just to say hello. They had a quick pretend dance on the way, then realising what he was doing, he said thank you very much and moved quickly up towards the disc jockey.

After talking to the DJ for a few minutes, and hearing his song start, he turned around to walk back to where his date was seated. He had to walk around a crowd of dancers in the middle and was horrified to see girl from the newsagent's being taken onto the dance floor by the very smartly dressed young lad that had previously been eyeing her up. He was even more horrified when he saw them dancing in a very tightly held clinch. When the song stopped the pair continued to dance together for the next three slow dances.

Allan sat patiently waiting for her to return. When she came back to where Allan was, he asked her what she was playing at, and she just looked him straight in the eye, and said, 'Well, that guy came over to me, and said I looked quite lonely on my own and dragged me up on the dance floor. When I looked for you, you seemed to be dancing with everyone on the way to the DJ, so I had no choice'.

Callum came over, and said, 'That's us going for a meal in the restaurant now. Are you bringing that girl you were talking to with us?'

'No', said Allan. 'I've kind of gone off her a bit, but will go for the meal anyway'.

As they wandered through to the restaurant they stopped to look at Basil, who seemed to be doing some kind of peculiar dance. As it happened, it was that in his drunken stupor he was trying to avoid the glitter-ball reflection on the floor. He wasn't quite as nimble and light-footed as he would have liked to have been, and ended up tying his legs in knots and falling in a heap on the floor which caused great merriment amongst his friends.

That was until he accidentally banged into one of the locals as he jumped to his feet. When he tried to say sorry, the lad he had banged into swung a punch, and Basil, not known for his calmness in a dodgy situation, immediately lashed out with a swift kick in the groin, as the other lad turned to go back to his seat. He forgot he wasn't in the student union ten years ago, but in an alien nightclub full of people he didn't know, and they were all on the side of the homester. Basil was immediately set upon, and Jerry Paul yelled to the others to come to his aid.

Almost immediately, a group of large bouncers appeared from nowhere to break the fight up. 'Right, you lot! I've been watching you since you came in. I know that you're in one large crowd, and I know whose fault it was. So, all of you – out now, and don't come back'. Yet again the lads fun night had been curtailed.

'Where can we go now?' asked Graham Sunderland, who was nowhere near ready for the night to end.

'Well, it's quite late now', said Allan. 'Maybe we should just make tracks for home'.

When they got to the taxi rank across the road each of the three taxi drivers said, 'No chance. You've just been thrown out the nightclub. You're not coming in my taxi', or words to that effect.

As they all set off on the long walk home, someone shouted out, 'I'm hungry now, since we didn't get our meal in the club. Let's have a Chinese!'

One old man was out walking his dog and looked startled when a group of young guys, all boisterous and full of beer, descended upon him to ask the whereabouts of the nearest Chinese restaurant. Pleased to see they were just a jovial bunch on a night out, he directed them to the Chinese, and they all started to run quite quickly, as the weather was beginning to get a bit colder.

The restaurant was not very busy, and the proprietor looked up and smiled when she saw some customers. 'I'm sorry', she said. 'It was very quiet tonight, so I sent the waitresses home, but we can do you a take-away if you'd like'. After much laughing and joking, and taking the mick out of the Chinese ladies accent, they all purchased a takeaway each, and decided to head for home.

In high spirits, and continuing their laughter along the road, with Andy Richardson impersonating being offered a fork for only 5p, they came to a park. Duncan Williams, a keen footballer, noticed a ball in the middle of a football pitch. 'Great, lads. Fancy a quick kick around just to warm us up a bit before we head back?' In the dark of the night, relieved only by moonlight when the clouds broke, they looked an odd sight using their bags of take-away and jerseys as goalposts.

'Well, that's me knackered', said Craig, and with the rest agreeing, they decided to crack on for home.

There was a small river running along the edge of the park which had a number of little dinghies all tied up at the edge. This site was too tempting for the lads, so they all piled in, and had a go in the dinghies until Grant noticed that the dinghies had been tied together, and the spare ones were now floating off downstream. 'Well, I think we had probably best stop this now, and make a quick getaway before anyone sees us, and calls the authorities!' shouted Grant.

Once they had all disembarked from the boats and watched them float away, Basil said, 'I'm going for a slash. I will just nip round the back of this hedge'. The rest joined him, and they all relieved themselves, until a scream was heard from Andy.

'Ayebassa! I never saw those tall jaggy nettles. That stings like hell'.

'Well, that will put you out of action for a while', shouted someone.

The laughter from everyone else was interrupted by another scream. This time it was Allan. He had moved to avoid a large group of nettles, and inadvertently slipped on the riverbank and was by now standing knee-deep in the river. 'Can someone pull me out?'

Callum shouted back, 'I can't. I'm afraid of water!'

'But you were in the NAVY!' said Graham.

'Correct, but the idea was to stay on the boat and out of the water, you eejit."

'I am becoming a bit fed up of all this', said Allan. 'Let's just crack on home, and eat our take-aways'.

By this time the weather had got much chillier, and so they all tucked their carry-outs under their arms rugby style and jogged home.

When a few raindrops started to fall, and they realised they still had a fair distance to go, they turned around to see a coach pulling up. Relieved, Basil said, 'Yes, please', when one of the occupants opened the door, and said, 'Would you like a lift? The weather looks like it may be getting worse'.

They were just about to jump on the bus, when one of the men they had fought with, in the nightclub said, 'Yes, we thought you would, but tough! See you around, loosers', and closed the door in Basil's face. The coach then sped off, with everyone on board making faces and rude gestures out the window.

At last, wet, cold and miserable, they reached Allan's house. Grant Michael said, 'Well, I never thought I would be so relieved to get back to this spooky creepy-looking old house. I am quite tired now anyway', as they all rushed in hoping for some refuge. By now, the carry-out had cooled down dramatically, so Allan tried to heat things up in the oven, after changing into something dry.

They all went through to the living room, and he came through from the kitchen, and said, 'Sorry, more bad news. I can't get the oven to work, so we will have to eat it the way it is, or leave it'. Most of the lads accepted this cheerfully, as they were discussing amongst themselves that, although it had been an eventful evening, they had all thoroughly enjoyed themselves and it had been good to catch up with everyone.

Just then, a flash of lightning lit up the night, followed by a loud clap of thunder, and the lights in the house all started flickering. 'All we need now is a wolf to howl', joked Ewan. Everybody looked up, and as someone made a scary ghost wooooooo noise, they all burst out laughing.

'Well', said Allan. 'I suppose, as Zebedee used to say, 'Time for bed'. Everyone agreed, and started to prepare to bunk down for the night. Locking the door and turning out the lights, Allan left them all to settle down, and headed upstairs to his own bed.

When Allan woke in the morning he lay in his bed, and as the house was silent, said to himself, 'Great! I'm first awake. I'll go downstairs, and make a big noise and annoy everyone'. The more noise he made going down the stairs the more his head pounded. 'But never mind, they'll all get a real shock'.

Bursting the living room door open, he shouted, 'Wakey-wakey, you drunken hoard of wasters!' Expecting to see a room full of thirsty headaches, Allan stopped in his tracks. The room was empty, neat and tidy! 'Was that a dream last night? There is no one here'.

Scratching his head in bewilderment, he went through to the kitchen, hoping for some signs of life. What he saw astonished him: there was no one there; only a pint of milk and some rolls. The kitchen was immaculate, and smelling as fresh as a daisy; there were no signs of carry-outs, or of life of any sort.

Just as he was about to put the kettle on, the front door burst open, and in rushed his missing mates. 'Oh, there you are', he said. 'I was beginning to get a bit worried'.

In subdued voices, they said, 'Oh, we've been up for a while, and have tidied everything up for you. We were just loading our gear back into the cars for the journey home, and Grant nipped over to bring you milk and rolls'.

'That was some night!' Ewan said, and they all agreed to do it again, soon.

Everyone shook hands, said goodbye, and quietly went on their separate ways, with Jerry agreeing to drop Ewan at the station, and Allan breathing a huge sigh of relief at the front door as he watched them all drive off.

CHAPTER EIGHTEEN

Séance

T he colleague who had been staring out of the window
for a while, turned to Allan, and said, 'What's that funny-
looking thing out there?'

Allan looked out, and said, 'What is it? I have no idea',

'Well I've been looking at it all morning, and wondering, "If
I half-inched it", what could I use it for?', said Ivan.

Their quiet consideration was interrupted when the Boss
came in, and said, 'If you two would stop carving up the
equipment on-site would you do something for me, Allan?
Take Irene and her friend back to the airport, and collect a
case of oak-smoked haddock from this address in Leith.
When you've done that just go home, and I will see you
tonight for the séance'. Pleased with the idea of seeing Irene,
but disappointed she was going back to France, he asked
some others in the office if they wanted any cases as well.
Then, he set off for the Bosses mansion and gave himself an
extra-large splash of the aftershave he always kept in the
glove compartment.

He was smelling like the cosmetic counter at Boots by now,
and feeling full of anticipation. Unfortunately, he got stuck
behind two slow moving tractors. As soon as the tractors
pulled into a field he put his foot down, as he was anxious

not to be late; the quicker he picked up Irene and her friend, the more time he had left to spend with them.

As he pulled up outside the Bosses house he could see the two girls at the upstairs bedroom window looking out, they waved and stepped back from the window to come downstairs. With one last check in the car mirror, he straightened his tie and carefully checking that no one was looking, skooshed some breath freshener spray into his mouth before stepping out of the car to collect the girls and their luggage.

As Allan opened the gate, he smiled and noticed a sign saying, 'Be aware of the dog!' A small, very yappy, Yorkshire terrier came hurtling down the winding path to meet him. As he bent down to pet the dog, and prevent it from jumping up and getting his trousers all dirty, a low, menacing growl from behind alarmed Allan and caused him to swiftly turn round, where he came face-to-face with what Allan could only describe as a cross between a bear and a wolf. 'Trixi!' shouted a female voice from the house. 'Leave him alone – come back!' Straight away, the fearsome-looking dog became a docile friendly pet and ran back to the house, allowing Allan to breathe a heavy sigh of relief and brush down his trousers. Annette, the Bosses wife, stood at the front door and said, 'That dog is just trying to scare you'.

'Well, it's wasting its time because I'm

scared already'. And started to walk up the long path through the very well-kept garden.

'Well, that's good timing, Allan', Annette said. 'Here are the girls, all ready for you with their suitcases, and a bag of something to eat on the way'.

As Allan picked up the luggage, the girls thanked Annette for her hospitality, and said that they would be in touch very soon. With the girls walking ahead of him, Allan struggled with their heavy suitcases while watching them go down the path, one of the girls shouted back, 'Do you need help with those Allan?' adjusting his grip on one of the cases, he shouted back, 'No, no!! they are all right' . After Allan put the suitcases in the boot, he took a few seconds to catch his breath, wiped his forehead, and got in the car. They all waved goodbye to Annette as she closed the front door, and they set off to the sound of the girls chattering to each other.

The traffic on the road was busy, but they journeyed at a good pace, and while they sped along the motorway and listened to the radio, they talked about what the girls had done during their visit, with Irene saying, 'That's a nice aftershave you have on'.

Pleased with this compliment, he immediately replied, 'Yes, I got it for my Christmas. You girls wear a nice perfume as well'.

They overtook a broken-down car at the side of the road, and Irene's friend Freida said, 'I'm glad you haven't stopped to help. We'll have more time to spend when we get there'.

Irene butted in, saying, 'Yes, I was hoping to get to spend more time with you while we were here, and thought we might have hired bikes and gone cycling, as I know you are a fitness fanatic'. Wishing he had spent more time with them, he remembered the fiasco he'd had with his bike.

When they saw some low flying aircraft in view ahead, Allan said, 'Well, that's us nearly there, girls. Give me your addresses so I can write to you'.

As they pulled into the car park they decided to have a cup of coffee in the cafe, where they talked further about what they had done. As they exchanged addresses, the girls got up to board their plane, and Allan pecked them on the cheeks, knowing he would never see either of them again. He watched the aeroplane soar into the sky, until he could see it no more, then turned to go back to the car, and headed to the address given to him for the fish.

A notice at the door of the warehouse said that, 'A maximum of 4 cases was the limit to individuals who did not have a wholesalers card'. In total, he had to buy seven cases, so he asked two girls at the gate, one tall with blonde hair and the other, petite and slim with auburn hair, if they would buy the extra he required. They were glad to do that they said, on condition that he dropped them off somewhere near Linlithgow if he was going that way. He wasn't exactly going that way, but said, 'No problem', as he welcomed the company.

They struggled to find room for seven cases of fish, a crab he bought for his Gran, and two herrings to take back to his Mum in the car and the boot, along with the girls' luggage. But with one girl keeping a case on her knee, they managed to get everything squeezed in. 'No room for any hitch-hikers this time', he thought, 'but these two will be good enough company'. As they chatted on the road back, it turned out the girls were just back from a holiday in Spain, with Allan complimenting them on their beautiful tans.

By the time they got to Linlithgow the smell of fish in the car was quite ripe, so Allan jumped out to carry the girls' bags up the path. 'Must get back quickly', he thought as he looked at his watch, and was almost bowled over by the smell in the car when he resumed at the wheel. Then, sped off quickly back home.

Knowing that he had plenty of time to spare, Allan went back to the office, hoping to unload some of the fish and to check up on the numbers for tonight. When he got there, he was met with a resounding, 'No, we'll pick it up from your house tonight. You're not leaving that in here just now!' One of his colleagues shouted, 'Hope that doesn't stink out your house for tonight''. Slightly disappointed, he headed back down to the car park.

Big Chic was just getting into his car, and looked quickly away when he saw Allan. 'Hi, Chic!' Allan shouted. 'Nice tie', he said, and grabbed the tie rubbing it between his fingers, with a smile on his face.

"Get off," he said in his usual manner.

Laughing, Allan replied, 'Nice car, Charlie, Japanese, eh?'

Turning away quickly, Charlie jumped into his car, and shouting over his shoulder, he said, 'You must be a very sad person having to use excuses like a séance to lure girls back to your house!' With that, Charlie took off down the road, revving the engine loudly and crunching the gears as he sped off to let his annoyance be known.

When Allan arrived home, he noticed that his next-door neighbour who had wanted fish was in, so he knocked on her door, and carried it into the house for her. 'My brothers were here a couple of week's ago; I hope they didn't bother you. They left early because of the noise of a dog', he said to her.

'No, they were no disturbance. But there are no dogs around here'.

'Don't forget I'm having a séance with some of the guys tonight, if you want to pop in?' Allan said.

'Well, I might just do that, even if it's only to get away from the smell of this, and the rest of the family moaning about it'.

After Allan had brought all the cases in, he just left them in the living room for easiness, and ran across to the precinct to buy an air freshener. The road was quite busy outside his house, after all, it was the main road, and it was time for everyone to leave their various jobs and offices.

Meanwhile, the Boss was still in his office alone, as he usually stayed later. Even though he was in first, he was always the last one to leave, as he enjoyed the quiet time while peacefully gathering his thoughts.

Eventually, he looked at his watch, and decided enough was enough for one day; it was time he moved off for Allan's house to meet the rest. As he sat there enjoying his last few moments of silent contemplation, there was an almighty bang! 'Just like a bullet'...

Jumping immediately to his feet, and running out of the office, he stopped when he heard no more noise. His trousers and shirt were all wet, and knowing it could not have been a bullet or anything else like that, he went back tentatively to his room.

Inside his office, he was amazed and a little amused when he realised what all the kerfuffle was; nothing sinister: it was the cork from the bottle of home-brew Allan had given him some week's prior. 'Well, obviously it's ready to drink', he thought. 'It's blown off the cork, and now the beer is still frothing from the exploded bottle'.

Knowing the cleaners would be in any minute, he set to tidying up as best he could, removing the bottle and cork, and blotting up as much as he could of the ale as possible with the newspaper, hoping the cleaners wouldn't know whose office it was, he turned to leave for home to get changed into some dry clothes.

On the way down the corridor, he said hello to the cleaners on their way in, and made a quick exit to his car. Knowing that his office would be stinking of beer when next he came in, he wound down his car window and drove quickly home.

Moving up his driveway, he waved to his wife at the kitchen window, and by the time he got back to the house, she had come to meet him. 'I thought you were going straight to Allan's?'

'Well, I was', he said, and then explained what had happened, cursing himself when he remembered he had brought a holdall with him to change out of his work clothes when he had got to Allan's.

He tooted his horn once, as he sped off to meet the rest. When he arrived at Allan's, and parked in the adjoining car park, he realised that he was actually the first one to arrive.

As the office next to the doctors started to empty, Allan parked his car in their car park, and said to the Manager as he left, 'Well, I've got a load of friends coming tonight. I've just told them to use your car park'.

With a reassuring nod, he added, 'You know that's fine. It's well worth the bottle of whisky you give me every year. What will you all be up to, anyway?' Allan told him, and the small bearded Manager shook his head and sucked air in through his teeth while saying, 'That's not a good thing to do. I wish you hadn't told me that'. Allan laughed, and armed with his air fresheners, ran back into the house. He just had time to phone Linda from the typing pool to remind her of the address, and then Carrie, who said she'd be around in half an hour.

As he sat down to pick up the kitchen phone, he was startled by a strange, but faint noise behind him. He froze temporarily, listening intently. 'What was that?' It sounded like tapping and scratching, but very quiet. As he strained to listen, the hairs on the back of his neck stood on end, and his blood ran cold when he thought he could feel two eyes piercing through the back of his head, searching and probing. Eventually, he plucked up the courage and gradually turned his head to see the fridge door slowly opening. 'That must have been what the noise was', he told himself. Feeling uneasy, and still trying to convince himself, he quickly shut the fridge door with his foot, then ran upstairs to get changed into some comfy clothes.

Just as he came back downstairs the doorbell sounded. Opening the door, he was faced by the Boss, who followed Allan in, and said, 'The rest are right behind me parking their cars where you told us to. I've had to go home to get changed because of that home-brew you gave me', and went on to explain what had happened.

When they went into the living room, the front door opened and a steady procession of workmates and others came in. So, they took a seat each and started on the booze. Some workmates had already met in The Drovers for a few drinks earlier, so were ahead of the rest.

When everyone was sitting there just waiting for the clairvoyant Carrie to arrive, one of the girls from the typing pool asked to be shown around the house. She said it looked like the one that was in the papers a few years ago. 'Maybe', Allan said.

As everyone rose to be shown around the house, before the telephone rang. 'Just you answer that, Allan', said someone. 'We'll look round ourselves if that's okay'.

When Allan picked up the telephone it was his mother. She did tend to speak forever on the phone repeating herself on several occasions, but Allan was used to this by now, and said, 'Look! Mum, I will have to leave you just now. I have some visitors 'Of course', she said, 'but wait 'till I tell you this though"', and she told him all about the new car she had bought.

'Oh, that's good, Mum, but I'll need to go now'.

'Okay', she said, 'but the last thing – we all went over to your Gran's last night'.

'No, no, your other Gran, and she was asking about your house. She wanted to come through, but your brothers put her off, so she won't be after all'.

'That's fine, then', said Allan, 'But I really must go now'.

'Well, what will you lot be doing there tonight?' she asked.

Wracking his brains to find something other to say rather than a séance, he welcomed someone shouting through from the living room, 'Are you coming through, or what? And that's your doorbell, anyway'. Allan took this opportunity to say goodbye, and open the door to let in Carrie.

Gemma said to Allan, 'I never ate anything when I left the office; I just came straight here, and with the smell of all that fish I am now starving'.

'Well, I'm hungry too', said someone. 'Let's send out for a takeaway'. After a brief discussion whether to have a takeaway now or to order it for later, they decided to have it later, and crack on now Carrie was here.

By that time, they had demolished most of Allan's stockpile of filled rolls and eaten all his biscuits, they decided to sit down and enjoy the proceedings. At this point, they had been drinking steadily since they arrived, and were now quite tipsy.

'Right, that's everyone here', said Allan. 'So, let's get started'. He made sure that he was sitting next to the typist Linda who he was to take to the wedding. 'I am looking forward to this wedding', he said to her. 'I have all the details on the card you gave me, along with your address and phone number, and I keep it in my wallet at all times, right next to my heart', as he patted his chest. He then had a quick look around the room to make sure none of the other girls had heard his cheesy comment.

The first person Carrie looked at was the Boss: 'I can sense that you're very sceptical about this, and only came under duress, but I see a promotion for you in the not-too-distant future and a house move'.

'Well, anybody could guess that', said David Plain. 'You don't need to be a spook to guess that one'.

Glancing up with an evil look in her eye, she said tartly, 'This is not a joke. Take it a bit more seriously. I see that you will be leaving us soon to go somewhere warmer'.

'Oh, do you mean I'm going to die soon and get cremated?'

'No, no, it's to do with your job'.

She went around the room, and one by one said everyone's future, and her interpretation of it.

'Can you warn us of something bad that's going to happen?' asked Allan.

'No', she said. 'I can't say anything bad'.

'Can you tell me what the lottery numbers will be this week, then?' asked someone, which brought a howl of laughter from everyone, except Carrie.

'Look!' she said, slamming her hand on the table. 'Either you take this seriously or I'm off'.

'Why? Could you not foretell we'd act like this?' At that, she sighed and shook her head.

'I was once at a reading where there was an ouija board', said Gemma. 'The spiritualist smashed the tumbler. She said she had done that for protection from the evil eye in the glass, whatever that meant'. Most of the assembled crowd gave a whistling sound which annoyed her even more.

'Right, that's your last warning!'

As things settled down, she turned to one of the girls, and said, 'You're going to meet someone on holiday who you will eventually marry'. This pleased the girl.

Carrie then turned to Gemma, and said, 'You're a very caring girl, and you care for your family and help them all as much as possible'.

'Yeah, that's right'.

A few other people were done, all being given a somewhat vague reading, and as she went around them, her voice got quieter and quieter, and very soft, with everyone straining to hear anything she said. When everyone was concentrating on what was being said, Tommy took his phone from his pocket, and sneakily punched in a number. By now, the spiritualist's voice was almost inaudible. Then suddenly her voice lifted, 'Is there anybody there', she cried. 'Is there anyone you want me to pass a message to?' she enquired, with eyes wide like saucers, and both of her hands in the air. She suddenly, wailed at the top of her voice, 'Speak to me! I demand you to speak to me, now!' she screamed. The room went silent until almost everyone screamed in horror when Allan's telephone rang. Tommy burst out laughing, and while he cackled to himself, everyone else tried not to laugh.

The living room door burst open, and looking at the startled faces before him, Curtis, who had just come down from the loo, asked pointedly, 'Who is the wisecracker around here, then? It's bad enough in that freezing toilet with the light not working, without some joker continually scratching at the door and trying the handle. It's a waste of time you guys trying to scare me; this place gives me the willies already'. Everyone looked at each other dumbfounded, as no one else had left the room.

Carrie said, 'Look, I warned you. That's it'. By this time, she had spoken to everyone, except Allan and Linda. 'Well, it's just us to go then we can call it a day', said Allan.

Looking over her specs, the spiritualist, taking a deep breath and shaking her head, clearly unhappy, said, 'No, I can't do you. I have to leave now', then picked up her overcoat, and hurried out. Everyone sat there slightly shocked at her hasty departure, but continued to drink and talk about the evening. Linda stayed for a few drinks more until she and Gemma decided to head off as well. The rest in the house, still smiling burst out laughing when they heard an ambulance go by, and everyone yelled out the old joke, 'He won't sell much ice cream at that speed'.

After a few more drinks, and many more laughs, one of the lads said, 'It's very cold now. Is there a window open?'

'No', replied Allan, 'it's always cold in this house, my bolshie wee sister keeps threatening to get a central heating engineer for me though'.

As it was by now getting quite late, Curtis said to Allan, 'Well, I think I best call it a night. Anyone else going out to look for a taxi? We can pick up our cars in the morning'. Remembering that taxis don't come to the house, they all nodded in agreement, put on their coats, and thanked Allan for a good evening.

Wandering the street in search of taxis, they saw Gemma crying and climbing into the back of an ambulance. They ran over to see what was going on and caught her just before they closed the ambulance doors.

'What's wrong?' asked Tommy.

'It's Linda, she was hit by a taxi. I'm going with her. It looks bad'. 'How did it happen?' asked Tommy.

'Well, she turned to me just as she stepped off the pavement, and didn't see the car. The last thing she was saying was how much she liked Allan, and was looking forward to going to a wedding with him'.

They stood there all speechless, not knowing what to do now, and shuffled from foot to foot in the cold night air, then walked over to a police car that had just pulled up. After taking some names in case they were required as witnesses, the police car sounded its siren, and with blue lights flashing, raced after the ambulance.

'Well, said the Boss, I suppose we should go inside and tell Allan what's happened, and phone our wives for a lift home'.

They stood and stared at the ever-disappearing ambulance and escort until it was no longer in view, then turned slowly, and walked up Allan's pathway.

All the noise had made a curious Allan come to the front door to see what was happening, and when he saw all their long, stunned faces, brought them back inside where, a clearly and very shaking Ivan, explained what had happened. Allan picked up the telephone that had started ringing, and the blood drained from his face. Then, with a sickening knot in his stomach, he whispered to the rest, 'That's Gemma phoning from the hospital... she's dead...Linda's dead!!!

CHAPTER NINETEEN

The Last Drop

Although it was a Saturday, Allan was awake as usual around 7 o'clock. At first, he was about to turn over and just listen to the radio for a good half an hour before getting up, then he suddenly sat bolt upright, and his heart sank. Linda was dead!

Every morning, since the accident, for the first few seconds he was awake, everything seemed fine, then it would hit him, that awful feeling that she was no more, she was never coming back. Then to make matters even worse, if that was possible, he remembered this was the day he had promised to work.

After stretching and very sluggishly climbing out of bed, he ran downstairs to switch the kettle on, then quickly made a cup of Instant Powdered Energy. It was never as good out of a tin or a jar as the real stuff in the office, but this would have to do for now.

He switched on the radio to hear the early morning news which he felt was really just an update of last nights, then decided he would have a shower, get dressed, and be back down in time to hear the weather report, and have his coffee.

On the way back upstairs to the shower, he made a mental note, 'My mates are quite right. This house is gloomy, but with all those years of emptiness it was only to be expected'.

He decided that when he got a spare minute or two at work on Monday he would phone around for quotes to have the stairwell decorated, and a new carpet for the stairs.

It would be good if he could convince some of the family to come through to help with the stripping of the wallpaper too,… and it would be cheaper.

Keen to get to work, he showered, and then contemplated what to wear. 'Should it be the usual suit and tie, or since it was the weekend, maybe just smart casual', as there would be no one else there.

As there was a possibility of bumping into some other sad person working on a Saturday, he decided on very smart casual, then ran back down for his coffee, frowning once again at his décor.

Coming out his front door, he said hello to the woman from two doors down, the one with the children. She was packing up her car for a day trip, and what looked like a picnic.

'Well, never mind, Allan. There's always some poor saddo that has to work', she remarked with a smile, as he headed towards his car. 'Don't work too hard now. See you later'.

As the neighbours got in their car, Allan shook his head and waved them off. 'Hope it bloody rains for their picnic',he muttered to himself and ran across the road for a newspaper.

The newsagent's shop was quite busy, so Allan held back and waited until it quietened down so he could get a word alone with the assistant.

'Well, that's me off to work now', he said, 'But maybe we could go out for a drink some night? If you are still open when I finish I may pop in'.

'Okay, you know where to find me', she said, as he waved her goodbye, and drove to his office.

It was strange turning up at work on a Saturday morning, with him being the only one there, and the Boss's car not already being in the car park. Once he had parked his car, there was no need to hang about for Gemma so he just went straight inside.

There was no inviting smell of coffee either, but he didn't make any as he was unsure how long he would be there today, and most of the time he would be in the main building, where there were plenty of free vending machines. He was also hoping there were, maybe, some filled rolls leftover from yesterday.

The first thing Allan did at his desk was to telephone the Boss to let him know he had arrived, or so he said, but really it was to interrupt his long lie. After the Boss made it clear that there had been no need for him to telephone, Allan put the files in his briefcase and set off for the main building.

Again, it seemed strange to him to see an almost empty car park except for a few of the engineers' cars. Normally it was a thronging, bustling set of offices, but today it was almost deserted. All that could be heard was the low, constant hum of the generators giving the whole place an eerie feel, almost like a ghost town.

Allan handed in the first report and chatted for a while with Matthew Wheeler, the engineer, then he went to the second office, and chatted at some length about what a waste it was spending Saturday morning at work. By the time they had finished speaking, the few engineers that had got the short straw to work the weekend were packing up, and going back home.

In the next office, he just left the report in the pigeonhole and decided to have a coffee from one of the machines and a leftover roll. While he was enjoying this roll, the last of the engineers appeared and said that they were finished and were off home now too.

'Enjoy your breakfast!' one of them shouted over his shoulder as they left. 'Just put the rest of the reports in the pigeonholes.

As he posted the last of that corridor's reports into the appropriate pigeonholes, he realised the whole building was almost empty now, and the only signs of life were himself and the gatekeeper-come-security man who would lock up later. Allan thought it was quite strange to be in this normally busy building when it is as quiet as this.

He walked along the corridor deliberately making a noise on the stone floor with the segs on his shoes, the metal tacks, like he used to do at school to annoy the teachers.

Listening to his shoes reverberating throughout the empty, silent building, he thought he heard a shuffling noise behind him, but there was no one there when he turned to have a look.

He only had two more corridors of offices to complete, but the noise continued as he moved on. Turning a corner, he looked behind him, expecting to see someone there. The noise of footsteps stopped, and to his horror! There was nobody there.

Surprised, Allan continued along the corridor, and the noise seemed to get louder and louder, and closer and closer. He spun around very quickly, and came face-to-face with... nothing! Nobody was there. 'Very strange', he thought to himself, 'But just a few more deliveries to make then am out of here'.

As Allan turned to head to the exit, the temperature suddenly dropped dramatically. 'The heating must go off at a certain time of day', he hoped, unless the door has been left open by someone in a rush to get home. Thank goodness I am about to go'.

Again, the shuffling started up behind him. As he slowed down so did the noise of footsteps behind, and when he speeded up again so did the noise.

As he stopped to listen, he could hear someone breathing behind him, but somehow did not feel the inclination to turn around and face whoever, or whatever it was, as he was now convinced that he could actually feel breath on his neck.

He just hurried up to get out quickly, as he felt that whoever it was, was almost within touching distance. The hairs on the nape of his neck stood to attention, and his back felt like someone had just put ice cubes down. He was breaking out into a cold sweat but decided that he would have to turn around and face up to his follower.

By now, he was unsure whether there was someone behind him or around the corner, so he turned back and looked to the right, and there he saw someone running away. It was a woman, and just as she was about to leave the building she turned around, tossed her head back, and cackled a horrible gurgling noise. Then she was off.

Allan decided it would be best to get out of here and home as quickly as possible, but the girl's face did look vaguely familiar to him and would be until his dying moments, indelibly etched in his mind.

As he pulled up outside his house, the girl from the newsagents saw him and waved. 'If you fancy that drink now, that's me finished', she said. 'Or, even better – my boyfriend has gone off for a boys' weekend, so I am all alone at home, so you can come around to mine, and just stay the night in the spare room if you want'.

When Allan explained that he had just had a rather disturbing experience so would've to decline, she said that she understood. With a mischievous grin, said she may come back to see him a bit later after he has had a rest, and got more energy. She then hurried away, leaving Allan to wonder.

Glad to get back home even though he was by now becoming depressed every time he entered that house, he made his tea, and settled down in front of the television with a large drink.

The news was the usual boring stuff about politics, strikes, and countries fighting with each other. Just as he was about to turn over to watch *Charlie's Angels* or *Bay watch* (one of his favourite programs), he was interested to hear that a convicted murderer in a nearby prison had escaped, and was heading back towards his home town of Dundee... of all places. 'Lucky I'm not going home as I may have picked them up as a hitch-hiker. I think I deserve an extra-large whiskey tonight', and poured himself another double, at least.

He was tidying up the living room when the doorbell rang. 'It will be that girl', he thought, with mixed feelings. When he answered the door his heart sank; it was a policeman from across the road. 'Sorry to bother you, Sir', he said. 'Nothing really to worry about, but I don't know if you saw that on the news; there is a prisoner that just escaped from up the road, and we believe he's trying to go home to Dundee. He suffers from sciatica and is in a lot of pain. We know he has not taken his medication with him, and so may break into a doctors surgery or chemist for painkillers. If you hear a noise next door, don't investigate, just call us'.

Relieved that the policeman did not think there was any connection to him, with him being from Dundee, and also that it wasn't the girl who said she may come to see him, he just smiled, and said, 'Do I look stupid? If it's a murderer there's no way I'll go near him'.

When the policeman left, Allan locked both doors and settled down in front of the TV with his drink. By now, his mind and imagination were working overtime: 'Should I sleep with my air rifle in my bedroom', he thought.

He was almost dozing off, when the telephone jolted him awake. It was his mother. 'Did you see that story on the news about the murderer?' asked his Mum. 'You be careful, and don't let anyone in. Keep your doors locked, and did I tell you about my new car?'

'Yes, a few times, Mum, but I've had a long day, so I'm just going to go to bed'.

'Well, it's still quite chilly. Take your bottle with you', she replied.

'I always take a bottle to bed, Mum', he said.

'Well, that's good. If you're tired, I'll let you go. Bye for now'.

Allan's overactive imagination made him think that maybe it would not have been such a bad idea after all if he had gone to that girl's house or if she had come here.

The living room was still a mess, so he thought he would leave it until morning, and just go up and watch TV in bed or listen to the radio. He decided to leave the front door unlocked after all, as he thought any intruder would not enter in full view of the police station across the road, instead, via the back door where they would be unseen. So, if he had to make a run for it, he could make a quick getaway without having to unlock the door.

On the way upstairs, every step he took seemed to make a creak louder than the previous step. Halfway up, he stopped and looked in the room where the piano was and thought to himself, 'This job started out great with so many opportunities, but I'm not so sure now. I haven't even learnt to play the piano in that room. That's another thing to put on my to-do list'.

Holding his hot water bottle close to his chest, and his other bottle in the other hand, he continued up the dark and dingy, noisy staircase, and into his bedroom. 'No wonder it's cold', he thought. 'The window is open'. Closing it, though he was sure he had done so this morning, he jumped into bed, and said mockingly to the picture, 'This is all your fault', and with a swig of his whiskey turned on the radio. He was pleased to hear the song playing was his recently discovered favourite, *'A Cry For Love'*. As he lay there contemplating an eventful day, and going over it again in his head, the doorbell went. 'Well, if it's that girl', he thought, 'she could not have picked a better time'.

Jumping out of bed, Allan ran downstairs to let the girl in, only to see three young teenagers laughing, and running away. Normally, Allan would have laughed at the kids' pranks, as he used to play this game himself when he was younger, but tonight he was not in the mood, just as he was about to slam the door closed, a passer-by said to him 'it was those young lads from down the road right, wee scallywags they are, It makes you smile though, we used to do that when we were that age' he said to Allan 'Well I never did!' replied Allan harshly as he closed the door with a loud bang and went inside.

He finished the bottle that was opened and took another one upstairs. The more he drank the more he became intrigued and intoxicated by that horrible picture.

There was a tap-tap-tapping sound coming from the window, and as much as Allan tried to ignore it, the louder it seemed to get. 'Well, it can't be someone trying to break in', he thought. 'Not up one storey, anyway'.

With a sigh and a few expletives, he went over to the window to investigate. Just as he was about to open the curtains, they lifted up into his face. 'Woh!' he shouted, as he jumped back quickly. Standing still for a second or two to come to grips with this, he smiled with relief, as it dawned on him it was just the blind being blown by the wind that was causing the noise; the window was open again somehow, and no matter how much he tried he could not get it to closed.

As a very bemused Allan was about to jump into bed, his telephone rang. 'Who on earth could this be at this time of the night? I've enough on my plate'.

He went downstairs to answer the phone, it was a heating engineer who said 'Hi, sorry to phone you so late, but it's the heating engineer from Kozi House Plumbers. I know you're trying to get in touch, I've been on holiday and a friend said, as a favour to her, I should please do your house as a matter of urgency, so I will be around first thing in the morning. I know where you stay, next to the doctors and opposite Crabby Archie's'.

'That's great', said Allan. 'I'll get back to bed now and sleep the sleep of the just. I can die a happy man now, see you in the morning'. Then ran back upstairs to bed.

No sooner had he got settled in bed, than the phone rang again. there was no one on the other end; all there was, was a dialling tone. 'Pain in the necks', he said, as he slammed the phone down, and went back upstairs.

This time a phone rang just as he was pulling the covers back. That sound is getting as annoying as the last orders bell in the pub. I'll just ignore it. It can't be anyone important now. So I just try for some sleep. He just lay in bed, trying to ignore it, but the phone still rang, and rang, and rang until eventually he could stand it no more, and thinking to himself that it must be important, he went back down swiftly. Again, it was just the dialling tone and no voice. This time when he replaced the handset, he waited for a good five minutes in case it started again. Then went back upstairs.

As he got to the bedroom door the phone rang again. This time, he ran down as quickly as he could, and when he just heard the dialling tone, he slammed the phone down, and in total exasperation wrenched it out furiously from the socket to prevent it from happening again.

'Right, now I will try to get some sleep!'

Back in bed, Allan took another large swig from his bottle, then lay back on his pillow hoping to relax, and possibly sleep. Suddenly, the bedsheets lifted from his bed, and landed flat back, covering him. As he lay there motionless, paralysed by the fear that had entered his body, he was too afraid even to take a breath. When at last he plucked up the courage, he gently pulled down the bedsheets and dared to steal another glance at the picture. 'This is getting more and more bizarre', he thought, as he lay there trying to make sense of things.

His eyes kept returning to the painting. As his vision got more and more blurry, and with the words of his mother about getting rid of the hideous picture echoing in his ear, he was just as he was about to get out of bed to wipe the pockmarks off after months of being annoyed by them every night, there was a loud slow creek on the bottom stair. 'Oh, just thermal contraction. Nothing to worry about', as he gently dropped his empty whiskey bottle on the floor. 'Well, I think I managed to squeeze the last bit out of there. That's probably why I hear and see strange things. I don't think I will touch the stuff anymore; that's me and alcohol finished for good'.

'What was that? said Allan, as the spare bedroom door slammed shut. 'Probably the draft from the open window', he thought. By now, Allan was too drunk or too tired to care anyway, but the picture still annoyed him. Eventually, he gave in and decided to get rid of the pockmarks by wiping them with some spit on a hanky. Turning quickly towards the top of the stairs, there was another creek when the wind hit the window, making a loud noise. Realising what the bang was, he returned his attention to the painting. As soon as Allan touched the painting, her mouth fell open, and Allan heard the cackle and gurgle he had heard before.

He immediately jumped two steps back, and stared at the painting, mouth agog, petrified, and temporarily rooted to the spot, as the lady stepped out the frame. The picture was of the same lady he had seen in the main building, but by this time Allan was running for safety.

As he got to the bedroom door, he could see she was walking towards him, and although it seemed in slow motion and he was going as fast as he could, she was still getting closer.

Allan was running down the stairs two at a time, and when he glanced again over his shoulder, to see the advancing apparition, his sore ankle went again, and he tumbled head over heels downstairs and landed heavily. The loud crack of his neck breaking was the last sound he ever heard. In a heap, he lay motionless on the floor. He was never to hear the policemen ringing the doorbell and coming in the unlocked door to tell Allan the escapee had been caught.

The older policeman radioed for an ambulance and then said to the young rookie, 'I've met this lad before, and funnily enough I told him that my very first job was a mysterious death in this house all those years ago. This is the same for you'.

'What's happened here?' he asked the lady, and under his breath, the rookie asked, 'And why is there a crab on the stairs?' They stared mesmerized at the crab as its pincers clutched vice-like to the fibres of the stair carpet and struggled inch by inch and step by step in its relentless pursuit of its goal. But she just cackled, threw her hair back, and went back into the bedroom. The policemen ran after her, but she was nowhere to be seen. They looked at each other in astonishment; the silence only being broken when the younger policeman shouted, 'Look!' and pointing to the painting, they noticed that, although the girl was nowhere to be seen, it was her picture in the frame.

Together, the policemen went straight over and studied the painting which had a plaque on it. The plaque read, '*To my darling, to say sorry, and as a reminder never ever to be unfaithful again*'.

The wind picked up and as a storm started to brew, a dog howled, and the lights flickered and went off in the bedroom. The policemen, very tentatively went downstairs as the sound of Moonlight Sonata played from the locked piano. When they reached the bottom of the stairs, they never noticed the lipstick-stained cigarette, stubbed out in the ashtray and opened the door to meet the ambulance men and the CID. The unplugged phone rang three times and then went dead.

THE END

The characters in this book are fictional although may bear resemblance to some people I have met in my life and therefore I apologise for any unintentional offence.

Printed in Great Britain
by Amazon

36480486R00158